The
Sweetest
Temptation

The Sweetest Temptation

ROCHELLE ALERS

ARABESQUE®

THE SWEETEST TEMPTATION

ISBN-13: 978-0-373-83102-9
ISBN-10:   0-373-83102-1

This is a work of fiction. Names, characters, places and incidents are either the product of the author's imagination or are used fictitiously, and any resemblance to actual persons, living or dead, business establishments, events or locales is entirely coincidental.

www.kimanipress.com

Printed in U.S.A.

The Whitfield Brides series

You've met Ryan, Jeremy and Sheldon—the Blackstones of Virginia—and now it's time to meet the Whitfields of New York. In this Arabesque trilogy, you will meet the wedding divas of Signature Bridals: Tessa, Faith and Simone Whitfield. These three women are so focused on their demanding careers that they've sacrificed their personal happiness. Within a year, though, each will encounter a very special man who will not only change them but change their lives forever.

In *Long Time Coming,* wedding planner Tessa Whitfield never imagined that opening the doors of Signature Bridals to Micah Sanborn would lead to their spending the next twelve hours together after a power outage hits her Brooklyn, New York, neighborhood. Her vow never to mix business with pleasure is shattered when the Brooklyn assistant district attorney offers Tessa an extraordinary friendship with a few special surprises that make her reevaluate everything she's come to believe about love.

Wedding cake designer Faith Whitfield, who owns the fashionable Greenwich Village patisserie Let Them Eat Cake, has all but given up on finding her prince, and refuses to kiss another frog. But when she least expects it, she discovers love in the passionate embrace of pilot to the rich and famous, and modern-day knight-in-shining-armor Ethan McMillan in *The Sweetest Temptation.*

After a disappointing marriage and an ill-fated reconciliation with her high school sweetheart, floral designer Simone Whitfield wants nothing to do with men. She's content to run her business, Wildflowers and Other Treasures, in the greenhouses on her White Plains, New York, property. In *Taken by Storm,* Simone witnesses an attack on a federal judge and suddenly finds her cloistered suburban life turned upside down when U.S. Marshal Raphael Madison from the Witness Protection Unit is assigned to protect her 24/7. Although they are complete opposites, Simone and Raphael come to share a heated desire and a love that promises forever.

Yours in romance,
Rochelle Alers

For Sean D. Young—
The ultimate wedding planner diva

His left hand is under my head and his right arm embraces me.

—*Song of Solomon* 8:3

Chapter 1

Faith Whitfield smiled at the doorman as he opened the rear door to the taxi and extended a hand. Grabbing her gloved hand, he helped her to her feet.

She'd come to record producer William "WJ" Raymond's West End Avenue high-rise river-view apartment to prepare the dessert menu for his daughter's engagement party. Tonight's menu would differ from the traditional one because most of the candies, cookies, cakes and tortes would be made with chocolate. And those familiar with Savanna Raymond knew she was a diehard chocoholic.

It was January eighth, and the number of projects Faith had committed to had increased instead of slowing down as they usually did during the postholiday season. It wouldn't have been a problem if Faith hadn't signed a contract with a major publisher for a book featuring her cake designs.

She'd admitted to her cousins Simone and Tessa Whitfield that she was tired, but the truth was that she was beyond tired. She was worn-out, done-in and completely exhausted. Faith's next projects included two cakes for afternoon and evening Valentine's Day wedding receptions.

Her smile was still in place when she stood on the sidewalk under the maroon canopy. "Thank you, Thomas," she said, reading the name tag pinned to his greatcoat.

The doorman touched the shiny brim of his cap. "You're quite welcome, Miss Whitfield."

His gaze lingered on her tall figure in a pair of jeans, low-heel boots and black wool wrap coat. He'd made it a point to remember the name of the incredibly beautiful dark-brown-skinned woman who'd come to see William Raymond. New York City luxury-apartment-building doormen were notorious gossips, and a housekeeper for the Raymonds had let it be known that Miss Whitfield had been hired to create a specialty wedding cake for their daughter's Valentine's Day wedding.

Thomas rushed to open the door to the lobby as Miss Whitfield strode by with an oversize black leather bag slung over her shoulder. "I'll call to let someone know you're on your way up," he said to her as she walked past him.

Faith nodded, refusing to dwell on how long it would take her to bake and decorate a large heart-shaped chocolate and red currant torte for Savanna Raymond as she stepped into the elevator and pushed the button for the penthouse. Her newly hired assistant, a recent graduate of a highly regarded New York City culinary school, had spent two days collecting and cleaning orange, bay, citrus and beech leaves, using them as templates for the chocolate leaves that would top the torte.

She'd baked everything, with the exception of the heart-shaped torte and chocolate-covered fresh fruits in her shop—Let Them Eat Cake—carefully packaging and labeling the contents before they were delivered to the Raymond residence the night before. The Raymonds had invited forty guests, and Faith had created a special gift for each: chocolate candies in edible boxes.

The door to the household staff entrance was open as Faith exited the elevator. A tall man standing a few feet away mumbled a greeting when he recognized her. He worked security for William Raymond.

A sensor set off a soft chiming as Faith walked through the door and into the stainless-steel kitchen reminiscent of those in restaurants or cooking schools. The Raymonds had employed a live-in chef who prepared gourmet meals for his employer and their guests. The smell of freshly brewed coffee reminded Faith that she hadn't had her morning cup of coffee.

Placing her leather bag on a stool in the corner, she made her way through the kitchen to an area with walk-in closets to hang up her coat. Selecting a white tunic and toque from a supply stacked on a shelf in another closet, she covered her blouse and hair.

Returning to the kitchen, she opened the bag and took out a plastic container with the chocolate leaves and several others filled with sliced kumquat, kiwi, strawberries, mandarin oranges, star fruit and bananas. After a cup of coffee with a liberal splash of cream, Faith busied herself arranging the fruit on platters. She stirred a mixture of sugar crystals and sugar syrup until the soft icing was the consistency she sought for a fondant she planned to flavor with a rum extract. In the two hours it took for the fondant to dry, she mixed the ingredients for the torte and placed the cake in a preheated oven. Working nonstop, she coated the strawberries with fondant before dipping them into couverture, placing them on parchment paper to set. She repeated the exercise with the other fruit, sans the fondant.

It was late morning when Kurt Payton strolled into the kitchen. The tall, lanky chef had soulful blue-gray eyes that were mesmerizing. His natural culinary talent had flourished only after he'd completed an apprenticeship under the tutelage of a tyrannical master chef at a three-star Boston restaurant. Kurt had eventually set up his own catering business, but had given it up twenty-two years later to work exclusively for William and Linda Raymond.

The distinctive lines around Kurt's eyes crinkled as he watched Faith Whitfield put the finishing touches on the torte. She'd spread a chocolate ganache over the top, sprinkled it with finely crumbled pistachio croquant, then topped it off with fresh raspberries on puffs of meringue.

"I bet you'll never eat chocolate again," he drawled lazily.

Faith looked up. A hint of a smile played at the corners of her generous mouth when she spied the chef in a white tunic, black pinstripe pants and a pair of black leather clogs. He'd concealed his wiry salt-and-pepper hair under a black bandanna.

"No lie, Kurt."

"Are you finished here?" He wanted to start preparing for the party.

She nodded. "I will be as soon as I put these in the refrigerator." She pointed to half a dozen parchment-lined trays filled with the fresh fruit confectionery. The chocolate-covered fruit were turned into candies because their natural sweetness harmonized well with the bitter chocolate when dusted with a sugar coating in the form of a fondant or the base of sweet almond paste.

Kurt moved over to the counter. He pointed to a tray. "What are these?"

"Kumquats. Take one and tell me if you like it."

He picked up one without the grated pistachios, popping it into his mouth. His eyes widened in surprise as he chewed thoughtfully. "You used an almond paste and orange liquor. Now, that's nice."

She curtsied as if he were royalty. "Coming from you, I'll take that as the ultimate compliment."

Kurt waved a hand. "If I'd met you a couple of years ago I would've asked you to work with me. We would've been a dynamic duo."

Faith lifted a tray and made her way to one of two walk-in refrigerators. "It wouldn't have worked," she said over her shoulder. "I prefer baking to cooking."

"You would've been my pastry chef." Kurt picked up two of the trays and followed her.

Faith pressed the foot lever on the refrigerator, and the door swung open. "I like working for myself." She liked being her own boss even if it meant working long hours. It was much more gratifying because she set her own hours and earned much more than she could've working for someone else.

Kurt's cell phone rang as he helped put the last tray into the refrigerator. Excusing himself, he walked out of the kitchen to answer the call as William Raymond III, affectionately called BJ, shuffled in drinking a bottle of beer.

. Faith watched him out of the corner of her eye as she washed her hands in a sink. He had on a pair of baggy jeans and nothing else. It was obvious he worked out because there wasn't an ounce of fat on his compact muscular frame. His shaved head, gold-brown coloring and trimmed mustache and goatee and strong features hinted of a sensuality that definitely wasn't lost on the opposite sex.

"*Waz-zup,* boo?" BJ asked, angling his head and leering at Faith.

"Hello," she answered as she dried her hands on a towel before retrieving her bag off the stool. She wanted to tell him she wasn't his peer, and definitely not his *boo.*

"Where are you rushing off to?" he asked when she headed out of the kitchen.

Faith decided it best not to respond to his query as she went to get her coat. She hadn't taken more than three steps when she found that BJ had come up behind her. Each time she moved, he also moved.

"*Excuse* me."

He leaned closer, the stale odor of beer wafting over her face. "Excuse you for what?"

Her attempt to sidestep him was thwarted when he came face-to-face with her. "Please step back."

A sneer pulled one side of his slack mouth downward. "Did anyone ever tell you that you have a sexy-ass mouth?"

Faith knew physically she was no match for Billy Raymond, yet she didn't want to give him the impression that she was afraid of him. She pushed against his solid chest. "Get out of my face!"

Propping an arm on the wall over her head, he dipped his head in an attempt to kiss her. She raised her hand at the same time an arm snaked around BJ's throat and jerked him back.

"You heard the lady, junior," crooned a soft male voice inches from his ear. "Get out of her face, and go sleep it off." The man held out a hand. "Give me the beer."

Billy's bravado fled with the soft-spoken warning. He pushed the bottle into the outstretched hand, turned and made his way down the hallway.

Faith hadn't realized how fast her heart was beating as she pulled off her cap and slumped against the closet door to collect her wits. She forced a smile. "Thank you."

Cursing softly to himself, Ethan McMillan watched his godson's retreat. Billy had begun acting out after his father ordered him back to New York from Florida. WJ had received a veiled death threat that targeted his son after WJ had signed a much-talked-about new artist to his label. However, Billy refused to allow his father's bodyguards to monitor his every move, and the nineteen-year-old sought to punish WJ by openly smoking, drinking and now sexually harassing women.

The rumors spreading throughout the hip-hop community claimed that WJ had lured an up-and-coming hip-hop phenom away from a rival record label by offering him an unheard-of sum with perks usually reserved for multi-platinum-selling artists.

William Raymond, Jr., had made a name for himself as a maverick in the music industry when he set up his own label to compete with Sony, Atlantic and Columbia Records before he'd celebrated his thirtieth birthday. In the two decades that followed, he'd signed artists whose debut albums went platinum while earning a Grammy for Producer of the Year three times. His prominence and wealth increased accordingly.

"Are you okay?" Ethan asked, turning around and looking at the woman for the first time. His eyes widened in astonishment as he stared at her. Although she hadn't worn any makeup, he found her breathtakingly beautiful.

Her flawless dark skin shimmered with a healthy glow. Her short hairstyle that wouldn't have worked for most women was perfect for her. Her large eyes, tilting at the corners, were hypnotic, and her short straight nose complemented a pair of high cheekbones and small chin. His admiring gaze lingered on her lush parted lips.

Faith patted her chest in an attempt to calm herself. "Yes." The word came out in a breathless whisper.

It was her turn to stare at the man who'd interrupted Billy Raymond's unsolicited advances. He was tall, at least six inches taller than her five-eight height, and startlingly attractive. She wasn't able to pinpoint his age, but his smooth tawny brown skin belied the profusion of gray in his close-cropped hair. His sparkling sherry-colored eyes reminded Faith of newly minted pennies. With his black suit, shoes, tie and white shirt, she wondered if he, too, was also a member of WJ's security team.

"Are you certain?" Ethan asked. His deep voice was low, soothing.

Faith smiled. "Very certain."

"Do you want me to speak to Mr. Raymond about his son?"

"No. That won't be necessary. I was just leaving." She opened one of the closets, unbuttoned the tunic and dropped it and the toque into a large wicker basket. Less than a minute later she'd belted her coat around her waist and slung her bag over her shoulder.

Ethan reached for her elbow. "I'll escort you downstairs."

Faith met his steady gaze. "That won't be necessary."

"I believe it is necessary, Miss…"

"Faith Whitfield," she supplied.

Ethan smiled, attractive lines fanning out around his

eyes and dimples winking in his handsome face like thumb-prints. He extended his hand. "Ethan McMillan." He wasn't disappointed when she placed her hand in his. "Ready?"

"Yes." Tightening his gentle grip, he led her back through the kitchen to the elevator.

Faith nodded to the guard. He returned her nod with one of his own, and waved to Ethan.

"You can let go of my hand now," Faith said softly once the elevator door closed behind them.

Releasing her hand, Ethan moved over to the opposite wall and pushed his hands inside the pockets of his trousers. "You're a chef." His question was more a statement.

"Actually I'm a pastry chef," she corrected. Ethan smiled again, and Faith couldn't believe how much the gesture transformed his face from stoic to irresistibly captivating.

"Yum, yum…the dessert lady. What did you make?"

She couldn't help smiling. "A little bit of this and a little bit of that."

Ethan's sweeping raven-black eyebrows lifted slightly. "Are you always this mysterious?"

"No. It's just that I'd like what I make to be a surprise."

"For whom?"

"For everyone attending the party."

His dimples winked again as Ethan lowered his head and stared at the toes of his highly polished shoes. "I suppose I'll have to wait to be surprised just like everyone else." The descent to the lobby ended and the elevator door opened with a soft swoosh. Cupping Faith's elbow, he escorted her to the lobby. "Do you have a car?"

"No. I'm taking a taxi."

"Where are you going?"

"I'm going home."

"Where's home?" he asked.

"The West Village." Normally she would've taken the subway downtown but not today. She wanted to go home and take a nap before tonight's party.

"Where in the West Village?"

"Patchin Place."

Ethan was familiar with the block of small, fashionable residences built in the mid-nineteenth century. He gestured to the doorman, who rushed over to the open the door. "Please hail us a taxi." The light above the canopy came on as Faith and Ethan waited in the lobby.

A brilliant winter sun coming through the glass doors revealed what Faith hadn't been able to discern in the penthouse's artificial lighting. Ethan was even more attractive than he originally seemed. His silver-flecked hair afforded him an air of sophistication without adding age to his unlined face. Her breath caught for several seconds when he lowered his gaze to reveal the longest, thickest pair of eyelashes she'd ever seen on a man.

"What time are you coming back?" Ethan asked when the doorman's shrill whistle signaled a passing taxi.

"I should be here around six-thirty." The cocktail hour was scheduled for six and dinner at seven.

A streak of yellow skidded to a halt at the curb on West End Avenue as the doorman quickly opened the taxi door. Ethan escorted Faith to the taxi, waiting as she got in. Reaching into his pocket, he took a bill from a silver clip, and handed it to the cabbie.

"Take the lady to Patchin Place in the West Village."

The address had barely left his lips when the cabbie took off in a burst of speed. Ethan stood on the sidewalk, oblivious to the frigid air coming off the Hudson River. Emotions he hadn't felt in years attacked him as he went back into the building, scowling. He'd thought himself immune to pretty faces, but it was obvious that his conversation with Faith Whitfield had proven otherwise. His frown deepened when he recalled the image of Billy harassing Faith. Once the teenager sobered up, he planned to have a man-to-man talk with his young cousin.

Faith leaned forward in her seat. "You can let me out here," she told the taxi driver as she handed him a bill through the open partition.

The cabbie, chewing on the stub of an unlit cigar, shook his head. "Keep your money, lady. Your boyfriend already paid me."

A frown furrowed her smooth forehead. "Boyfriend?"

"Yeah, lady. The guy who put you in my taxi." He shifted on his seat and glared at Faith. "Are you getting out, or do you want me to take you somewhere else?"

"I'm getting out," she said as she pushed open the door, got out and closed the door behind her.

She walked to the entrance of a three-story walk-up, unlocked the front door and made her way up three flights to her studio apartment. Her cousin Simone complained about the high rent Faith paid to live in Manhattan, but she loved historic Greenwich Village with its bohemian life-style, quirky residents, charming row houses, hidden alleys and narrow streets. It was after dark that the Village truly came alive with late-night coffeehouses, jazz clubs and cafés. Her apartment took up less than a thousand square feet of living space, but she'd learned to maximize every foot, and the result was inviting as well as charming.

She opened the door, and warmth curled around her

like a rising mist. When she flipped a wall switch, two table lamps flooded the apartment with soft yellow light. She'd lived in the building for three years, and there was never a day when she didn't have heat or hot water.

Her home had become a retreat where she came to relax, eat and sleep. A compact utility kitchen ran the length of a brick wall, and a cushioned window seat with storage drawers spanned the width of three tall, narrow windows providing the perfect place for her to curl up to read or while away hours watching her favorite movie on the flat-screen television on its stand resting on a bleached pine drop-leaf table. The pale color was repeated in the other furnishings: a claw-foot pedestal table with four matching petit-point-cushioned pull-up chairs, an antique sleigh bed in an alcove that had been a walk-in closet, an antique-white armoire and a love seat covered with Haitian cotton.

Former tenants hadn't removed the shelves in the converted closet, so Faith stacked them with books, linens and a collection of priceless crystal vases. An antique clothespress doubled as a bureau and vanity for items that normally would've been stored in the minuscule bathroom that had been updated to include a basin, commode and shower stall.

The telephone rang as she slipped out of her coat. Hanging it on a coat tree, Faith picked up the cordless receiver off the kitchen countertop. She smiled when she saw the name on the display. "Yes, Tessa. I'm hosting Monday's get-together."

Her cousin's sultry laugh came through the earpiece. "For you information, Miss Smarty Pants, I'm not calling about Monday night."

Cradling the receiver between her chin and shoulder, Faith leaned over and pulled off her boots. "What's going on, Tessa?"

"Are you free to go to Mount Vernon with me tomorrow?"

"What's happening in Mount Vernon?" she asked as she made her way into the bathroom to wash her hands.

"I'm bringing Micah with me so he can meet the family."

She paused drying her hands. "What aren't you telling me, cousin?"

"I got engaged last night!"

Faith hadn't realized she was screaming until Tessa pleaded with her to calm down. "I don't believe it, Tessa! Did he give you a ring? When am I going to meet your manly man?" Simone, who'd met Micah, described him as a *manly man*.

"Yes, he gave me a ring. Come with me tomorrow and you'll meet him."

Reaching for a towel, she dried her hands and walked out of the bathroom. "I can't make it tomorrow. I'm having brunch with Peter Demetrious, and I can't change the date or time because he's only going to be in New York for the weekend."

Faith had thought herself blessed when Tessa convinced the celebrated photographer to take pictures of her cake designs.

"What about tonight?"

"Tonight I have Savanna Raymond's engagement party. Why don't you bring Micah with you when you come Monday?"

"No, Faith. Mondays are for the girls, not girls and guys."

"Is it going to be that way after you're married?"

"My marrying Micah shouldn't change our bimonthly

get-togethers. Don't forget our mothers still get together with their girlfriends once a month without their husbands."

"You're right, Tessa. Nothing should change that drastically, just because you're changing your name."

"I'm not changing my name to Sanborn."

"You plan to keep your maiden name?"

"No, Faith. I'm going to hyphenate it like Micah's sister did. She's now Bridget Sanborn-Cohen, and when I marry Micah I'll become Theresa Whitfield-Sanborn."

"How is baby girl doing?" Faith knew within minutes of meeting Bridget Sanborn for the first time that she'd been spoiled *and* indulged. And it was obvious that her new husband would continue to indulge her. When Bridget and Seth sampled fillings and conferred with each other about the overall design for their wedding cake, Seth had always deferred to Bridget.

"Micah said Bridget and Seth are still honeymooning in Tahiti. After two weeks they're going to Fiji for another week."

Faith smiled. "Nice." Her smile faded. What she would give for a few days in a warm climate. It didn't have to be the South Pacific. A weekend in the Caribbean, or even South Florida would do quite nicely.

"Bridget gave me a gift to give to you. I'll bring it when I come Monday."

"She didn't have to give me anything. After all, I charged her top dollar for the cake and the individual cakes she gave as favors."

"She said it's just a little token for making her day so special given such short notice."

Faith smiled again. Tessa had successfully coordinated a formal New Year's Eve wedding in only ten weeks. "Isn't that what Signature Bridals do? You've established a reputation of performing wedding miracles."

"I couldn't have done it without you and Simone. You know I want you to design my cake."

"Have you set a date?"

"We've decided on the last Saturday in June. And of course it will be held at Whitfield Caterers."

Faith nodded even though her cousin couldn't see her. Their fathers were closing their catering business at the end of August to open a bowling alley the following spring. "You know Daddy and Uncle Malcolm have been waiting a long time to host another Whitfield wedding."

"Well, they won't have to wait too long because June is less than six months away. I'm going to let you go because you have a party tonight. I'll see you Monday."

"Monday," Faith repeated before ending the call. She turned off one of the table lamps.

Walking over to the alcove, she set the alarm on the radio, undressed and got into bed. She couldn't believe it. Her cousin was getting married. Tessa, who hadn't dated in years, had fallen in love and planned to marry the brother of one of her clients. At least one of them had found her prince.

A groan escaped Faith's lips as she turned her face into the softness of the pillow. The instant Edith Whitfield found out that another one of her nieces was getting married, Faith was going to have to put up with her mother's constant haranguing about why couldn't she find "a nice boy to settle down with."

She'd lost count of the number of times she'd informed her mother that she didn't want a *boy* but a *man*. And just because they were male and over eighteen, that didn't necessarily make them *men*.

At thirty, she'd had more than her share of dates and a couple of what she'd considered serious relationships. In fact, she'd kissed so many frogs trying to find her own prince that she was afraid she'd get warts.

Her dating woes ended the year before when she made a resolution not to date again until she found Mr. Right. She'd tired of the Mr. Right Now or Mr. for the Moment. And if she never found her prince, then she was content to live out her life as an independent single woman.

All thoughts of princes and marriage faded when she drifted off to sleep.

Chapter 2

Faith walked out of her building and came to an abrupt stop when she recognized the man leaning against the bumper of a late-model Lincoln Town Car. Her eyes widened as he straightened and came over to meet her.

"What are you doing here?" she asked Ethan.

He flashed his sensual, dimpled smile and reached out to take her arm. "I've come to drive you uptown."

"Did WJ tell you to pick me up?"

Ethan steered her over to the car and opened the rear door. Waiting until Faith was seated comfortably on the leather seat, he closed the door and came around to sit behind the wheel. It wasn't until he left the narrow street and pulled out into traffic that he spoke again.

"Yes, he did."

She stared at the back of his head. "I could've just as

easily taken a cab." Faith wondered if Ethan had told WJ about his son's attempt to kiss her.

"What happened to 'thank you'?"

"Say what?"

"Isn't door-to-door car service in Manhattan better than trying to hail a cab at night in the middle of winter?"

The heat from her blush intensified. Ethan McMillan had just verbally spanked her. "Thank you, Ethan."

Ethan schooled his features to stop the grin parting his lips. "You're welcome, Faith." He glanced up at the rear-view mirror. "Your face looks very nice."

She couldn't stop the blush heating her cheeks. "A little makeup can work miracles."

He shook his head. "A miracle cannot improve perfection. I'm sure men have told you that you're very beautiful."

Faith stared out the side window. "Men have told me a lot of things."

"Do you believe them?"

"No."

"Why don't you believe them?" Ethan asked, slowing down and stopping at a red light.

"Because it's easier for them to lie than admit the truth."

"So, you have trust issues with men?"

If she'd taken a taxi uptown she wouldn't be having this conversation with her driver. She didn't know Ethan McMillan, and she had no intention of spilling her guts to a complete stranger.

"I'd rather not answer that question."

"You don't have to, Faith. The fact that you don't want to answer it tells me that you do." He drove several blocks in silence then asked, "Why did you decide to become a pastry chef?"

Faith smiled. The conversation had segued to a topic less personal in nature. "After graduating culinary school I worked in a restaurant for two years."

"Did you like it?"

She shook her head. "Even though I liked cooking what I hated was the frenetic pace of cooking for hundreds every night. There was always chaos when a dish didn't turn out right or when the head chef got in our faces because we weren't working fast enough. One night I decided I'd had enough. I handed in my resignation and went back to school to specialize in cake decorating. Now I work at my own pace and if I ruin something I can usually salvage it."

"If the icing doesn't come out right, don't you throw the cake away?"

"No. I usually remove it and start over."

"How long does it take to decorate a wedding cake?"

"It depends on the size of the cake, the decorations and accessories. However, making bows, flowers and ribbons are the most time-consuming."

Ethan concentrated on driving as he detected a thawing in Faith's tone. It was no longer guarded, but soft and seductive as she talked about cakes with specific themes. The ride ended much too soon as he maneuvered into the building's underground garage.

Once inside the elevator, he inserted a key into the slot for the penthouse. Leaning against a wall, he stared openly at Faith's enchanting profile, finding everything about her breathtakingly stunning. Her short curly black hair hugged her head like a soft cap, and the light dusting of makeup served to enhance the rich, dark hues of her satiny mahogany skin. Mascara, flatteringly applied eye shadow and a glossy wine-colored lipstick on her sexy, lush lips held him hypnotized.

She'd replaced her jeans, boots and wrap coat with a bottle-green, three-quarter shearling coat, a navy-blue pencil skirt, ending at her knees, matching sheer hose and suede pumps that added another three inches to her dramatic height.

The elevator stopped at the penthouse, and he moved forward as the door opened. Ethan looped an arm around her waist as if he'd performed the gesture countless times and led her past the small crowd waiting to get into the penthouse. The Raymonds had mailed out specialized invitations with bar codes that were scanned upon arrival.

"This is why WJ wanted me to pick you up," he whispered close to Faith's ear.

Smiling up at him over her shoulder, she mouthed a thank-you.

He escorted her past the kitchen to the hallway where she could hang up her coat. The distinctive, soulful voice of a new artist who'd signed with WJ's record company floated from speakers concealed throughout the penthouse. The Raymonds had planned for a sit-down dinner, followed by Savanna opening her gifts, then dancing under the stars in the enclosed solarium.

"Will you save me a dance?"

With wide eyes, Faith halted unbuttoning her coat. "No!"

Ethan leaned closer, his warm breath sweeping over her ear. "Why not?"

She shrugged out of her coat. "Have you forgotten that I'm not a guest but hired help?"

"Then that makes two of us, Faith Whitfield. Hired help need fun, too." He ignored her soft gasp. "All I want is one little itty-bitty dance."

"No. Not here, Ethan."

"Where, Faith?"

Why, she thought, was Ethan pressuring her to dance with him? "I'll let you know." She saw a glimmer of anticipation in his eyes at the same time a smile softened his generous masculine mouth.

He winked at her. "Okay."

Faith smiled up at him through her lashes. "Now, get out of here so I can get some work done." William and Linda Raymond had paid her quite well to prepare the desserts for their daughter's party.

Ethan gave her a sharp salute, took a step backward and spun around on his heels like a soldier at a dress parade, leaving Faith smiling at his retreating ramrod-straight back.

Wearing a white tunic over her white silk blouse, Faith walked into the kitchen but quickly backpedaled to avoid being knocked over by a waiter hoisting a tray on his shoulder. Other waiters followed with trays of hot and cold hors d'oeuvres. Another carried a crate filled with bottles of wine and fruit juice.

A young woman tapped her arm. "Are you Faith Whitfield?"

"Yes, I am. Why?"

"Mr. Payton asked that you see him as soon as you arrived."

"Thanks for letting me know."

She entered the kitchen to find Kurt with a towel slung over one shoulder, peering at the meat thermometer inserted into a generous cut of prime rib. "You wanted to see me?"

The chef let out an audible sigh. "Thank goodness you're here. I need you to fill in as my sous chef tonight.

Please, Faith," he said quickly when he saw her stunned expression. "The person I'd hired to assist me called about half an hour ago to tell me he has the flu." He grabbed her hand, kissing the back of it. "I wouldn't ask you if I weren't desperate. I'll pay you—whatever you want, just please help me out here."

"It's been a long time since I've—"

"It's like riding a bike or having sex," he interrupted. He kissed her hand again. "You never forget."

Faith rolled her eyes at him. "Let go of my hand, Kurt. I need to cover my head."

"Bless you, my child."

"The hand, Kurt," she warned softly.

Kurt was right. After removing her desserts from the refrigerator and placing them on a cart that would be rolled into the dining room later that evening, Faith found herself at the industrial stove braising, sautéing and stirring as if it were something she did every day. She saw another side of Kurt's easygoing personality. The chef ran his kitchen like a drill sergeant, barking orders to the waitstaff. However, his tone softened whenever he asked her to prepare something for him.

She'd finished filling gravy boats when a waitress rushed in, wringing her hands. "We don't have any fish plates."

Kurt mumbled a savage expletive under his breath. He'd been so busy serving meat and chicken that he'd totally forgotten about those who'd requested fish. "Faith, can you get the tray of fish from the refrigerator and prepare a sole meunière?"

"Are they marinated?" she asked him.

"Yes."

The fact that the fillets were seasoned would save time in preparing the fish dish served with a butter and lemon sauce. She took the tray from the refrigerator, heated a pan with unsalted butter, then placed them skin side up and fried each side until they were golden brown; she placed them on a heated plate. All of Faith's culinary training returned when she drained off the butter for frying, wiped out the pan with a towel before returning it to the heat. Chilled cubed butter was cooked until golden and frothy. She removed the pan from the heat, adding the juice of fresh lemons. While the mixture still bubbled, she spooned it over the fish. A quick garnish with parsley and lemon wedges and the dish was ready to be served.

"How many want fish entrées?" she asked the waitress who'd stood off to the side waiting for her to finish.

"Six."

Reaching for six plates, she quickly spooned slices of fish onto them, adding lemon wedges and a garnish of parsley to each.

Then she lost track of time as she assisted Kurt slicing prime rib, halving Cornish hens, adding a medley of steamed vegetables and seasoned roasted potatoes to plates as the waiters loaded their trays with the entrées. And it wasn't until all the guests sitting in the formal dining room were served that she found a stool in a corner, sat down and dabbed her damp face with a cloth napkin. The smell of brewing coffee overpowered the scents left from the beef, fish and chicken.

Kurt was right about her not forgetting her former training, but it was the noise and chaos that went along with working in a restaurant that reminded Faith why she'd elected to become a pastry chef.

The chef handed her a bottle of chilled water. "You're fantastic, Faith Whitfield. I told you we would work well together. How would you like to be my on-call assistant?"

Faith took a long swallow of water, the cool liquid bathing her throat. She gave Kurt a withering look. "No."

"No?"

"Which part of the word don't you understand?" she asked.

He moved closer. "It would be no more than twice a year. WJ usually hosts an open house for the Super Bowl and a pre- or postcelebration Grammy Award get-together."

"No, no and no. I run a bake shop, I have personal clients and I'm involved with my cousin's wedding business. I couldn't assist even if I wanted to."

Kurt winked at Faith. "You can't blame a bloke for trying." He patted her back. "I'm going to fix us something to eat while there's a lull. What can I get for you?"

"Chicken and veggies."

Faith was still sitting in the kitchen when Ethan walked in. He'd removed his tie and suit jacket. And, despite the lateness of the hour, his shirt was completely wrinkle-free. She couldn't pull her gaze away from the way his trousers fit his slim waist and hips as if he'd had them tailored expressly for his lean physique.

"Have you eaten?" she asked softly.

Ethan forced himself not to stare at Faith's long legs. She sat on the high stool, legs crossed at the knees and her skirt riding up her thighs. The heat in the kitchen was stifling, yet the sheen on her face made her skin appear dewy, satiny.

"I was just coming to get a plate."

"What do you want, Mac?" Kurt asked as he reached for a clean plate for Faith.

"What do you have?"

"Prime rib, chicken and fish."

"I'll have the fish."

Kurt turned on an exhaust fan and prepared plates for Faith, Ethan and himself. The three moved over to a serving table and sat down.

Ethan bit into a tender piece of fish. He nodded to Kurt. "The fish is delicious."

"I can't take credit for the fish. You have to thank Faith."

Ethan looked at her as if she were a stranger. "You cooked?"

The slight frown that'd formed between his eyes deepened as Kurt explained his dilemma. "Savanna's guests would still be waiting to eat if Faith hadn't stepped up to the plate to help me."

Ethan lowered his head, his gaze fixed on his plate. "WJ hired her to bake, not cook." There was a silken thread of censure in his statement.

"I'll pay her for her time," Kurt countered angrily.

Ethan waved his hand. "Don't bother. WJ will take care of it."

Faith listened intently to the interchange between the two men. They were discussing her as if she were invisible. "I didn't help out because I expected to be paid."

Ethan glared at Faith. He'd just left Billy's room after reading him the riot act as to how he could've been charged with sexual harassment. His young cousin had refused to leave his room, saying that his sister "had enough people grinning up in her face," and because his parents hadn't wanted to have a family row and spoil Savanna's engagement party they'd left him sulking in his room.

When WJ informed him that Billy wouldn't be joining the

family, Ethan told WJ that he would talk to his younger
cousin. At first Billy refused to unlock the door, but when
Ethan told him that if he had to kick open the door, then
William Raymond III would be forced to prove his manhood.
Within seconds of his threat Billy opened the door.

At thirty-eight, Ethan was twice Billy's age, and even
though he hadn't fathered any children, in that instant he'd
become a surrogate father, listening to his teenage cousin
blame his namesake for screwing up his life.

Ethan didn't say anything until Billy finished spewing
his venom, then promised him that he would talk to his
father in an attempt to come up with a strategy that would
prove amenable to both William Raymonds. So far, he
hadn't thought of anything because his thoughts were
occupied with the image of Faith Whitfield—her face,
voice and body.

He turned his attention to Faith. "Whether you expected
to be paid is irrelevant. You *will* be paid for cooking." He
finished eating, rose to his feet, looked at Kurt, then Faith.
"Thank you for dinner."

"I'm sorry you had to get caught up in this," Kurt said,
apologizing to Faith once they were alone.

She leaned closer. "Why is Ethan blowing this up when
it's not even necessary?"

"Maybe because he's family."

Her curving eyebrows lifted. "Family?"

Kurt almost laughed when he saw Faith's expression.
"You didn't know that Mac and WJ were related?"

A rush of heat stung her face. "But…but he told me that
he's hired help."

This time Kurt did laugh. "You, me, the housekeepers
and the guys you see standing around packing heat are

hired help. Ethan McMillan and William Raymond, Jr., are first cousins."

Faith recovered enough to ask, "What's with Ethan playing chauffeur?"

Kurt shook his head. "I know nothing about that arrangement. Mac showed up the day after the news got out that someone was out to whack Billy Junior."

She wanted to question Kurt further about Ethan McMillan but held her tongue now that she was aware that Ethan was related to her client. He'd told her that he was hired help, yet something should've alerted her when he came up behind Billy and defused what could've become an embarrassing scenario. Billy hadn't challenged Ethan when he probably would've defied one of his father's employees.

She wanted to know more about the mysterious man with the X-rated dimpled smile who'd asked that she dance with him. She didn't know whether he was married or single, a father or a baby's daddy, but that wasn't important, because after tonight she probably would never see Ethan McMillan again.

Faith never saw a bride on her wedding day, or interacted with her family members. Most times she scheduled a delivery for the wedding cake hours before the reception. Many of her cakes, baked in tiers, were packaged separately and then painstakingly put together with the assistance of one, and sometime two, of her employees.

She'd scheduled a time with the banquet manager at Tavern on the Green to set up Savanna Raymond's three-tiered cake at noon for a two o'clock reception. Later that afternoon she would deliver another cake to a Long Island country club for a wedding ceremony scheduled for six in the evening. No, she mused, the world wasn't going to stop spinning on its axis if Faith Whitfield didn't give Ethan McMillan his "one little itty-bitty dance."

All too soon the calm ended when the waiters returned to the kitchen. Dinner was over.

Chapter 3

Savanna Raymond's fiancé touched her arm to get her attention as the dessert cart was rolled into the dining room. She covered her mouth with her hand when the large heart-shaped chocolate-and-red-currant torte was placed in front of her. Platters of candies with exotic fillings, butter cookies, truffles, chocolate-covered fruit and petit fours were set on the tables, much to everyone's delight.

Savanna, a very pretty, full-figured, twenty-five-year-old elementary schoolteacher with a flawless café-au-lait complexion and glossy black chemically straightened shoulder-length hair, stared numbly at the profusion of chocolate confectionery, her eyes welling with tears.

Her fiancé shook his head in amazement. Tall, studious-looking geneticist Dr. Roland Benson threw back his head and laughed loudly. "Baby, you're going to OD on all this chocolate."

Linda Raymond smiled at her future son-in-law. "Don't worry about Savanna overdosing, because she's going to have plenty of help." Linda and Savanna looked more like sisters than mother and daughter, while Billy was a younger version of his father. There came a chorus of "amen" and "you ain't lying" from several of the invited guests.

Faith leaned over and handed Roland a sharp knife. She'd covered the handle with a napkin. "Why don't you and your fiancée get in some practice making the first cut? Then, I'll take it from there." She'd made the torte large enough to serve at least forty. Savanna placed her hand atop Roland's and the moist blade of the knife sliced cleanly through the layers of ganache, frozen raspberry and white cream filling and sponge cake.

Faith took the knife from them. "I have gift bags you can give to your guests before they leave. They're chocolates in edible packaging wrapped in cellophane." It'd taken countless hours and skill to make the rectangular pieces of chocolate, then assemble them, using tempered couverture in a pastry bag to glue them together. All the tops were striped with either dark or white chocolate.

"I also made one for you and your fiancé to share with your parents," she continued in a hushed tone. The smaller rectangular boxes each contained eight pieces of candy made with walnut caramel, while the larger round box held sixty in various shapes that were filled with mocha and nutty creams.

Pushing back her chair, Savanna stood up and hugged Faith tightly. "Thanks so much, Miss Whitfield. I can't tell you how special you've made this day for me."

"This is only the dress rehearsal for your big day."

Savanna fanned her face with her hand. "I just hope I make it."

"Don't worry, you'll make it," Faith reassured Savanna as she picked up the torte, turned and walked in the direction of the kitchen.

Leaning against one of the massive columns separating the living room from the dining room, Ethan crossed his arms over his chest and watched Faith with Savanna. Everything about her radiated confidence—of herself and her place in the world. She claimed she preferred baking to cooking, yet her fish entrée was extraordinary.

He'd found her utterly feminine, something that was missing in the women with whom he'd become involved since his divorce. And although Faith Whitfield looked nothing like his ex-wife, there was something about her that reminded him of Justine. What bothered him was that his attraction to both had been instantaneous.

He occasionally dated women who tried too hard to impress him, while the ones with the pretty faces and gorgeous bodies were usually too insipid to keep his attention for more than a few hours.

Waiting until Faith left the room, Ethan made his way over to William Raymond. "I need to talk to you," he said in a low, quiet voice.

William patted the empty chair his wife had just vacated. "Sit down, Mac." Ethan complied. Vertical lines appeared between the deep-set dark eyes of the man who'd amassed a small fortune because of his innate gift for recognizing musical talent. "You've heard something about…?" His words trailed off.

William had spent most of his life avoiding trouble, but at fifty-four trouble had come knocking at his door in the form of a rival who'd threatened his son. It wouldn't have unnerved William if the threat had been directed at him. He'd grown up on New York City's mean streets, learning how to survive well enough to avoid becoming a statistic. But someone had gotten to him, struck his Achilles' heel when they put his son's life—heir to his music empire—in jeopardy.

"What's up, Mac?"

"What do you think of sending Billy to Cresson to stay with my folks? He could transfer his credits from Bethune-Cookman to Mount Aloysius and get his degree there." Billy had just completed the first semester of his sophomore year. A look of uncertainty crossed William's face as he and Ethan regarded each other.

"Aloysius isn't a historically black college," Ethan continued, "and west-central Pennsylvania isn't Florida, but I don't think anyone would think of looking for him in the Allegheny Mountains." He'd made the suggestion because his parents were professors at the college.

William's face brightened as he ran his fingers over his mustache and goatee. Nodding, he crooned, "It could be you're on to something."

"It's only a suggestion."

"I like your suggestion, Mac. Now, all I have to do is convince my son that sending him to live with his great-aunt and -uncle would be in his best interest."

Ethan patted his cousin's hard, muscled shoulder under a custom-made silk and wool blend suit jacket. "I believe it would go better if I talk to him." He knew Billy resented his father too much to listen to anything he had to say right now, even if it meant protecting his life. He leaned closer. "There's something else you should know."

The music mogul listened to his younger cousin, then

nodded in agreement. "Thanks for letting me know. I'll take care of it."

Ethan felt a measure of satisfaction. He'd come up with a plan for his godson, but if Billy rejected his suggestion, then he would have to come up with an alternative solution. And he knew if WJ hadn't been so focused on seeing his daughter married, he would've come down hard on Billy for his behavior.

Ethan hadn't come to stay at the West End Avenue penthouse to protect his godson from what was potentially a real threat, but rather from his father's explosive temper. Growing up, he'd witnessed the hurt WJ had inflicted on anyone who'd dared to cross him.

Faith slipped into her coat and gathered her handbag. She was ready to go home. She managed to slip out without encountering Kurt or Ethan, taking the elevator to the lobby. Someone was exiting a taxi as she walked out of the building. The doorman's whistle stopped the driver from pulling away from the curb.

She got in, gave the bearded man her address, closed her eyes, then settled back against the seat for the short ride to the Village. The cabbie drove as if he was training for the NASCAR circuit, and Faith didn't draw a normal breath until she found herself on terra firma outside her building.

The harrowing experience came close to making her swear off riding in New York City taxis for a very long time.

The ride, the lingering smell of the food clinging to her body and the image of Ethan McMillan's sensual smile were forgotten when she brushed her teeth, showered and crawled into bed.

Other than an early-morning jog, attending mass and

sharing brunch with Peter Demetrious, Faith planned to take advantage of the rest of her Sunday to do absolutely *nothing!*

Sunday dawned with an overcast sky and below-freezing temperatures. Dressed in a pair of sweats, a baseball cap, short jacket and running shoes, Faith inserted earbuds in her ears and began walking north, increasing her pace each time she crossed another street until she was jogging at a pace that didn't leave her feeling winded. Although she preferred reading a book to listening to them, she made the exception when jogging.

As the narrator read a fairly explicit love scene, it reminded Faith why she'd stopped reading romance novels. What she didn't want was to be reminded of her resolution not to date, because if she kissed one more frog she would swear off men altogether. The reason she'd downloaded the audio book to her iPod was because it was advertised as a mystery. But, damn! she mused, did the author have to be so descriptive when the female detective, having denied having feelings for her partner, finally went to bed with him? By the time Faith reached the next block the erotic scene was over.

She jogged to Chelsea, stopped at a Starbucks to sit and enjoy a latte before retracing her route. Every time she jogged she varied her route. Most times she stopped in Soho, Tribeca, Chinatown, Little Italy, the East Village or the Lower East Side.

When the heat and humidity became too oppressive to jog, she set off on leisurely walks. For someone who'd grown up in the suburbs, the bright lights, large crowds, noise and pulsing energy of New York City enraptured her in a magical world that she never wanted to leave.

Even if she'd wanted to move out of the city she couldn't because she'd invested too much money in Let Them Eat Cake, and the small patisserie, conveniently located three blocks from her apartment building, was now showing a profit. She also had to consider her employees—two full-time clerks, part-time baker and now her assistant. Six months ago she'd expanded the shop's hours of operation from four to five days a week. However, she did make an exception for weeks during Thanksgiving, Christmas and Valentine's Day. The only time she opened on Sunday was for Mother's Day.

Faith returned home in time to shower and make it to the twelve o'clock mass. She'd attended an all-girl private Catholic school from grades one through twelve, and going to mass was a ritual that had become as natural to her as breathing.

Sleet had begun falling when she left the church to hail a taxi to take her to the Ambassador Grill, a restaurant in the United Nations Plaza Hotel, touted to serve an extraordinary Sunday lobster-and-champagne brunch buffet. The restaurant was a favorite of Peter Demetrious. He was waiting for her when she arrived, and within minutes they were shown to a table.

He was shorter in person than he appeared in photographs, his full head of hair a shocking white, and the minute lines crisscrossing his weather-beaten face reminded her of a map. Faith had researched his background on the Internet and learned that the celebrated photographer, the only child of a Greek father and Italian mother, was born in San Francisco, and currently made his home in Southern California. In several articles written about him he admitted his obsession with photography began when an uncle gave him a

Brownie camera for his eighth birthday; half a century later his passion hadn't waned.

Over flutes of mimosas and fluffy omelets, Faith outlined the concept for the coffee-table book as Peter Demetrious studied her face as if she were a photographic subject, his sharp, penetrating black eyes missing nothing.

"When's your deadline?" he asked.

"June thirtieth," Faith replied.

Peter removed a small leather-bound diary from his jacket pocket, flipping pages. The creases in his forehead deepened. "How many cakes do you want me to photograph?"

Faith touched a napkin to the corners of her mouth. "I'm not certain. What I'd like to do is separate the book into themes—birthdays, holidays, weddings and special occasions like sweet sixteen, engagement, new baby and anniversaries. Then there are the religious themes—christening, communion, bar and bat mitzvah."

"Give me a number, Faith."

"I estimate between eighty and one hundred. The publisher has projected a 240-page book, and that includes text, recipes and credits."

Peter stared at the pastry chef as if she'd suddenly taken leave of her senses. "You're going to bake one hundred cakes before the end of June?"

She nodded, smiling. "It's not impossible. If I bake five or six a week, then there's no reason why I wouldn't be able to make my deadline." Faith knew it wasn't impossible now that she had an assistant. "Do you have a date for the shoot?"

Peter stared at a page in his diary. "I'm going to be back in New York for several weeks in late April." He flipped a few more pages. "And I also have a full week in mid-June."

Pulling her cell phone from her handbag, Faith turned

it on. She'd missed a call because she always turned it off before entering church. Activating the calendar feature, she scrolled through the months. The end of April meant that she had at least sixteen weeks to bake and decorate the cakes. A smile softened her mouth. Peter had given her plenty of time.

"I'll have them ready for you," she confidently.

"Will they keep?" the photographer asked.

Faith nodded. "Yes. They'll be frozen solid and definitely not fit for human consumption, but I'll spray them with a waxy substance before you photograph them to give them a fresh look."

"Where are you going to store them?"

"Some I'll store in the freezer in my shop, and the others in the freezer of a friend's restaurant."

She'd called a friend who owned and operated a restaurant before she signed the book contract to ask if she could rent space in one of her walk-in freezers to store the cakes.

Peter's dark eyebrows lifted with this revelation. "It looks as if you've done your homework."

"Would you have agreed to collaborate with me if I hadn't done my research?"

"No, Faith. I'm too busy, and to be honest I don't need the money. I agreed to collaborate with you because I've never done anything like this, and I owe your cousin Tessa for contracting me to photograph the Fyles-Cooper wedding, which by the way will be in the next *InStyle Wedding* book."

If Peter owed Tessa, then Faith owed Tessa—big-time—for getting him to agree to photograph her cake designs. Tessa and Simone Whitfield were the sisters she'd never had, but somehow she got along better with Tessa than Simone.

"Where are you going to photograph them?"

Resting his elbows on the table, Peter leaned closer and lifted his bushy eyebrows. "I'll make arrangements to shoot them in a photography studio in Tribeca."

"Do want to take any outdoor shots?"

"No. The studio is filled with stock art and set decorations that we can use for interior and exterior shots."

Raising her flute, Faith touched it to Peter's. *"Cheers!"*

He raised his glass, grinning broadly. *"Il saluto!"* he countered in Italian.

They lingered at the restaurant for another half an hour, then Peter settled the bill and suggested they share a taxi. He got out in Tribeca while Faith continued on to the West Village.

It was exactly four when Faith walked into her apartment, ideas as to what cake designs she wanted Peter to photograph crowding her mind. She'd tried imagining what the book would look like on bookstore shelves or on coffee tables, and until she decorated the first cake the notions remained that—just a notion.

She'd grown up a dreamer—a weaver of fairy tales. Her parents thought she was going to be a writer because of the number of notebooks she'd filled up with childish stories. The day she celebrated her sixteenth birthday she wrote down three wishes in her diary: become a chef, write a cookbook and marry a prince before she turned twenty-five. Long ago she'd accepted the truth that not all dreams come true as scheduled, but she was satisfied knowing that two of the three had manifested.

Faith changed out of her pantsuit and into a pair of well-washed faded jeans, a long-sleeved tee and a pair of thick cotton socks. She checked her home phone for messages. Nothing. Then she remembered the missed call on her cell phone. Retrieving it, she tapped in her password and folded her body down onto the cushioned window seat.

She listened to the recorded message: "Faith, this is WJ. I was told that you helped Kurt in the kitchen last night. I wanted to speak to you but you were gone. I'm sending someone over to your place this afternoon to deliver a little something to show my gratitude for all you've done to make my daughter's engagement party so spectacular. The person should be at your place at four-thirty. If this is not a good time for you, then call me…"

The sound of the doorbell eclipsed the voice coming through the earpiece. Faith took a quick glance at the clock radio. It was 4:33. Whoever WJ was talking about was standing on the other side of her door.

She crossed the room and peered through the security eye. William Raymond's *someone* was no other than Ethan McMillan.

"Who is it?" she asked.

"Ethan McMillan."

Faith unlocked the door, coming face-to-face with the man with the sexy smile and seductive voice. He was dressed down in a pair of faded jeans, pullover sweater, lined bomber jacket and brown suede oxfords. Her pulse quickened. The man should've been arrested for exuding that much masculinity.

Her smile was slow in coming. "Hello, Ethan."

Ethan returned her smile, dimples winking at her. "Hello, Faith. Did WJ tell you I was coming?"

"No. He said *someone* was coming."

Ethan angled his head. "Well, I'm that someone."

"Do tell," she teased.

"I would've rung your intercom to let you know I was downstairs, but one of your neighbors let me in."

Faith opened the door wider. "Please come in."

Wiping his feet on the straw mat outside the door, he walked into warmth. Ethan glanced around the apartment. "This is really nice."

Closing and locking the door, she turned to stare at Ethan surveying her apartment. "Thank you. It's a little small, but I like it." Why, she chided herself, was she apologizing to him about the size of her studio?

Ethan shook his head. "It really isn't that small. There are plenty of New York City studio apartments half this size."

He turned to stare at Faith. It was if he were truly seeing her—all of her for the first time. Her jeans hugged her body like a second skin, outlining the sensual curves of her hips. She was slender, but not a raw-boned slender. With her height, face and body she probably was mistaken for a model.

Faith met Ethan's stare with one of her own. There was something about him that intrigued her, and she wanted to know more about him: his age, what he did for a living, other than being related to William Raymond, what was his association with the record mogul?

She blinked as if coming out of a trance. "You lied to me, Ethan McMillan."

His expression mirrored confusion. "What are you talking about?"

Folding her arms under her breasts, Faith gave him a saucy smile. "You told me you were hired help when in reality you're WJ's cousin."

A hint of a smile tugged at the corners of Ethan's mouth. "I didn't lie to you."

"Why didn't you tell me you and WJ were related?"

"You didn't ask," he countered.

Faith refused to relent. "And if I had asked would you have told me?"

"Why not? I may deny a few things, but never family."

"Lie or deny?"

"Deny, Faith." A slight frown distorted his handsome face. "It seems as if we're back to the topic of you not trusting men."

"This is not about me, Ethan," she retorted.

"Then exactly who is it about? It certainly can't be about me," Ethan said, answering his own question. "I was raised to tell the truth, and rather than lie I just won't say anything." He gestured to her. "Come on, Faith, ask me something."

"What do you do for WJ?"

"I'm his driver." He angled his head. "Now, may I ask you to do something for me?"

Something told her not to ask, but she did anyway. "That all depends what it is."

Ethan pointed to the coffeemaker on the kitchen's countertop. "Would you mind brewing me a cup of coffee? I've been on the road for the past twelve hours and I need a double shot of caffeine to keep my eyes open before I drive to New Jersey." He'd been awake for thirty hours, and he couldn't remember the last time he'd been that sleep deprived.

He'd talked to Billy about attending college in Pennsylvania, and much to the elder Raymond's shock, he'd agreed. It was only after Savanna's guests retreated to the rooftop solarium that Ethan and an armed bodyguard escorted Billy down the stairwell to the underground garage and into the Town Car.

Ethan had called his parents en route to let them know that their grandnephew would be staying with them until he completed his education or whoever had threatened his life was apprehended. He made it to Cresson, Pennsylvania, in record time, stayed long enough to see Billy settled in, then got back into the car for the return drive to New York.

He'd returned to his cousin's penthouse, shaved, showered and packed his clothes. Once he informed WJ that he was returning to his Englewood Cliffs, New Jersey, town house condo, his cousin asked that he deliver a letter to Faith Whitfield.

Faith saw a trace of fatigue etched on his face for the first time. His eyelids were drooping and his speech was slower. "Of course I don't mind. Let me hang up your jacket." He shrugged out of the leather jacket, handing it to her. He swayed before righting himself. Instinctively she reached out to steady him, but drew her hand back. "Why don't you lie down on the bed before you end up on the floor, and there's no way I'll be able to lift you."

A tired smile pulled one corner of Ethan's mouth upward. "Thanks."

He headed for the large bed in the alcove covered with a white comforter, shams, throw pillows and dust ruffle trimmed in lace. If he hadn't been so tired he would've turned his nose up at the frilly bed linens, but now it was like an oasis to a thirsty traveler.

He sat on the side of the bed, removed his shoes, then lay on the unabashedly feminine bed and exhaled a sigh of relief. Englewood Cliffs was right across the river from New York but as he lay staring up at an eave above the bed he doubted whether he would've been able to make the drive without being a danger to himself or other motorists.

Ethan closed his eyes, his chest rising and falling in a deep, even rhythm. "Would your boyfriend mind if I took you dancing?"

Faith was barely able to control her gasp of shock. She stopped pouring coffee beans into the grinder. Within seconds she recovered enough to say, "No."

"No, what? You don't have a boyfriend, or you don't want to go out with me?" His voice seemed to come from a long way off.

Her cheeks warmed with heat. "No to both."

Her answer pleased Ethan. He was more interested in knowing if Faith Whitfield had a boyfriend than taking her out, because if she was involved with someone, then that meant he'd have to retreat honorably.

"Thank you." The two words came out slurred.

Shifting, Faith stared at the tall man reclining on her bed. To say he was an enigma was putting it mildly. He'd asked her to go dancing with him, then acted as if she'd given him a reprieve when she turned him down.

"Thank you for what?"

"For your honesty and…"

"And what, Ethan?" There was no answer. "Ethan?" She called his name again and was greeted by soft snores.

Resting her hands on her hips, she glared at the figure lying sprawled across her bed, unable to believe he'd come to her apartment to sleep. If he was that tired, then she would've given him the address to several hotels in the area. He could've checked into the Washington Square Hotel for about one-fifty a night, or if he wanted luxury then there was the Marriott Financial Center at three to four hundred a night.

Faith smothered a curse under her breath as she pressed

a button on the grinder. The tantalizing smell of fresh coffee filled the air. She'd come home to relax, but that was thwarted because Ethan McMillan had commandeered her bed. She programmed the coffeemaker to begin brewing in three hours. That was all the time she was going to give the man sleeping in her bed before she'd wake him to send him on his way.

Chapter 4

Faith opened the window shutters, sat down on the window seat and stretched her legs along its length. The width of the seat was one of many reasons why she'd decided to rent the apartment. It provided additional seating, and the windows overlooked an alley wide enough to park at least half a dozen cars. During the warmer weather she opened them and sat out on the fire escape. It wasn't a traditional balcony or terrace, but served the same function.

Resting her back against an overstuffed pillow, she closed her eyes. What was it with the men who came to the homes of Whitfield women for the first time and ended up sharing their bed? She opened her eyes, staring at the falling snow piling up on the fire escape. Ethan *was* in her bed, even if she wasn't sharing it with him.

Tessa admitted that she'd shared her bed with Micah Sanborn the night he'd come to her home because of a blackout, and within a week knew that the Brooklyn A.D.A. was her prince.

Reaching for a book, Faith opened it to the last page she'd read. She chanced a quick glance at Ethan McMillan and shook her head. He wasn't a prince, but then he wasn't exactly a frog, either. He was more like a bad penny that kept turning up when she least expected. Focusing on the book, she forgot about the man in her bed and lost herself in the lives of the novel's characters.

The smell of brewing coffee wafted in Ethan's nostrils as he opened his eyes to semidarkness. The only light in the room came from a floor lamp near the windows. Sitting up, he swung his legs over the side of the bed, his gaze widening when he saw Faith on the window seat with her head at an odd angle.

His feet were silent on the floor as he neared her. A book lay open in her lap. It was apparent she'd fallen asleep while reading. Guilt assailed him when he realized he'd put her out of her bed. Checking his watch, he realized it was almost eight o'clock. When he'd asked Faith if he could lie down to wait for coffee, he hadn't thought he would end up sleeping for hours.

Ethan stood over Faith, staring openly at her and seeing up close what he hadn't noticed the day before. Her hands were delicately formed, the fingers long with tapered nails. There was a tiny beauty mark on her temple near her left eye. The yellow glow from the lamp highlighted the gold undertones in her flawless dark skin, which reminded him of minute particles of gold dust mixed with smooth dark milk chocolate.

His gaze moved lower to the rise and fall of her breasts

under the T-shirt, and within seconds he felt like a pervert spying on an unsuspecting woman. The sound of the coffee brewing was unusually loud in the quietness of the apartment. A gurgling noise indicated the brewing cycle had ended. Turning away from Faith, Ethan made his way to the kitchen to fortify himself with a cup of the brew that was certain to keep him alert long enough to make it home.

He found a large mug in an overhead cabinet, filling it to the brim. Resting a hip against the countertop, he sipped the steaming-hot coffee, the heat burning his throat and settling in his chest and belly like a soothing blanket.

Ethan hadn't lied to Faith when he'd told her that he liked her apartment. The pale colors and her choice of furnishings gave the space a lived-in look, unlike his that had been decorated by an interior-design firm. Once he'd closed on the luxury two-bedroom condominium, he hadn't had the time nor the patience to visit stores or shops looking for tables, lamps, beds or the other accessories that determined a room's personality. He told the decorator what he didn't like, and she took it from there. There were times when he felt as if he were walking into a furniture showroom, but for all of the time he spent there it was more than adequate.

He felt rather than saw Faith move, and he straightened from his lounging position. Smiling, he watched her come awake with the grace of a cat. He knew he'd frightened her when a small cry escaped her parted lips.

Blinking, Faith stared at the man standing in the shadows. "You woke up."

"So did you." Ethan gestured to the coffee in the carafe. "Would you like a cup?"

Faith couldn't believe his audacity. He was offering her *her* coffee in *her* own home! "You're really ballsy, aren't you?" When Ethan glanced down at the front of his jeans she wanted to disappear on the spot. "I didn't mean it that way."

Ethan didn't move. "How do you want me to interpret ballsy?"

"What I meant is cheeky, audacious and—"

"I get your meaning, Faith," he said, putting up a hand and cutting her off. "Now what have I done for you to get your back up?"

Swinging her legs off the window seat, Faith walked over and stood less than a foot from Ethan. His warmth and the lingering scent of his cologne had become an aphrodisiac, pulling her to him when the opposite was what she wanted. She wanted Ethan McMillan out of her home because everything about him was a sensual assault.

"I do the serving in my home."

"Now, that's a very selfish approach, Faith," he chastised in a soft tone. "If you were in my home I'd permit you to do whatever you wanted."

"That's where we're different, Ethan."

"You think so?"

"Yes."

He shook his head. "Wrong, Faith. We're more alike than dissimilar."

"Why would you say that? You don't know anything about me, or vice versa."

"What I do know and what I see I like."

This time Faith had no comeback. Clamping her jaw tightly, she refused to give him the satisfaction of admitting the same. Despite all of her protests, she also liked what she saw and what he'd shown her—arrogance notwithstanding.

"WJ said he gave you something to give me," she said instead, deftly changing the topic of conversation.

Ethan set his mug on the counter and went over to get the envelope from his jacket hanging on the coat tree. Retrieving it, he handed it to Faith. "Thank you for the use of your bed *and* the coffee." He winked at her as he walked over to the bed to get his shoes. "I believe I can make it home okay now."

"Are you sure you'll be all right?"

Sitting on the edge of the mattress, he stared at her. "Are you inviting me to spend the night?"

"No. It's just that it's snowing and…"

His eyebrows lifted when she didn't finish her statement. "I'm touched that you're concerned about my well-being, but I can assure you that I'm able to maneuver in snow."

Faith gave him a facetious grin. "Of course. After all, you are a chauffeur."

"Right," he said after a lengthy pause. Driving wasn't his livelihood or career, but that wasn't something he would disclose to her. Bending over, he tied his shoes. Rising from the bed, he closed the distance between them. "You still owe me a dance," he whispered close to her ear.

Faith's eyes narrowed. He was like a dog with a bone. "What if I put on some music and we dance here?"

"No, Faith. You should've danced with me last night, but you cut and run like a candy-ass."

Her delicate jaw dropped before she recovered. "Now, that sounds like military jargon. Were you in the military?"

"I'll tell you, but under one condition."

Faith registered the teasing quality in his voice. "What's that?"

"Because you forfeited the chance to dance with me last night, now it will have to be someplace else."

"What on earth are you talking about, Ethan?"

"Let me know when you're available to go out."

She stared wordlessly as a shock flew through her. "Are you asking me out on a date?"

"No, Faith. It's not going to be a date."

"If my going out with you is not a date, then pray tell what is it?"

"You making good on your promise for one little itty-bitty dance, and in turn I'll tell you about my military experience."

Faith saw the beginnings of a smile crease the skin around his eyes. She didn't know whether he was teasing or serious about taking her out. Now she had another adjective to add to his personality—persistent.

"What are you trying to do? Wear me down?"

"Nope," Ethan countered. "All you have to do is say yes."

"But what if I say no."

"Then I'll be forced to wear you down."

She shook her head. "Please don't. Not only am I worn down but also worn-out."

"What say you, Faith Whitfield?"

She couldn't stop the smile softening her mouth. "I say yes, Ethan McMillan."

Leaning over, he pressed a kiss to her cheek. "I'll call you."

"But you don't have my number," she said to his back when he walked over to get his jacket.

Slipping his arms into the sleeves of his jacket, Ethan turned and looked at Faith. "I'll get it from WJ." He gave her a snappy salute, turned and opened the door. It closed and locked automatically behind him.

Faith stared at the door, unable to believe what she'd just committed to. Ethan wanted to take her out for "one little itty-bitty dance," and to her that translated into a *date*.

Glancing at the envelope in her hand, she returned to the window seat, sat down and opened it. WJ had enclosed a business card. She flipped it over, smiling. He'd scrawled the word *thanks,* his signature and drawn a smiley face. Her smile faded when she peered into the envelope to find a stack of crisp one-hundred-dollar bills. She removed them from the envelope and began counting. She stopped at eight hundred. William Raymond's little something added up to more than a thousand dollars.

Tucking the flap into the envelope, she stood up, crossed the room and opened the doors to the armoire and secreted the money in a sachet-scented lined drawer cradling her lingerie. The Raymonds hadn't blinked when she quoted a figure for the dessert menu for Savanna's party, a figure that was near the top of her price list because of the amount of chocolate she'd ordered from a renowned confectioner who imported raw cocoa beans from South America, Java, Grenada, Mexico and Gabon.

Faith knew any attempt to return the cash would be construed as an insult by WJ, so she had to devise another plan to thank him for his extraordinary generosity or pass his gratitude along to her employees in the form of a bonus when they put in long hours to accommodate the customers who crowded into Let Them Eat Cake for the specially prepared candies, tortes and cookies for Valentine's Day.

Blowing snow and an accident slowed traffic to a crawl. Ethan was less than three miles from his home, but it could've been three hundred because of the "lookie-loos" craning their necks to stare at the two men waving their arms and yelling at each other because of a fender-bender. Someone blew a horn, prompting a cacophony of horn blasts until the congestion eased and he maneuvered past the scene of the accident and drove to an industrial area where he would park the Town Car and pick up his own car.

The windows to MAC Elite Car Services, Inc., were dark, which meant his office manager had followed his directive to close because of the weather. Kenneth Mobley would've remained in the office until his shift ended, taking calls and instructing drivers to pick up clients who were partial to door-to-door car service. He'd also instructed Kenny to call the drivers to tell them to come back to the garage after their last drop-off, because the lives and safety of his employees were more important than the bottom line.

Punching in a series of numbers on the remote device attached to the limousine's visor, Ethan waited until the door to the bay opened where he'd left his car. Within minutes he'd backed out a late-model Mercedes-Benz coupe, maneuvered the Town Car into the space and driven the short distance to the gated community and his town house condominium.

He parked in an attached garage, unlocked the door leading directly into the kitchen. Not bothering to check the stack of mail the cleaning woman had left on a side table in the living room, he climbed the staircase to his second-floor bedroom. The large numbers on the clock on a bedside table glowed eerily in the darkened space. Not bothering to turn on a lamp, Ethan undressed, leaving his clothes on a leather-covered bench at the foot of the king-size bed. All of his actions were mechanical as he pulled back the comforter and sheet, got into bed and let out a sigh of relief.

It was the first time since he'd moved into the house that he truly appreciated his bed. The last thing he remembered before sleep claimed him was Faith Whitfield's face with a pair of dark eyes, pert nose and incredibly sexy mouth, a mouth he wanted to sample, to discover if it tasted as delicious as it looked.

Faith woke late Monday morning, feeling more rested than she had in weeks. Let Them Eat Cake, closed on Sundays and Mondays, didn't require her going into the shop, so the only thing on her agenda was cleaning her apartment and preparing dinner for her bimonthly get-together with her cousins.

Looking through her freezer, she took out several bags of shrimp: medium Gulf white for stir-fry with snow peas, jumbo for shrimp cocktail and Maine shrimp for shrimp chowder. She had most of the ingredients on hand for her seafood menu with the exception of the snow peas, scallions, garlic, potatoes, leeks and chives, and that meant she would have to make a trip to Balducci's, her favorite gourmet grocery at 14th Street and Eighth Avenue.

Fortified with a cup of coffee, she turned on the radio to a station featuring the latest R & B, pop and hip-hop, singing along and dancing to a few of her favorite artists. Snow accumulations measured three inches, not enough to close schools, but enough to make walking hazardous for pedestrians trying to jump over mounds of snow created by sanitation department plows.

Faith emptied the laundry hamper, stripped her bed and changed the towels in the bathroom, putting everything in two bags. Although there was a self-serve Laundromat on the avenue around the corner, she was loath to spend hours in the place, waiting for a washer or dryer, then having to fold up clothes and carry the bags up the three flights of stairs to her apartment. The owner of the laundry offered pickup and drop-off. She willingly paid for the additional service.

She called the laundry for a pickup, cleaned the bathroom and kitchen, dusted all the furniture and changed her bed. She hadn't thought of Ethan again until she recognized the lingering scent of his aftershave on one of the pillows.

Faith wasn't certain what it was about the man who'd appeared to have more than his share of ego, a trait she didn't particularly like in a man, yet she didn't find it repulsive. She'd dated men who were so aggressive that their behavior bordered on bullying. One had insisted because he wanted her that she would eventually surrender to his will. What he failed to realize was that Faith Vinna Whitfield surrendered to no one—especially a man. She might not have known what she wanted, but she knew without a doubt what she *did not* want, and that included men who took rejection as a personal affront and those who were so full of themselves that they were unable to fathom that a woman might not want to have anything to do with them.

They were nothing more than insufferable, egotistical, nauseating frogs! She would go out with Ethan McMillan, but if he exhibited even the slightest indication that he was like the rest of her past dates, then he would also be relegated to frog status.

The downstairs bell chimed, and Faith glanced around the apartment before going over to the intercom. Depressing a button, she spoke into the tiny speaker next to the door. "Who is it?"

"We're here," the sisters said in unison.

Tessa had called to let Faith know that she and Simone were meeting at the West 4th Street Washington Square subway stop. Both had decided to leave their cars in Brooklyn Heights and White Plains respectively, and take the subway and railroad.

Smiling, Faith pressed the button that would release the lock on the outer door. She was ready for her Monday-night get-together. It'd been several months since her cousins had come to Manhattan for their bimonthly dinner because she hadn't been available. Unlocking the door, she opened it slightly before walking over to the refrigerator to remove a bowl of salad. She'd even included her shrimp theme in the salad.

"Something smells good," Simone announced, sticking her head through the slight opening in the door. At the same time she removed her boots, leaving them on the thick straw mat.

Faith smiled at Simone. "I made one of your favorites." She knew how finicky her cousin was when it came to food.

Petite, hazel-eyed, with a profusion of red and gold-streaked curly hair falling down her back, Simone Whitfield had been blessed with a natural seductiveness that was startling and breathtaking at the same time. The talented, divorced, thirty-three-year-old floral decorator always shocked men when she revealed her age because she looked as if she were barely out of her teens. While most women would've given anything to look years younger without help from a plastic surgeon, Simone complained that she was still carded when ordering a drink.

Simone walked into Faith's apartment, set a shopping bag on the floor, removed her coat and hung it up. Her eyes widened when she saw a quartet of shrimp perched around the rim of crystal cocktail glasses filled with cocktail sauce at each place setting.

"Thank you, Faith," she crooned, moving over and hugging her cousin.

Faith returned the hug. "You're welcome." She didn't get along with Simone as well as she did Tessa because of Simone's occasional dark moods. Simone blamed her mercurial disposition on seasonal affective disorder, but Faith attributed most of it to her on-again, off-again relationship with her shiftless, trifling ex-husband.

"Everything looks nice," Tessa said, walking in and closing the door. She slipped out of her coat, draping it over a hook on the coat tree.

There was no mistaking Tessa and Simone for sisters, although Tessa's hair, eyes and complexion were darker than Simone's. Thirty-one-year-old Tessa had become a preeminent wedding and event planner in the four years since starting up Signature Bridals and Event Planners, Inc. with her sister and first cousin. Tessa owned sixty percent of the company, while Simone and Faith shared equally in the remaining forty. The company had afforded the thirty-something Whitfields a very comfortable lifestyle.

"Thanks. I love your haircut, Tessa," Faith said, smiling. She was surprised to see that Tessa had cut her hair. For years she'd affected a flyaway hairdo that was a modified throwback to the Afro of the seventies. The shorter style was a combination of punk and chic.

"Enough chitchat," she said, extending her hand to Tessa. "Let me see it." Tessa held out her left hand. Prisms of light sparkled from a magnificent cushion-cut diamond with round and baguette diamonds set in platinum. Faith turned her hand over. There were pavé diamonds on the band. "It is exquisite, Tessa." There was no mistaking the awe in Faith's voice. She placed her arms around her cousin's neck and kissed her cheek. "You deserve all of the good things coming to you."

"Stop, Faith, before I start crying. And I did enough of that yesterday to last me a lifetime."

Simone removed a cellophane-wrapped bouquet of pink hydrangeas and grape hyacinths and a bottle of white wine from the shopping bag. "Tessa had everyone crying, Mama, Daddy and Aunt Edie. Even Uncle Henry wiped away a tear or two."

"Did your soon-to-be, manly man brother-in-law cry?" Faith teased.

"No. In fact, he seemed rather amused. I can't wait to see what happens when we go to Franklin Lakes this coming Sunday to have dinner with the Sanborns. And please, Faith, don't tell me you have something on your calendar for Sunday," Simone drawled facetiously.

A slight frown appeared between Faith's eyes. "I don't believe I do."

"Go check!" the sisters chorused.

Hiding a grin, Faith crossed the room and picked up her PDA from the bedside table and scrolled through her calendar. "I'm good." She hadn't planned anything for the day, but she would've used the time to bake and decorate a couple of cakes for her book.

"I'll call and let you know what time Micah and I will pick you up," Tessa said. "And if it's not raining or snowing, then dress casually. And bring a change of clothes," she added cryptically.

"Why?"

"That's because the Sanborns get together to play touch football on Sundays."

Faith shook her head while waving a hand. "Forget it, Tessa. I don't do sports."

"Neither did I before I got involved with Micah," Tessa admitted reluctantly.

"I love rolling around in the dirt," Simone said, as she filled a vase with water and skillfully arranged the colorful blooms.

Faith gave her cousin an incredulous look. "That's because to you dirt equals money."

"No lie," the floral decorator quipped.

"And, by the way, the flowers are beautiful." Simone knew she was partial to pink flowers.

Affecting a curtsey, Simone flashed a wide grin. "Thank you." She'd just signed a contract with a well-known White Plains law firm to deliver floral arrangements for their reception area and conference rooms. She'd built a greenhouse on a portion of her property where she grew and cultivated herbs and flowers year-round. She'd grown her business, Wildflowers and Other Treasures, selling bouquets and corsages for birthdays, holidays and proms. Her involvement with Signature Bridals expanded into specialty wedding bouquets, and now she'd added her first corporate client. She set the vase of flowers on the table, glancing around the studio apartment.

"Tessa's right. Your place does look nice." Soft music flowed from concealed speakers, lighted lemon-scented votives and the lowest setting from the three-way bulb in the floor lamp provided a calming, subdue setting for laid-back dining pleasure. "You should be entertaining a man tonight, not your cousins," Simone said in a quiet tone.

Faith rolled her eyes upward. "I've dated more men than the two of you combined, so please don't mention entertaining a man."

"But how many have you slept with, Faith?" Simone asked.

She lowered her gaze. "Not many."

"How many is 'not many'?" Simone questioned.

"I'm not going to tell you that!" Faith said in protest. Although she'd dated a lot of men, she hadn't slept with them. "And that's because most of them weren't worth taking off my clothes to even consider sleeping with them." Faith looked at Tessa. "I know you're getting your freak on with Micah, but you, Miss Simone Whitfield, are a different story. Once you fell under Anthony Kendrick's spell you never looked at another man." She cupped a hand to her ear. "How many men, other than Tony, have you slept with in the past…" She paused. "How long has it been— seven or eight years?"

"Eight," Simone mumbled. "But that's over and done with, and Tony knows it."

Faith blinked once. "You told him?"

Simone nodded. "Yes. Tessa is my witness."

"Yes!" Faith said through clenched teeth. "I know I've kissed a lot of frogs, but with all you have going for yourself, Simone, I always thought you could do so much better than that…Tony," she said, biting back the criticism she usually reserved for her cousin's highly educated, bum-ass ex-husband.

Tessa smiled at her sister and cousin. "Now that we're done discussing men, I'm going to wash up so we can eat. I'm starved."

Both pairs of eyes, one light and the other dark, stared at Tessa. "Are you sure you're not pregnant?" Simone asked.

Tessa gave her a saccharine grin. "I know I'm not." She headed for the bathroom.

"Do you and Micah plan to have children?" Faith said as Tessa retreated.

Tessa smiled over her shoulder. "Yes."

Simone winked at Faith before following her sister into the bathroom. "Hot damn! We're going to be aunties."

"I'm going to spoil my niece or nephew!" Faith called out.

"You better not," Tessa called out.

"Try and stop me, Theresa Anais Whitfield."

Tessa stuck her head out of the bathroom. "Oh, no, you didn't call me by my full name."

"Yes, I did." Faith returned to the kitchen area to turn off a simmering pot of shrimp chowder. She added a Thai peanut dressing to the salad, tossing the crisp greens and crispy-fried popcorn shrimp, placing the bowl on the table next to the floral centerpiece. She planned to begin the five-course meal with shrimp cocktail, followed by soup, salad, an entrée of shrimp and snow peas with white rice and a dessert of frozen cassata—a vanilla ice cream cake that incorporated the flavors of an Italian cannoli filing: ricotta, chocolate, pistachios and orange peel.

The sisters returned. Tessa offered to uncork the bottle of wine while Faith ladled the steaming chowder into soup bowls. Her cell phone rang, and before she could tell Simone not to answer it, she'd picked it up.

"Good evening, Let Them Eat Cake." Simone knew Faith used her cell phone exclusively for business.

"May I please speak to Faith Whitfield," said a deep male voice.

Simone's eyebrows lifted slightly. "Who shall I say is calling?"

"Ethan McMillan."

Simone covered the mouthpiece with her thumb. "It's Ethan McMillan."

Faith's breath caught in her chest before she let it out slowly. "Ask him if he can leave a number so I can call him back."

Simone repeated Faith's request. "Hold on while I get something to write with." She gestured for something to write, and Faith handed her a pen and paper from the magnetic pad attached to the side of the refrigerator. Simone wrote down the number, then repeated it for accuracy. She was smiling when she ended the call. "Who's the brother with the X-rated voice?"

Faith schooled her expression not to reveal what she was feeling at the moment—a rush of excitement for a man who'd managed to affect her more than she wanted, a man whose very presence disturbed and piqued her curiosity.

"How do you know he's a brother?" she asked Simone as they sat down.

"Don't play yourself, cousin," Simone drawled as she placed a cloth napkin over her lap. "Only brothers are blessed with voices that deep."

Tessa peered closely at Faith. "Who is he?"

Faith knew that if she didn't give the two a plausible explanation, then they would pester her throughout dinner. She could lie and say he was a client, but she'd never lied to her cousins and didn't want to start now.

"He's someone I promised to go out with."

Tessa shared a smile with Simone. "I'm going to ask you one question, then I'm going to get out of your business." Faith nodded. "Is he what Aunt Edie would call 'potential husband material'?" Faith's mother had lectured them sternly once they'd begun dating, saying, "Every man you date should be considered a potential husband. If not, then don't waste your time."

Faith filled the wineglasses with the pale wine rather than meet Tessa's questioning gaze. "I'll reserve comment. First I have to find out whether he's a frog."

"Ribbit!" Simone croaked.

Faith and Tessa burst out laughing, setting the tone for an evening of good food and a closeness that had begun with earlier generations of Whitfield women.

Tessa pushed back her chair and stood up. "I forgot to give you Bridget's gift." She retrieved her purse and took out a small gaily wrapped box, handing it to Faith.

Simone and Tessa stared at Faith as she removed the paper, opened a small black velvet box and stared numbly at a pair of thirteen-millimeter Tahitian pearl earrings suspended from a drop clasp of bezel-set diamonds.

"Oh, my!" Faith gasped in awe. "They *are* stunning!"

"I got the same pair," Simone said.

Faith smiled at Tessa. "I'm going to wear them at your wedding."

"Speaking of weddings, Faith," Tessa began softly, "I'd like to ask you if you'd be my maid of honor."

A rush of tears filled Faith's eyes. She blinked them back before they fell. "I'd be honored, Tessa. How many attendants do you plan to have?"

"That's going to depend on Micah. He's asked his father to be his best man, and his two brothers will be groomsmen. You'll be my maid of honor, Simone a bridesmaid and I'm thinking of asking Micah's sister-in-law whether her teenage daughter can be a bridesmaid."

Faith wrinkled her pert nose. "Isn't it going to feel funny planning your own wedding?"

"I'm not," Tessa admitted smugly. "Simone's going to be my wedding planner."

"You're kidding, aren't you?" Faith asked, an expression of shock freezing her features.

Simone shook her head. "No, she's not."

A blush suffused Tessa's face. "Micah and I have decided to begin trying for a baby as soon as we're married. And if that happens, then I'd like to have a backup person in case of morning sickness, bloated ankles and when I'm too fat to bend over to tie up my shoes."

Faith waved her hand. "Please, Tessa. Knowing you, you'll probably design a wardrobe that will make you Brooklyn's most tricked-out mother-to-be. Speaking of Brooklyn, do you still plan to live there after you're married?"

Tessa nodded. "Yes. Micah sold his Bronx condo to Bridget and Seth, and he only has six months left on his Staten Island rental. I've put a lot of money into the brownstone, so I've decided to keep it."

Reaching for her wineglass, Faith raised it in a toast. "To Tessa and Signature Bridals."

Simone and Tessa followed suit, touching glasses in a toast to Signature Bridals.

Chapter 5

Faith couldn't believe how quickly time had slipped away when she closed the door behind her cousins. They'd talked nonstop about Tessa's upcoming June nuptials, and would've still been talking if Simone hadn't had to go to Grand Central Station to catch a train to White Plains, before she had to wait hours for one or they stopped running altogether until the following morning. Tessa had invited her sister to spend the night with her, but Simone turned her down, saying she had to deliver flowers to patients at a local hospital.

Faith had filled a large container with leftover chowder for Simone. Her artistic cousin grew and arranged beautiful flowers, set an exquisite table, but couldn't cook worth a damn! When their paternal grandmother decided it was time her granddaughters learned to prepare some of the recipes that had been passed down through countless generations of Whitfields, Simone was nowhere to be found. And when she finally showed up hours later, she was dirty and sweaty from playing ball with the neighborhood boys.

Clearing the table, Faith stacked dishes in the dishwasher, and then she saw it. It was the paper with Ethan's number. How could she have forgotten that he'd called? Picking up the cordless phone, she dialed his number. He answered after the fourth ring.

"Good evening."

Smiling, Faith cradled the receiver between her chin and shoulder. "Good evening to you, too. This is Faith Whitfield returning your call."

A deep chuckle caressed her ear. "I knew it was you, dessert lady, because your name and number came up on my caller ID."

"Did you make it home all right last night?"

"It took a little longer than I'd expected, but yes, I made it home safely. Thank you for asking."

"You're welcome."

"Do you have your calendar nearby?"

A slight frown appeared between her eyes. "Why?"

"I'd like to see when you're available to go out with me."

"Before I get my calendar, I'd like you to answer one question for me."

There was a pause before Ethan said, "What do you want to know?"

"Are you married?" She'd noticed the gold signet ring on the pinky of his right hand.

There came another pause, this one longer than the previous one. "Do you think I'd ask you to go out with me if I was married?"

"I can't answer that, Ethan."

"And, why not?"

"Because I've been asked out a few times by married men."

"Well, I'm not married, so are you still willing to go out with me?"

Tearing a sheet off the pad, she picked up a pen, drawing a line down the center of the page. She jotted down Ethan's initials and labeled the columns Frog and Prince. She checked off Prince.

"Yes. Hold on, let me check my calendar." Retrieving her PDA, she clicked on the current month. "I'm free Thursday and Saturday."

"It would have to be Saturday because I'm taking you to the Rainbow Room for dinner and dancing."

"The Rainbow Room," she repeated.

"Rockefeller Plaza, sixty-fifth floor."

"I know where it is, Ethan."

"Well…"

"Well what?" he asked.

"Okay."

"Okay what, Faith?"

She let out a sigh. "I'll go to the Rainbow Room with you for dinner and dancing."

"Why does it sound as if you're doing me a favor?"

Faith smiled. "That's because I am, Ethan McMillan."

He laughed again. "I'll pick you up at seven-thirty."

"I'll be ready. Good night, Ethan."

"Good night, Faith."

She ended the call, her smile still in place. Faith was tempted to give him another check, but decided to wait until Saturday.

* * *

When Faith unlocked the door to Let Them Eat Cake early Tuesday morning she was met with the tantalizing smell of baking bread. She'd hired Oliver Rollins the year before because some of the regular customers who frequented the patisserie had requested freshly baked bread. Oliver made the ubiquitous white, rye, wheat and pumpernickel, then one day he added onion-dill rye and maple-pecan breakfast loaves. The nontraditional varieties became so popular that Faith and Oliver decided to forgo the traditional loaves. On Saturday mornings a line of customers stretched down and around the block as they waited patiently to get into the tiny shop to purchase loaves of bread, rolls, cake, candies and delicate pastries for the weekend.

During the warmer weather, the selections varied when Faith made beignets, diamond-shaped donuts made famous in New Orleans where they're traditionally eaten warm with café au lait. Foccacia had become an instant favorite the first time it was offered, along with pesto swirl bread. A delicious layer of pesto spread on light whole-wheat dough rolled up and baked into a tasty loaf was the perfect complement for soups, salads, pastas and grilled meat and fish.

Let Them Eat Cake's reputation hadn't flourished from the exotic pastries and desserts offered to their customers but from the individual-size portions on display in the showcases. Someone wishing to purchase a black forest cherry cake as dessert for three was given the choice of buying three individual-size cakes rather a whole cake that would serve eight to ten. It took more time to create the smaller cakes, but customers were more than willing to pay extra for the more precise portions. Those who'd admitted being on diets expressed their gratitude because of the all-natural ingredients and size proportions.

Locking the door behind her, Faith made her way to the rear of the shop. The heat of an industrial oven felt good after her brisk three-block walk. It was five o'clock, and it would be at least another hour before sunrise and two before Let Them Eat Cake opened for business.

"Good morning, Mr. Rollins."

Oliver Rollins, closing the door to the oven, glanced over his shoulder to give Faith a wide, gap-toothed smile. "Morning, missy." He'd confessed that he wasn't very good with names, so he referred to every woman as missy. "You're in early this morning."

Storing her coat in a narrow metal locker, Faith returned his friendly smile. Oliver had been a baker with the Silver-cup Bread Bakery in Long Island City for more than twenty years before the plant was sold and converted into movie studios. He'd worked odd jobs over the ensuing years, and because of his appearance was hired as a department-store Santa during the Christmas holiday shopping season. Faith considered herself blessed when, only two days after placing a Help Wanted sign for an experienced baker in the shop's window, Oliver Rollins applied for the position.

"I want to bake a few birthday cakes today."

She'd decided to begin her book with the ever-popular birthday cake. She slipped on a bibbed apron, covered her hair with a hair bonnet, then washed her hands in a sink. Faith had thought it ironic that the kitchen was twice as large as the shop's selling area, yet had decided to forgo having an architect reconfigure the space's design because that would've meant getting approval from the building's owner, obtaining the necessary permits from the city and closing down for several months. Her only other alternative was to relocate to another building in the West Village. One major drawback was that a bigger space in a more up-to-date building translated into higher rent, and because she'd just begun to realize a profit, she was reluctant to operate in the red again.

A buzzer rang in the kitchen, and Oliver and Faith glanced up at the wall clock at the same time. It was exactly six o'clock. Oliver took off his latex gloves. "I'll see who it is." Walking over to a panel on the door that led to the alley behind the shop, he pressed a button. "Yes?"

"It's Ranee," said a nasal voice through the speaker. Faith and Oliver shared a glance. It was the assistant pastry chef, Ranee Mason. The classically trained pianist had turned down a full scholarship to Juilliard to pursue her dream of becoming a pastry chef.

"Let her in," Faith ordered in a quiet voice, wondering why her assistant had shown up two hours earlier than her regularly scheduled time. She didn't have to wait long for an answer when Ranee raced into the kitchen.

"I need you to sample something I made last night!" Her dark eyes were filled with an excitement that Faith hadn't seen since the day she told the recent graduate that she was hired. Ranee thrust a plastic-covered container at her boss before she pulled a hand-knitted cap from her braided hair.

Oliver walked over to Faith, peering into the container when she removed the top. He liked Ranee's ebullient, outgoing personality. Her enthusiasm for baking was spontaneous and contagious. She reminded him of the dolls on display during the holiday shopping season, with her round dark eyes, smooth brown skin and tiny nose and mouth. Even her diminutive height made her appear doll-like.

Faith stared at three tart-size cakes. Ranee had baked two cheesecakes: blueberry, raspberry and a mousse made with a chocolate pastry shell, a white chocolate filling and drizzled with dark chocolate.

She smiled. "They look too pretty to eat."

Ranee pressed her palms to her chest over her coat. "Please taste them."

Faith, who'd almost given up eating desserts after taste-testing so many of them over the years, removed the cakes from the container. Reaching for a knife, she cut them in two. She handed Oliver a half of the chocolate mousse.

"Two sets of taste buds are better than one," she remarked as she took a bite of the cake. Eyes widening in surprise, Faith tried to identify the ingredients. She recognized the distinctive taste of white chocolate and vanilla extract, but the other ones weren't overtly recognizable. The mousse was delicious.

Oliver chewed and swallowed his portion, bushy white eyebrows lifting as he angled his shaved head covered with a white baseball cap. "It's fantastic."

"I agree," Faith said, as she searched her mind to identify what Ranee had mixed with the white chocolate. "Okay, Ranee, I give up. What did you use for the filling?"

Ranee grinned like a Cheshire cat. "I added powdered gelatin to superfine sugar, vanilla extract, eggs and plain yogurt."

Faith shook her head in surprise. "That's it! The yogurt makes it light and not too sweet."

Ranee unbuttoned her coat. "It's a Greek chocolate mousse tartlet. Now, please try the cheesecakes." She watched intently as Faith and Oliver sampled both cheese-cakes. "What do you think?"

Faith's impassive expression did not reveal what she was feeling at that moment. Ranee Mason was not only a gifted musician, but pastry chef, as well. "I believe you may have matched Junior's." The Brooklyn-based landmark restaurant on Flatbush and DeKalb Avenues had earned the inimitable reputation as the home of New York's best cheesecake.

Ranee beamed like a child whose fervent wish had been granted. "I made the blueberry shell with ground hazelnuts and varied the strawberry with a French tart pastry."

Wiping her hands on a towel, Faith met her assistant's gaze. "Congratulations, Ranee. Your cakes will be added to the showcase of *staff favorites.*"

Clapping a hand over her mouth, Ranee did a happy dance before hugging Faith, then Oliver. "Thank you," she crooned over and over, her apparent joy boundless.

Customers who visited the shop always stopped to peruse the showcase with the recommended items, and the result was usually a sellout before closing time. Faith, while a pastry chef apprentice, had been encouraged to come up with her own creations, and she'd done the same with her baker and assistant pastry chef.

If the patisserie was forced to move to a larger space, then there was no doubt Oliver Rollins and Ranee Mason would assume supervisory positions. Faith's long-term plans for her business did not include renting, but building ownership.

Faith, hopping on one foot to the door to answer the intercom, was in the process of multitasking as she pulled up the strap of her shoe over her heel while talking into the cell phone cradled between her chin and shoulder. It was definitely time for her to get a hands-free device. It was seven-thirty, and there was no doubt it was Ethan McMillan who'd rung her bell.

"Please hold on, Mrs. Fiori," she said to her caller.

She wouldn't have answered the call, but Tomasina, Tommi to her close friends, Fiori was one of her best clients; she wintered in Palm Beach, Florida, and divided her summers between her Park Avenue penthouse and a Mill Neck, Long Island, beachfront estate. The wealthy widow, relaxing in the Florida sunshine, wanted her to come to Florida to bake a cake for her ten-year-old grand-daughter. The Valentine's Day party, which included a guest list of seventy-five, was to be a surprise for the over-indulged child.

Placing her thumb over the mouthpiece, Faith pressed the talk button on the intercom. "Who is it?"

"Ethan." Her pulse quickened when she heard his deeply modulated voice. How, she thought, had she forgotten the rich timbre, that his voice was merely an integral compo-nent of his overall blatant virility?

She depressed another button, disengaging the lock on the downstairs door, then unlocked the one to her apart-ment, opened it and waited for Ethan to walk up three flights. She moved her thumb. "It's impossible for me to come to Florida because I have two wedding receptions on that day," she said, resuming her conversation with her client. This year the lovers' holiday fell on a Saturday. "Do you mind if I suggest an alternative?" Faith asked at the same time Ethan walked through the door.

Her breathing faltered slightly when she stared at the ex-quisite cut of his black cashmere topcoat over a tailored dark-gray suit he'd paired with a stark spread-collar white shirt and gunmetal-gray silk tie. He looked like a million dollars! Smiling, she inclined her head, and she wasn't disappointed when he returned her smile with a seductive dimpled one. Her gaze fused with his until he turned and closed the door.

"What are you suggesting, Miss Whitfield?" asked Mrs. Fiori.

"I can ship you the cake."

"I don't trust the post office, Miss Whitfield. Either it'll arrive too late, or when I open the box it will be to a pile of crumbs."

"I'm not talking about using the postal service. I use a shipping company who take special care with fragile items."

"Special care or not, I'm not willing to tempt fate."

Faith knew the woman wouldn't relent, while she looked forward to going out with Ethan. Other than her bi-monthly get-togethers with her cousins her social life was nonexistent.

She stared at Ethan watching her, wondering what was going on behind his sherry-colored gaze. "I'll check my calendar again, Mrs. Fiori, and I'll call you Monday morning."

Ethan couldn't pull his gaze away from Faith Whitfield when she continued her telephone conversation, her expression registering exasperation. He hadn't realized until he walked into her apartment that he'd spent the week attempting to recall the sound of her voice, the incredible slimness of her body, which was curvy *and* feminine, and her natural beauty that had enthralled him the moment he saw her face.

Tonight, instead of her curly hairdo, Faith had applied a gel and brushed her short hair until there was no hint of a curl, and she'd replaced her jeans and T-shirt with an off-the-shoulder, drop-waist, long-sleeved black bodice-hugging dress that ended midway to her shapely calves. His gaze moved lower like a river of slow, red-hot lava to her legs and feet in sheer black nylons and matching satin, sling-back stilettos. Her accessories were a pair of diamond studs and four narrow diamond eternity bands stacked on the middle finger of her right hand.

Waiting until she ended her call, Ethan came to her, lowered his head and kissed the side of her long neck. "You look fantastic for a dessert lady." The smoky shadow on her eyelids had changed her into a mysterious, alluring siren.

"Pastry chef, Ethan," Faith said softly, correcting him.

He winked at her. "Okay, pastry chef."

Resting her hands on the lapel of his coat, Faith smiled up at him. "And you look pretty good for a chauffeur."

Ethan didn't want to move, and if possible he didn't want to leave Faith's apartment because after seeing her he wanted her all to himself. Jealousy, an emotion he'd never experienced before, swept over him. He didn't know why, but he didn't want other men staring or lusting after his date.

He put on an impassive expression. "Does it bother you that I'm a chauffeur?"

He didn't tell Faith that he'd become his cousin's driver after WJ suspended the services of his regular driver while he took steps to ensure the safety of his son. He also wouldn't tell her that he was the president of a company with two corporate jets and a car service with a half-dozen luxury cars.

A slight frown formed between her eyes. "No. Why would you ask me that?"

"Some women will only date Wall Street brokers, doctors or lawyers."

Faith's frown disappeared. "I'm going out with you, aren't I, so that should answer your question. But didn't you say that we weren't actually going out on a *date!*"

Lowering his head, Ethan stared at Faith's slender feet in the stilettos that put the top of her head at eye level with his. He liked that she was comfortable with her height. His head came up and he stared into twin pools of liquid brown eyes.

"Yes, I did. I'd like to think of tonight as a brief encounter that could lead to a possible date."

Faith mentally gave Ethan another check under the Prince column. His ego wasn't so inflated that he just assumed she'd go out with him again after tonight. She affected an attractive moue, bringing his gaze to linger on her burgundy-colored lips.

"We'll see," she said, unwilling to commit to going out on a real date with the impeccably dressed man who'd promised her a brief encounter of dining and dancing.

Faith walked over to the love seat and picked up a tuxedo-style mink jacket at the same time Ethan reached for the fur garment, holding it while she slipped her arms into the sleeves. Gathering her evening purse and keys, she smiled at him over her shoulder. "I'm ready."

Ethan waited for Faith to lock the door to her apartment, wondering if she was ready for him, because he certainly was ready for her. Too often his "brief encounters" ended before they actually began, but within several hours he would know whether he was attracted to Faith Whitfield because she was just another pretty face, or if she was *the* woman with whom he could have a mature ongoing relationship free of angst and drama.

Reaching for her hand, he led Faith down the three flights and out to the street. An all-day rain earlier in the week had washed away the mounds of dirty snow, and the temperatures had risen steadily to the midforties, but New Yorkers weren't so gullible as to believe warmer temperatures signaled the end of winter. There was still the rest of January, all of February and March, the most unpredictable month of the year.

Tightening his hold on her gloved hand, Ethan steered Faith to the corner. "I'm parked in the alley behind your building."

"This must be your lucky night." Parking in Manhattan was a feat unto itself.

Patting the hand tucked into the bend of his elbow, Ethan smiled. "It is," he said confidently. He considered himself very lucky to have met Faith Whitfield when he'd rescued her from his cousin's unwarranted advances, and even luckier when Faith agreed to go out with him.

Pressing the button on a remote device, he unlocked the doors to the coupe parked in the cobblestone alley. Opening the passenger-side door, he seated Faith, waited until she was belted in before circling the vehicle. He took off his topcoat and suit jacket, placing them across the rear seats before taking his place behind the wheel.

"Would you like some music?" he asked Faith when he started up the engine.

"Anything soft would be nice."

Faith didn't know why, but something about Ethan's profession didn't sit right with her. She wanted to know how many chauffeurs drove top-of-the-line luxury cars for their personal use—not unless the car belonged to their employers. And the black-on-black Mercedes-Benz coupe with a six-figure price tag was the same color and model driven by her father, Henry Whitfield. Who else, she wondered, other than William Raymond did Ethan work for? And how much could he possibly earn in a year transporting wealthy clients?

A jazzy number by the Brand New Heavies came through the speakers, filling the interior of the vehicle with incredible sound as Faith stared out the windshield. She was confused by the man sitting beside her, because first she'd been taken aback by his attire and now his car. It wasn't just the style of his wardrobe, but the quality.

When she'd hosted the Monday gathering and when her cousins discussed the upcoming Whitfield-Sanborn wedding, the focus had been on what to wear. Tessa had insisted on simplicity with her gown and Micah's suit, and as a professional fashion designer she always kept up with the changing styles. She talked about the more slimming silhouette of the contemporary man's suit with a two-button closure, narrow lapels in a high-notch or peak style, high armholes, narrowly set and thinly padded shoulders, low-waist and slim-cut pants with hems that did not touch the top of shoes.

The man who'd stood in the middle of her living room wore the suit Tessa spoke of, a suit that was priced in the two-thousand-dollar range. His shirt and shoes probably cost close to five hundred dollars each and his tie about one hundred. She couldn't begin to imagine the cost of his cashmere topcoat. Ethan had admitted to being a chauffeur, and it was apparent he was paid well for his services, or, she wondered, was he into other *things?*

She didn't want to jump to conclusions or prejudge the man, but Faith knew she had to be very, very careful, because she didn't want to become involved with someone who walked the fine line between legal and illegal.

"Do you mind if I ask you another question?" she asked, when Ethan stopped for a half a dozen teenage girls crossing the wide avenue against the light.

He gave her a sidelong glance, his face awash from lights on the dashboard. "What do you want to know *now?*"

"You don't have to say it like that."

"Like what?"

"You make it sound as if I were a bother."

Ethan flashed an easy smile. "You may be a few things, but never a bother."

Her eyes widened. "Do you mind elaborating on that?"

Returning his attention back to the road, Ethan took off in a burst of speed to make it to the next green light. He'd driven in Manhattan enough to be able to time the lights so that he'd cover at least half a mile before having to stop for a red one.

"You're the most incredibly beautiful woman I've met in the past ten years."

Faith's eyebrows lifted with his disclosure as she shifted slightly on her seat to look at his distinctive profile. "What happened to her?"

There came a slight pause. "I married her."

"You married her." Her question was a statement.

He nodded. "Yes. It was a mistake and we both knew it."

"How long were you married?"

"We managed to make it to eight months before calling it quits."

Faith turned away to look out the side window. "I'm sorry."

"Sorry doesn't figure into the equation, Faith. Divorce

was preferable to destroying each other." A thread of hardness had crept into his normally soft voice.

"I said I'm sorry because I'm in the wedding business *and* I believe in happily ever after."

"Have you ever been married?"

"No"

"Isn't it somewhat ironic that you're in the wedding business, you believe in fairy-tale endings, yet you're not married?"

Careful, Mac, she mused, *because you're about to get your first Frog check.*

"No, it's *not*," she said.

Faith knew she sounded defensive, but she didn't much care. She wasn't going to marry any man because she was thirty and in a few years her biological clock would start ticking loudly enough for everyone to hear. And, no matter how much her mother complained about wanting grand-children, Faith refused to succumb to pressure and marry the first man who flashed his cuspids at her.

She pressed the back of her head to the headrest. "I never figured you for someone who'd be so superficial."

Ethan gave Faith a quick glance. "You think I'm super-ficial?"

"Yes. Are a woman's looks that important to you?"

He lifted a shoulder under his white shirt. "That's all I have to go on until I get to know her better. For example, if we'd attended the same party and I spotted you across the room, it would be what you look like that would prompt me either to turn away or attempt an introduction. And after the introduction, then other factors would come into play—your voice, body language, manner of speech and above all how you conduct yourself in a social setting. I have to assume it's the same for you when you meet a man."

"Somewhat," she admitted reluctantly. "To me manners are much more important than physical attraction."

"By manners, do you mean home-training?"

"Yes, I do."

"I have to assume you have a criteria of do's and don'ts."

"Yes." Faith wanted to tell Ethan they weren't do's and don'ts, but categories relegated to frogs and princes. "Don't you?"

"We'll continue this over dinner," Ethan said as he maneuvered into a parking garage at 48th Street between Sixth and Seventh Avenues.

The parking attendant opened the driver's-side door. "How long are you staying, sir?"

"At least four hours."

Ethan stepped out and reached into the pocket of his trousers to give the young man a generous tip.

"Thank you, sir. I'll park it on the lower level."

Ethan nodded before reaching in to retrieve his jacket and coat. Once he left the restaurant, he didn't want Faith to have to wait outside in the cool night air while the attendants brought his car from the garage's upper level.

He rounded the coupe to assist Faith. He'd made a dinner reservation for eight o'clock, and the entertainment from a live big-band orchestra went on until one in the morning. He'd had the promise of one brief encounter with Faith Whitfield, and before it ended he hoped it would lead to an actual date.

Taking her hand, he held it as they navigated their way down the crowded sidewalk. People were getting out of cars and taxis in front of Radio City Music Hall as others were filing into the landmark theater.

They entered 30 Rockefeller Plaza, rode the elevator to the sixty-fifth floor, walked into the Rainbow Room and checked their coats. Faith didn't know whether it was the sound of the orchestra playing a seductive tango, or the elegantly dressed dancers gliding on the revolving dance floor in the center of the dining room, the panoramic views of north, south and east Manhattan, or the man holding her to his side, but she felt like a princess in one of her childhood fairy tales.

If she and Ethan were only going to share a brief encounter, then it was her intent to enjoy her time with him.

Chapter 6

Ethan and Faith were shown to a table, the maître d'
stepping back to permit Ethan to seat her, given menus and
informed that their waiter would be with them momentarily.

Rather than study the wine listings, Ethan stared across
the table at his dining partner. Faith had accused him of
being superficial because he'd admitted he was attracted to
her face. What she failed to realize was that any normal-
sighted man would be drawn to her because of her natural
beauty, and if that made him superficial, then he was.
However, it wasn't only her face and body that sent his libido
levels off the chart. Faith Whitfield as the total package.

In the short time he'd interacted with her he recognized
her intelligence, talent, independent spirit, ambition,
spunkiness and dependability. In other words, she was
perfect—almost too perfect, and he wondered why some
man hadn't put a ring on her finger.

Ethan stared at the extensive wine list offering red, white, dessert wines and champagne from France, as well as sparkling wines from Italy and California. "Will you share a bottle of wine?" he asked.

"What do you prefer?" Faith asked, perusing the list.

Looking up, he met her eyes before his gaze moved lower to her parted lips. "I'm partial to champagne."

Faith lifted a perfectly arched eyebrow. "Then champagne it is."

"Which one do you want?"

"You choose."

Shaking his head slowly, Ethan leaned forward. "Tonight is your night, Faith. I'm just here to try to make it special for you."

It was Faith's turn to shake her head. "That's where you're wrong, Ethan. Tonight is your brief encounter, so I'm here for you. We also wouldn't be here if I'd given you your one little itty-bitty dance at your cousin's penthouse."

A rush of color flooded Ethan's tawny-brown face, and she found the gesture both surprising and endearing. The added color made his short-cropped graying hair appear lighter than it actually was. He compressed his lips and the elusive dimples winked at her.

"You're right, Faith. I knew I wanted to see you again, so I came up with the excuse that I wanted to dance with you." Her delicate jaw dropped at his candid admission.

Faith closed her mouth, shocked by Ethan's candidness. "And what if I'd danced with you at your cousin's place? Would you've devised another plan to get me to go out with you?"

Ethan inclined his head. "Yes."

"What?" The single word came out in a hushed whisper.

Reaching across the table, he placed his left hand over her right, his thumb caressing the rings stacked on her slender finger. "Tell me what you want to hear, Faith. Would you've preferred that I lie to you?"

Her eyelids fluttered wildly. "No."

He smiled. "Good. I'm not a very complex man, so what you see is what you get."

"And just what is that?" she asked.

"I find myself quite taken with the woman sitting across from me. It's as if you've cast a spell over me."

"I possess no magical power to cast spells."

"Perhaps you're unaware of your power."

"I have no special powers, Ethan. In fact, I'm quite ordinary."

Ethan gave her hand a gentle squeeze before releasing it. "Define *ordinary* for me."

Faith felt a rush of warmth sweep over her as her gaze met Ethan's. Why did she find him so vaguely disturbing? What was there about him that sent her pulses spinning, her heart slamming against her ribs and her response to him so bewildering that it frightened her?

"I'm single, thirty and I have no children. I worked briefly as a model, but gave it up to go to culinary school. I'm a professionally trained pastry chef and I own a tiny patisserie known as Let Them Eat Cake."

"Where did you grow up?" Ethan asked.

"Mount Vernon."

"Do you have any brothers or sisters?"

"No. I'm an only child, but I have two first cousins whom I think of as my sisters. Any other questions?" she asked after a comfortable silence.

"No. But I beg to differ with you, Faith. You're anything

but ordinary. In fact, I'd think of you as quite extraordinary because you must be very good at what you do or you never would've met my cousin. WJ is anything but impulsive. He told me that he had you checked out thoroughly before agreeing to become your client. He showed me a list of recommendations from your clients that include A-list actors, hip-hop artists, high-profile athletes and the Euro-elite."

The heat in her face intensified. "You had me checked out?"

"No, Faith. WJ had you checked out. I'd never do that because that would've destroyed your mystique. When I asked WJ for your number he launched into a monologue about how you'd exceeded what you'd proposed in your contract. I believe it was the edible souvenir boxes that did it."

"He paid me well for my services."

"But you didn't include the souvenirs in your contract."

"That's my personal trademark," Faith said, smiling. "I try to include a little extra something for my clients. Enough talk about me…" She didn't finish her statement when the sommelier approached the table. Ethan ordered a bottle of 1996 Taittinger Comtes de Champagne Rosé. As soon as the sommelier left, their waiter came over and introduced himself. His slight Italian accent was music to her ears.

Faith focused on the dinner menu with specially created dishes highlighting Northern Italian cuisine. She ordered breaded tuna steaks with peas and artichokes with prosciutto. Ethan chose lasagna with pesto sauce and a capon salad with walnuts.

Leaning back in his chair, Ethan angled his head. "Where did you learn to speak Italian?" Faith had ordered in Italian.

Faith took a sip from her water goblet, peering at him over the rim. "I'm not that fluent in Italian."

"But you ordered in Italian."

"I spent some time in Italy and France to perfect my knowledge of Italian and French cuisine, so I picked up a few words." She'd returned to Rome last spring to attend the wedding of a childhood friend to an Italian restaurateur. She took another sip of water. "I have a confession to make." Sitting forward in his chair, Ethan stared at her. "I went to twelve years of parochial school, and—"

"You studied Latin," he said, completing her statement. "I'm also a product of a parochial school education. In fact, my parents teach at a Catholic college in Pennsylvania."

"Did you attend a Catholic college?" Faith asked.

Ethan picked up his goblet and drank deeply before setting it down on the cloth-covered table. "No. I went to a military academy."

Propping her elbow on the table, Faith rested her chin on the heel of her hand and wrinkled her nose. "I knew you were a military man."

He frowned at her. "You don't have to sound so smug about it. Now, if you can guess which one I went to, you'll get a gold star."

"I want more than a gold star, Ethan," she crooned.

Ethan's gaze was riveted on his date's face as the invisible wall she'd erected to keep him at a distance suddenly vanished with her seductive teasing. "What do you want?"

Faith knew she'd stepped into a trap of her own choosing as she asked herself the same question. What did she want from Ethan? Did she want from him what she hadn't gotten from the other men she'd dated?

"If we go beyond tonight's brief encounter, then I want…"

The seconds ticked off as Ethan waited for Faith to finish her statement. "You want what?"

"I want trust. I want to be able to trust you."

Ethan hadn't realized he'd been holding his breath. He didn't know why, but he felt like shouting. What she was asking was possible and doable. "And you will," he said after an interminable pause. Raising her goblet, Faith touched it to his. Smiling, he followed suit, touching her glass. "We will not lie, steal or cheat, nor tolerate among us anyone who does. Furthermore, I resolve to do my duty and live honorably, so help me God." Throwing back his head, he laughed softly when he saw an expression of confusion freeze her delicate features. "It's the U.S. Air Force Academy's honor code."

Faith recovered quickly. "Don't tell me you're a flyboy?"

"Hel-lo. The proper term is pilot, dessert lady."

Her eyes narrowed. "You just blew it, Ethan McMillan. I was going to bake you something special but—"

"Please don't punish me, sweetness." He put his forefinger to his lips before touching hers. "I'm sorry I called you dessert lady."

A sensual smile tilted the corners of her mouth. "Apology accepted."

They were the last words they exchanged as the sommelier returned with a bottle of chilled champagne and a crystal bowl filled with ice. Reaching for a corkscrew, he quickly and expertly uncorked the bottle, poured a small amount into a flute and handed it to Ethan. He repeated the gesture with Faith, who sipped the premium wine, holding it in her mouth for several seconds before swallowing.

She stared at her dining partner. He still hadn't sampled the champagne. "It's good."

"We'll take it," Ethan said to the sommelier. The wine steward filled the flutes, then backed away from the table. Holding the stem of the wineglass between his thumb and forefinger, he extended it toward Faith. "To trust."

She nodded. "To trust."

Faith couldn't remember the last time she'd enjoyed sharing dinner with a man. Her former dates were predisposed to monopolize the conversation by extolling their virtues, believing she was impressed with their achievements. A few times she'd sat silently, counting the number of times they used *I* or *me* repeatedly. One had used the pronoun more than two hundred times in less than ninety minutes. And when he called to invite her out again he couldn't understand why she'd rejected his offer of another date.

However, it was not the case with Ethan. It appeared as if he was reluctant to talk about himself. It was only after her subtle urging that he disclosed he was thirty-eight, the middle child and an only son of college professor parents. He told her that he'd graduated from the air force academy, trained as a fighter pilot at Andrews Air Force Base and had flown sorties in the Middle East. There came a swollen silence before he admitted to leaving the air force to become a commercial airline pilot; however, he'd remained a reservist until he celebrated his thirty-fifth birthday, retiring with the rank of major.

Faith glanced up at him through her lashes. "Do you still fly?"

"I do occasionally," he admitted truthfully. He'd piloted corporate clients for a while until he reconnected and hired two former air force pilots with whom he'd graduated flight school. "Do you like flying?" Ethan asked Faith.

Her head came up and she met his eyes. "It's okay."

"Just okay, Faith?"

"It's the fastest mode of transportation when you want to get somewhere in a hurry."

"That it is," he agreed.

Ethan put down his fork and touched the corners of his mouth with his napkin. He stared out the window at the lights in the many office buildings towering above the streets, avenues and canyons that made up Manhattan island rather than at the woman sitting across from him.

"Would you like to learn to fly?"

"No!"

He turned to look at her, seeing a flash of fear in her eyes. "I'd make certain nothing will happen to you."

"Can you guarantee it one hundred percent?" Faith retorted.

Ethan shook his head. "No, I can't."

"Then, my answer remains the same. No."

He and Faith made a toast to trust, and that was what he wanted her to do—trust him. Trust him not to cheat on her if they were to have a relationship, and trust him to keep her safe whenever they were together. Placing his napkin on the table, Ethan extended his hand. "Come, let's dance."

Faith, waiting until he stood up and came around the table, placed her hand in his outstretched palm. The orchestra was playing a slow number that had everyone up on the dance floor. Within seconds of finding herself in Ethan's embrace, she felt as if she belonged there.

The arm around her waist tightened until their bodies were molded from chest to thigh. His tailored clothing concealed a lean but hard muscular body. Her body went completely pliant as she sank into the tall, athletic physique. She was suddenly jolted into an awareness of how long it'd been since she'd permitted a man to hold her. What she refused to think of was how long it'd been since she'd slept with one. And, if she were truly honest with Simone, she would've admitted to having only two serious relationships.

The first one had been with a male model, and the second was her pastry chef instructor. What made their relationship more palatable *and* ethical was that the much-older man had waited until she graduated, then approached her. He was fifteen years her senior, and two years after they'd lived together, Faith decided it was time to end their liaison because he didn't trust her. Whenever she interacted with a younger man or men, her lover turned into someone she didn't know or recognize. Rather than risk becoming the statistic from a crime of passion, she moved out of his Upper East Side apartment and into the Greenwich Village studio. It was another three years before she agreed to date again, but with disastrous results. It was as if all of the losers had lined up to take a number to date Faith Whitfield.

"What perfume are you wearing?" Ethan asked close to Faith's ear.

"Why?" There was laughter in her query.

He spun her around and around in an intricate dance step. "You smell scrumptious." This time she did laugh, the soft tinkling sound sending a shiver of wanting over him. "What's so funny?"

"To me *scrumptious* translates into *delicious*." She smiled. "Only food can be delicious."

"I beg to differ, sweetness."

"You're going to have to make up your mind, Ethan. Am I sweet or delicious?"

Ethan stared at Faith's face, committing everything about it to memory. He recalled her saying that he was superficial, but he was past caring what she thought. What he felt, was beginning to feel for Faith Whitfield had surpassed his obsession to become a pilot. Once he'd mastered flying a single-engine plane, then it'd become a fighter jet. He'd set goals and achieved most of them, but this was the first time in his life that the objective was a woman. His head came down slowly.

"What are you doing?" Faith whispered seconds before his mouth covered hers in a soft kiss. It'd happened so quickly that she would have thought she'd imagined it, if not for his quickened respirations.

A knowing smile parted Ethan's strong, masculine mouth. "I just had to see whether you're delicious or sweet."

The kiss, though lasting mere seconds, left Faith's mouth burning for more. She rested her head on his shoulder rather than meet his omnipresent gaze. "What did you decide?"

"You're both," he whispered, his breath hot against her ear.

"You're not playing by the rules, Ethan."

"Why would you say that?"

"Because brief encounters don't include gratuitous kisses."

Without warning, he dipped her, her head inches from the floor, his mouth inches from hers. "What if we change the rules?"

Smiling up at him, Faith shook her head. "That can only happen by mutual agreement." Gracefully, as if he were a professional dancer, he eased her up and they stood in the middle of the dance floor smiling at each other. "The music stopped, Ethan," she whispered.

He didn't move. "I hadn't noticed."

Faith glanced over his shoulder to find everyone staring at them. "Ethan!" she gasped, totally embarrassed.

He blinked once, as if coming out of a trance. Looking around he saw countless pairs of eyes staring at him. The music started up again as the orchestra segued into another slow ballad. His entrancement with the woman in his embrace intensifying, Ethan rested his hand on the curve of Faith's waist and pulled her closer. He lost track of time as they glided across the floor. It was only when the music changed into an upbeat tempo that he led her back to their table. All of his motions were fluid as he seated her, lingering over her head longer than necessary.

"Thank you for dancing with me."

Staring up at him over her shoulder, Faith met his stare. "It was my pleasure."

Reaching for her right hand, Ethan held it firmly within his grasp and rounded the table, not letting her go, because although they weren't dancing he didn't want to let Faith go. He sat down, meeting her gaze. They'd spent nearly three hours at the Rainbow Room drinking champagne, sharing an exceptional three-course dinner and dancing together. Dining sixty-five stories above the pulsing, electrifying, crowded pedestrian and vehicular Manhattan traffic was like being whisked away to a make-believe world where only the two of them existed.

Her lashes lowered and he noticed Faith glancing at his watch under the French cuff of his shirt. "Are you ready to leave?"

She nodded. "Yes."

Pushing back his chair, he rounded the table and eased her to her feet. "I hope you enjoyed our brief encounter."

An intimate smile trembled over Faith's lips as she leaned into Ethan's warmth and strength. "What do you think?"

Ethan went completely still. The woman he wanted to kiss until he lost his breath, the woman who'd unknowingly twisted him into knots had become a teasing siren that made him feel a stirring of desire he was unable to ignore.

"Would you think me a superficial buffoon with an over-inflated ego if I said yes?"

"No, I wouldn't." She held up a hand. "And, before you ask me, the answer is yes, I will go out with you."

He bit back a smug grin. He wanted to tell Faith that he felt good when he was with her, and that he wanted to spend more time with her. "Thank you." The two simple words conveyed an emotion so foreign that he wasn't able to identify or explain it. Curbing the urge to kiss her, Ethan took a step backward. "Let me settle the check. Then I'll take you home."

Ethan opened the door and glanced around. The lowest setting on the lamp on the bedside table cast a soft glow throughout the Greenwich Village studio apartment. Reaching for Faith's hand, he pressed the keys to her palm, pulled her gently inside, closed the door and eased her to his chest.

"May I call you?"

Faith stared over Ethan's shoulder before she closed her eyes. He felt so good, smelled so good. She smiled, wondering why he sounded so tentative because she'd told him that she would go out with him again.

"Yes, you may."

"I'm going to be on the West Coast next week, but I promise to call you—"

"You don't have to call me until you get back," she said softly, cutting him off.

Easing back, Ethan stared down at Faith staring up at him. "Is that what you want?"

There came a beat of silence before she answered his query. "No, Ethan, it's not about what I want but what's practical. There's the three-hour time difference, and I don't want you to feel that you're obligated to call me." A mysterious smile curved her mouth. "I'll be here when you get back."

His smile was slower in coming, dimples slashing lean cheeks. "You're not going to accuse me of neglecting you?"

Justine had complained constantly whenever he was scheduled for a bicoastal or international flight, because it meant he'd be away for days. Her continuous badgering that he wasn't giving her enough attention or that she was fearful to be left alone forced him to check into a local hotel whenever he returned home rather than attempt to explain why he spent most of his waking hours in the air.

Faith rolled her eyes at the same time she sucked her teeth. "Of course not. I don't need you to entertain me."

"I knew there was something I liked about you when I first saw you."

"Yeah, I know," she drawled.

"But you don't know," Ethan countered, his smile still in place. "It's not only your face and *other* obvious assets, but also your spunkiness and independence."

Faith wanted to ask Ethan what *other* assets he was referring to, but decided not to broach the subject. She didn't know Ethan and he didn't know her, and she didn't want to say or do anything to upset their fragile association. She'd admitted to wanting to date him because he presented himself as the total package. Not only was he good-looking, but intelligent *and* socially adept. A man's looks weren't as important to her as intelligence and manners.

It'd been drummed into her head by Edith Whitfield that if a man didn't possess a modicum of home-training then she should keep walking. And it didn't matter the size of his bank account, level of education or social standing because to her mother good manners was the defining factor when forming a relationship with the opposite sex.

Edith, a former showroom model, who'd recently celebrated her thirty-fifth wedding anniversary to Henry Whitfield, professed she knew she was going to marry Henry the moment she was introduced to the tall, handsome man who was Malcolm Whitfield's identical twin brother. Her prediction was manifested because two months later they drove to Virginia and eloped, much to the consternation of her new mother-in-law, who refused to address Edith directly until after she'd presented her with another grandchild.

Looping her arms around Ethan's neck, Faith pressed a light kiss to his cheek. "Thanks for the compliment, but I'm going to have to say good-night because I have to get up early."

"Do you have to work tomorrow?"

She shook her head. "No. The shop is closed on Sunday and Monday."

Lowering his head, Ethan kissed Faith's forehead. "Try to relax."

"Yes, Doctor," she teased, smiling.

"On that note, I think it's time I take my leave. Good night, Faith."

Faith's smile was still in place after she closed and

locked the door. Their brief encounter had gone well, and she'd promised Ethan that she would go out with him.

Unknowingly Ethan McMillan had earned another check as a prince.

Chapter 7

Faith eased a pair of jeans over her hips, pulled up the zipper and buttoned the waistband. Surprisingly they fit. She'd bought the pair six months before, and after washing several times, discovered they were too tight. There was no doubt that she'd lost weight she could ill afford to lose. Tessa had remarked about her weight loss, and her explanation was that whenever she was stressed or overworked she neglected to eat. This year she'd made only two resolutions: to take better care of her health and not to date any frogs.

She'd gotten up earlier that morning and gone into Let Them Eat Cake to bake desserts to take with her to Franklin Lakes, New Jersey. Tessa had called to inform her that Edgar and Rosalind Sanborn had invited their guests to join them for a festive Super Bowl party; they'd also extended the invitation to include spending the night to join in celebrating Dr. Martin Luther King's birthday the following day. Her cousin had disclosed that Micah's parents met for the first time as law school students when they'd joined thousands of other students traveling south to march and sit-in at segregated lunch counters, bus and train depots.

Walking over to the window seat, Faith sat down and pushed her feet into a pair of black leather low-heel boots. She glanced around her apartment, mentally noting if she'd forgotten anything. She'd charged her cell phone; her overnight bag sat by the door; boxed cakes and cookies and her purse were on the dining-area table. The downstairs bell buzzed noisily like an annoying insect and she glanced at the clock. It was exactly nine o'clock. Crossing the room, she pressed a button on the intercom.

"Yes?"

"It's Tessa."

Faith pushed another button, disengaging the lock on the downstairs outer door. Reaching for a waist-length wool jacket, she slipped her arms into the sleeves. She put a hand into one of the pockets, making certain she had her wool cap. If she was to play football in the dead of winter, then she wanted to make sure she was dressed for the below-freezing temperatures.

She opened the door to Tessa's knock and came face-to-face with Micah Sanborn for the first time. There was something so inherently male about the district attorney that she found herself staring and holding her breath at the same time. His large, deep-set eyes took in everything in one sweeping glance. Faith noticed his close-cropped hair was flecked with a few gray strands at the temples. To say he was tall, dark and handsome was definitely an understatement. And Simone was right when she'd referred to him as a manly man.

She smiled. "Please come in."

Tessa turned, smiled at her fiancé, extending her hand. "Pay up, darling." Reaching into the pocket of his sheep-skin-lined bomber jacket, Micah Sanborn took out a dollar and placed it in Tessa's hand.

Faith rested her hands on her slim hips. "Would you mind telling me what you'd made wagers on?"

Tessa approached Faith and hugged her. "I told Micah that you would make something to take to his parents' place."

She glared at her cousin. "Tessa Whitfield, you know good and well that we were raised not to go to anyone's house empty-handed."

"You're right, cousin. I'm sorry, but I'm forgetting my manners." Taking two steps, Tessa reached for Micah's hand. "Micah, this Faith Whitfield. Although we're cousins, we think of ourselves as sisters. Faith, Micah Sanborn."

Faith extended her right hand, but Micah ignored it as he swept her up in a strong embrace. "Welcome to the family," she gasped, as he kissed her cheek.

"Thank you. Welcome to my family," he said softly. He released Faith, smiling. Grooves in his lean jaw made him more attractive with the gesture. "What do you want me to take downstairs, Faith?"

"You can take the boxes on the table. Be careful not to tilt them too much."

He stared at the boxes. "How on earth did you transport my sister's wedding cake from New York to New Jersey without it ending up in a mess of crumbs?" Micah asked as he stacked one box atop another.

"I packed it very carefully, then assembled it once I got to your parents' house. What also helps is that I use a delivery company that utilizes special bins and crates to transport fragile items, so even if the driver hits a bump the cake is still protected."

Tessa picked up the overnight bag on the floor near the door. "What else do you need to get?" she asked her cousin.

"That's everything." Gathering her keys and purse, Faith locked the door and followed Tessa and Micah down the three flights of stairs and out to the street. Their breaths were visible in the cold air as a light rain began falling. She caught up with her cousin. "I hope it snows," she whispered, sotto voce.

Tessa quickened her pace and gave Faith a sidelong glance before she stared at her fiancé loading the rear of her SUV with the boxed desserts. "I listened to the Weather Channel this morning, and they're predicting a snowy mix," she said low enough so that Micah wouldn't overhear their conversation. "When Micah asked why I couldn't stop grinning, I didn't have the heart to tell him about the weather forecast. You'd think watching the Super Bowl should be enough football for one day."

Faith rolled her eyes upward. "Girl, please. You're preaching to the choir. One thing I'm not is a fan of football."

Without warning, Micah turned and looked at the two cousins, successfully concealing a smile behind an expression of indifference. He'd overhead them complain about playing touch football, which had become a Sanborn Sunday-afternoon tradition. It permitted everyone to get together after brunch for an hour of noncompetitive physical interaction.

He stared at Faith Whitfield, silently admiring her natural beauty. Although she and Tessa did not look alike, there was something inherent in them that indicated they were related. However, there was no doubt that Tessa and Simone were sisters.

"Did Tessa tell you about our Sunday-morning football game?" he asked innocently.

Faith went completely still, wondering whether Micah had overheard her talking to Tessa about not wanting to play football. "Yes, she did."

His expressive eyebrows lifted slightly. "Are you ready to play?"

"No."

"No?" Micah repeated, his eyes widening in disbelief.

"I'll help with cooking and cleaning, but no football." She'd use any excuse she could to get out of rolling around on the ground.

Opening the side door to the second row of seats, Micah assisted Faith into the vehicle. The first time he'd invited Tessa to his parents' house she'd also complained about playing touch football. It was apparent the Whitfields were girly girls.

"We'll see," he mumbled under his breath after he'd closed the door. He helped Tessa up into the passenger-side seat, then rounded the SUV and sat behind down behind the wheel.

Once he left New York and crossed the state line for New Jersey the rain turned into snow. Glancing up into the rearview mirror, he smiled at Faith. "It looks as if you got your wish."

"What's that?" she asked, staring at the back of his head.

"It's snowing."

"Don't tell me you heard me?"

Glancing quickly over his shoulder, Micah gave her a smug look. "Yes, I did."

A wave of heat swept up Faith's chest, settling in her face. "You must have ears like a bat."

Micah rested his right hand on Tessa's knee. "I've told Tessa that I have special powers, but she doesn't believe me."

Tessa emitted an unladylike snort. "You wish."

Faith closed her eyes, pressed her back to the leather seat, listening to the easy banter between Tessa and her fiancé. She had no doubt that falling in love with Micah had changed her cousin. She now appeared less guarded, and her laughter was spontaneous, not forced.

The gentle motion of the vehicle and the heat coming through the vents lulled Faith into a state of complete relaxation where she forgot about her coffee-table book, the two Valentine's Day wedding receptions and her "brief encounter" with Ethan McMillan until Micah activated a button on his visor's remote to open the iron gates to the Sanborns' Franklin Lakes property.

Faith recognized Simone's truck parked behind several SUVs and minivans, which meant her parents, aunt and uncle had arrived before them. The first time she'd come to Franklin Lakes it was to assemble the four-tier cake for Bridget Sanborn and Seth Cohen's wedding.

Simone had come the day before and decorated the living and dining rooms and ballroom with baskets filled with white calla lilies, cosmos, orchids, gardenias and deep magenta roses that were repeated in Bridget's bridal bouquet. And in the time it took to assemble the cake, a team of workers had arrived to set up tables and chairs for eighty-three wedding guests, while the catering staff filed into the larger of the two kitchens as she climbed into the rental van to return to New York.

Faith had celebrated the beginning of a new year cloistered in her apartment, watching television as the ball dropped in Times Square. She'd been invited to several parties, but had elected to stay home rather than put up with the crowds of raucous partygoers who'd believed it was all right to overindulge because it was New Year's Eve. Her parents had invited her to go to Mount Vernon to celebrate the holiday with them and her other relatives, but she'd also declined their invitation because she found that she wanted to be alone to reflect on the course her life had taken. At thirty, she'd revised her wish list for the next decade. It'd become a practice for her to update her wish list every ten years.

Micah, balancing the boxes in one hand, opened the door to the three-story manor-style house, and she and Tessa walked into a great room with a ceiling rising upward to three stories. The massive chandelier, floor and table lamps were aglow, offsetting the shadowy gray light coming through the many tall windows.

A teenage girl with a fall of black curly hair caught up in a ponytail and earbuds in her ears skipped down the winding staircase. "Grandma, Uncle Micah and Aunt Tessa are here!" she screamed at the top of her lungs as she crossed the marble floor and launched herself at Micah, who fortunately had placed the cake boxes on a table in the entryway.

Micah stared at his niece as if she'd taken leave of her senses. Reaching for the thin white wires, he removed them from her ears. "Dial it down, Marisol."

She placed a hand over her mouth when Rosalind Sanborn came to see what the shouting was about. "Sorry about that," she mumbled in apology.

Rosalind's face lit up when she saw Micah with his fiancée and her cousin. Arms extended, she hugged and kissed Micah, Tessa and then Faith. Eyes the color of brilliant blue topaz crinkled attractively. Casually dressed in a pair of running shoes, sweatpants and shirt with a fading college logo, she looked nothing like the elegantly attired woman who'd been mother of the bride three weeks before. Although petite and slender, there was something about the woman with the coiffed short silver hair that radiated a strength that didn't compromise her femininity. Even without makeup her porcelain complexion was flawless.

"Welcome, Faith," Rosalind crooned softly.

"Thank you for inviting me, Mrs. Sanborn."

"It's Rosalind," the older woman admonished softly.

Faith nodded. "Okay, Rosalind."

"Where's everybody, Mom?" Micah asked.

"They're in the kitchen." She motioned to her granddaughter. "Marisol, take Tessa's and Faith's bags up to Bridget's room." Smiling at Tessa, she said, "I hope you don't mind sharing the room with Simone and Faith."

Tessa shook her head. "No, I don't mind." She'd lost count of the number of times she, Simone and Faith had shared a bedroom when growing up. And even now in their thirties they still had occasional sleepovers.

Rosalind pressed her palms together. "I'll show you where you can hang up your jackets." Turning on her heel, she followed Micah to the kitchen. "The men have volunteered to do the cooking today."

Faith shared a knowing glance with Tessa. Malcolm and Henry learned to cook when their parents opened one of the first take-out-only restaurants in the Mount Vernon–New Rochelle Westchester County communities, and they'd continued the reputation of concocting the finest Southern-inspired cuisine when they established Whitfield Caterers for weddings, family reunions, sweet sixteen and retirement celebrations. One year they had the distinction of catering a high school prom. Although their fathers owned a catering establishment, the brothers hadn't cooked in years because they'd hired and trained a staff of talented chefs whose culinary skills had become legendary throughout Westchester County.

She and Tessa stored their jackets in a large closet off the kitchen. When they walked into the kitchen they were met by a cacophony of voices competing to be heard as three generations of Sanborns mingled comfortably with two generations of Whitfields.

Faith's father, Henry Whitfield, wasn't only identical to Malcolm, but also a mirror image. Henry was right-handed to Malcolm's left-handedness. Tall and slender, both men had affected salt-and-pepper trimmed mustaches and goatees. The facial hair added character to their khaki-brown faces, and with close-cropped curly graying hair and hazel eyes they presented as handsome middle-aged men.

The brothers, along with Micah's father, a former judge who now taught courses at Princeton Law School, all wore white bibbed aprons. When Tessa had told Faith about Micah's mixed-race, multicultural family, she'd found the information intriguing until Tessa had explained that Rosalind's inability to have children of her own led her and Edgar to adopt children who were abandoned, born to drug-addicted mothers and one with a physical disability. With an infinite amount of patience and love the Sanborn offspring had thrived and excelled far beyond anyone's expectation. Micah had become a lawyer and Bridget a children's book editor; one brother had become a biblical historian and the other a pharmacist.

Reaching for Faith's hand, Rosalind turned to Tessa. "Please introduce Faith to everyone."

As if on cue a swollen silence filled the enormous

kitchen and Faith saw curious and familiar stares directed in her direction. She smiled when her father winked at her. Tessa began with Edgar Sanborn, who with his rich baritone voice and mane of patrician salt-and-pepper hair could've passed for an aging matinee idol. Smiling and repeating the appropriate "my pleasure," or "nice meeting you," she was introduced to Micah's brothers William and Abram, his sisters-in-law Melinda and Ruby and his identical-twin, ten-year-old redheaded nephews Isaac and Jacob. She continued with fifteen-year-old Marisol and lastly two-year-old Kimika, who clung to Simone's neck as if she were her lifeline.

Marisol approached Faith once the introductions were over. "I'll show you where you can wash up." Leading her to a half bath off the kitchen, she closed the door. "Mommy and Daddy promised to give me a sweet-sixteen party next year. With my uncle marrying your cousin we're going to be family and…" A rush of color darkened her face, and, seemingly embarrassed, she let her words trail off.

Turning on solid brass faucets, Faith adjusted the water and soaped her hands with a vanilla-scented soap gel. She smiled at the spontaneous adolescent. "You want me to make your cake." Her query was a statement.

Marisol bit down on her lower lip as she struggled to contain her enthusiasm. "Will you?"

"Of course I will."

Pumping her fists, she spun around on her toes of her running shoes. "Yes!" Throwing her arms around Faith's neck, she pulled her head down and kissed her cheek. "Thanks, Aunt Faith."

I'm not your aunt, Faith mused as Marisol slipped out

of the bathroom. If the two families were joined when Tessa married Micah, then she and Marisol would become cousins through marriage.

She rejoined the others in the kitchen. Her mother, aunt and Rosalind were carrying plates and serving pieces into the formal dining room. Although the table in a corner of the kitchen seated ten, it still wasn't large enough for the eighteen who would sit down for Sunday brunch. William and Abram were chopping ingredients for omelets, while Ruby and redheaded, freckle-faced Melinda rolled out dozens of chive and cheddar biscuits.

One of the twin boys patted Edgar's arm to get his attention. "Grandpa, can you make green eggs and ham?"

Edgar, who was cracking eggs into a large aluminum bowl, stopped and exchanged glances with Henry and Malcolm, both of whom lifted their shoulders.

"You can make them with chive butter," Faith said in a quiet voice. Isaac and Jacob, who'd inherited their father's olive-brown coloring and their mother's curly red hair, cheered loudly, while Kimika patted her chubby hands in response to the cheering.

Simone rubbed noses with the toddler. "Do you want green eggs and ham, too?"

Throwing back her neatly braided head, Kimika shrieked, "Kimmie want eggs!"

Faith smiled at Simone's antics, and suddenly it hit her. Simone had married a man she thought was the love of her life, but unfortunately Anthony Kendrick was either too spoiled or too lazy to work, so their union ended before it could begin. And Faith knew Simone wanted a child. Seeing her usually sullen cousin with Kimika made it all the more apparent.

Henry put down a knife, wiped his hands on a towel and motioned to Faith. "Come, baby, and do your thing."

"Daddy, you know how to make chive butter," Faith insisted.

"It's time I set up the warming trays, or we're going to eat cold food."

Ruby pointed to the walk-in refrigerator. "You'll find the chives in a container on a lower shelf."

Faith hadn't come to Franklin Lakes to cook, but it was preferable to playing touch football in the dead of winter.

Faith lay across the bed in Bridget's old bedroom with Tessa, while Simone reclined on a daybed with Kimika cradled to her chest. The little girl, thumb in mouth, had fallen asleep. After what had become a fun-filled three-hour brunch, everyone had retreated to their respective bedrooms to relax.

"I can't believe I ate so much," Tessa crooned sleepily.

"Do the Sanborns eat like this every Sunday?" Faith asked, not opening her eyes.

"With the exception of the sirloin steaks and fried chicken and waffles, yes," Tessa said. Her father had suggested the chicken and waffles, and the Sanborns' response to the crispy fried chicken drizzled with honey over crisp Belgian waffles was overwhelming.

"Damn," Simone whispered, "it's no wonder they play football to work off the calories."

"I'm not complaining, because everything was delicious," Faith said, smiling.

Tessa turned over to face Faith. "The steak with the chive butter was working."

"You have to teach me how to make it," Simone said.

"Don't tell me you want to learn how to cook now," Faith teased.

Simone pushed out her lower lip. "I know how to cook, but what I make isn't fancy like yours and Tessa's."

Sitting up, Faith leaned on an elbow. "Anyone can throw a steak on a grill, but when you take the time to marinate it beforehand that's what makes it above average."

Tessa also sat up, supporting her back on a mound of lace-trimmed pillows. "You have to take the time to make it fancy, Simone."

Simone angled her head. "Is that how you snagged Micah, Tessa? Once you cooked for him he couldn't resist you?"

Tessa shook her head slowly. "No. Micah's no neophyte when it comes to cooking."

"Unlike Tony, who couldn't boil water for a cup of tea," Simone spat out.

Faith met Simone's angry stare. "What was your cockroach ex-husband good for aside from looking pretty?"

Vertical lines appeared between Simone's large hazel eyes. "Now that I'm finally able to step back and assess what went wrong with my marriage—not much."

"I hope he was good in bed," Tessa said with no emotion in her voice.

Simone sucked her teeth loudly. "He even struck out in that department, too."

"No!"

"Damn!"

Tessa and Faith had spoken in unison.

"That's some kind of pathetic, Simi," Faith said, shaking her head. "Anytime a man gets a failing grade in everything, and that includes lovemaking, then it's time to show him the door."

"Speaking of men," Simone said. "What's happening with you and Ethan McMillan?"

"Is he a prince or a frog?" Tessa asked, running her fingers through her short hair.

Faith felt a warm glow flow through her. "So far he hasn't earned any ribbits."

Simone's smile was dazzling. "Good for you."

Faith felt comfortable telling her cousins about her date with Ethan, and the more she talked about him the more she realized just how much she looked forward to going out with him again.

The softly falling snow had changed over to sleet, then finally rain, and it was the hypnotic tapping against the windows that finally lulled everyone to sleep.

Chapter 8

Faith, a towel wrapped turban-style around her head and a bath sheet swathing her body, walked out of the bathroom to answer the phone. The two days she'd spent with the Sanborns that were relaxing and fun-filled had set the stage for the week. The weather changed, and seemingly the pace of the city quickened with the warmer weather as afternoon temperatures topped out in the mid- and lower sixties; however, New Yorkers were not fooled by spring-like weather, so they enjoyed it while they could.

She and Ranee had baked and decorated more than fifteen cakes for her book, bringing the total to twenty. Faith had decided to use piping bags to make the realistic-looking flowers, colorful characters and lifelike animals rather than mold them by hand, which would've taken many hours to complete one flower. Ranee photographed each cake with a digital camera and later that evening Faith downloaded the pictures onto her laptop, then typed up recipes and descriptions for decorating each cake. It was the last week of January and she'd completed one-fifth of her book project.

Picking up the receiver without glancing at the caller display, Faith rested a hip against the kitchen's countertop. "Good morning," she said cheerfully into the mouthpiece.

"Is it really a good morning?" asked the deep male voice on the other end of the connection.

Faith froze, her heart beating a double-time rhythm. "E-than?" She hadn't realized there was a quiver in her voice.

There was a pause before he said, "Are you all right, Faith?"

She recovered quickly. "Yes…yes, I am. I just didn't expect to hear your voice."

"I did promise to call you."

Her heart settled back to its normal rhythm. "Yes, I know."

"Are you sure you're all right? If this is a bad time or if you have company, then I'll call back another time."

"I don't have company, Ethan McMillan."

"If you're going to be pissed off at me, then you should use my full name, Miss Faith Whitfield."

"What is it?"

"Ethan James McMillan."

A hint of a smile played at the corners of Faith's mouth. "For your information, Ethan James McMillan, I'm not angry with you. It's six-thirty in the morning, I just got out of the shower and I hadn't expected to answer my phone and hear your voice."

His sensual chuckle caressed her ear. "Now that we've gotten that out of the way, how was your week?"

"It was wonderful. And yours?"

"Other than a little residual jetlag, I'm good. I called to ask you whether you'd go out with me tomorrow night."

Faith smiled. "It just so happens I'm free tomorrow night." She'd gotten up early to go into Let Them Eat Cake to complete decorating a cake that resembled a teddy bears' picnic for a bank president's daughter's sixth birthday.

"Do you like jazz?"

"Yes, I do." She'd grown up listening to her father and uncle playing their favorite jazz performers on vinyl records.

"Good. I'm going to take you to a club that's off the beaten track in Philly. It's a little seedy, but the food and live music more than make up for the lack of ambience."

Faith wanted to ask Ethan why rule out the celebrated Greenwich Village jazz venues to drive to Philadelphia to hear live jazz but held her tongue. If they survived the encounter to set up another date, then she would suggest one in her neighborhood.

"What time should I be ready?"

"I'll pick you up at six. By the way, dress is casual."

"Okay. I'll see you tomorrow."

"I can't wait," Ethan said softly.

Stomach muscles contracting, Faith bit down on her lower lip. "Hang up, Ethan," she whispered.

His sensual chuckle reverberated in her ear again. "Did I embarrass you, sweetness?"

"Goodbye, Ethan." Depressing a button, she ended the call.

Removing the towel from her damp hair, Faith chided herself for getting flustered because a very sexy man had admitted that he couldn't wait to see her.

Although not vain about her looks, Faith knew men

were attracted to her face and—those who preferred slim women—her body. She'd grown up believing her mother was the most beautiful woman in the entire world, unaware that she and Edith Whitfield looked exactly alike. Her body eventually filled out, and girls whom she'd considered her friends turned into *heifers* when she secured her first modeling assignment and shattered her fairy-tale world where everyone and everything was good. The realization that her face and body set her apart from her peers made her uncomfortable when it should've empowered her.

If Ethan couldn't wait to see her, then the truth was she also couldn't wait to see him again.

Ethan shifted the pillow beneath his head and turned over on his side. He'd been counting the hours and number of miles it took for him to return to the East Coast, because he'd left Faith's telephone numbers in New Jersey. Calling her from California had become a temptation he wasn't certain he'd be able to resist.

Everything about Faith Whitfield was tempting: her face, body, smell, voice and the way she lowered her head slightly to glance up at him from under her lashes. He doubted whether she was aware of the seductiveness of the gesture because she executed it with a spontaneity that was effortless.

Ethan admitted to Faith that he was undergoing jet lag when what he felt went beyond circadian rhythms gone awry. He was exhausted. William Raymond had asked that he fly him to Las Vegas for pre-Grammy parties before traveling on to Los Angeles for the actual ceremonies. WJ, surrounded by a cadre of bodyguards and trailed by reporters and photographers from the major entertainment tabloids and magazines, never seemed to tire from the nonstop parties, blasting music and the forced laughter from those who hadn't had enough sleep, food and definitely had too much to drink. He suspected the frenetic energy of the partygoers was fueled by illegal substances that made them forget who they were and what they did, hours after they came down off their high. Cognizant that his cousin didn't drink or take drugs, Ethan marveled that WJ hadn't exhibited any signs of exhaustion until he collapsed within minutes of boarding the jet for the return flight. He slept throughout the flight, waking when the aircraft landed on a private airstrip near Newark Airport.

If his client had been anyone other than his cousin, Ethan wouldn't have made the cross-country flight. He closed his eyes and took deep breaths to slow his respiration. Minutes later he drifted off into a deep, dreamless sleep, and his last images were those of the face of a woman who'd occupied his every waking moment.

For the first time in his life Ethan found himself at a loss for words. The woman standing on the other side of the door looked as if she'd just stepped off the catwalk or off the set for a photo shoot. This time she hadn't brushed her hair, but left it natural. The short black curls softened her delicate features, making her look much younger than thirty. Dark shadows on her lids and arching eyebrows above her wide-set eyes drew his rapt attention.

"Please come in."

The sound of her smoky voice broke the spell as he stepped into Faith's apartment. Dipping his head, he kissed her cheek. "How are you?"

Faith felt a shiver shake her body when she inhaled the

scent of Ethan's cologne that was intensified by the heat from his body. He was casually dressed in black cashmere: jacket, modified V-neck sweater that bared his strong throat and slacks.

"I'm good, thank you." She turned to find him staring at her with a strange expression on his face. "Is something wrong?"

Ethan blinked as if coming out of a deep trance. "No. I just can't believe that you could improve on perfection. You look incredible."

Faith wore a long-sleeved black sweater over a pair of matching cuffed black stretch slacks that hugged every curve of her slender body. Black sheer hose and a pair of black patent-leather peep-toe pumps completed her winning look. There was no doubt she was quite comfortable with her height to wear three-inch heels. Her only accessory was a pair of large yellow-gold hoops in her pierced lobes.

Lowering her head and peering up at Ethan through her lashes, Faith gave him a demure smile. "Thank you."

He shook his head. "Don't thank me, Faith. I had nothing to do with the way you look. What I will thank you for is agreeing to go out with me."

She wanted to tell Ethan that he looked incredible, but didn't want to turn it into a mutual admiration competition. Reaching for a lined leather jacket, she handed it to him. He held it while she slipped her arms into the sleeves. Then she gathered a small purse and her keys.

"I'm ready."

Are you really ready? Ethan wanted to ask Faith. Was she ready for him? Ready for what he'd planned for them? It'd been a long time since he'd found himself so enthralled with a woman that he felt as if he were embarking on his first solo flight. He, who'd flown an F-16 "Viper" armed with six air-to-air sidewinder missiles or cluster bombs, was about to embark on his most important mission where he hoped to get Faith Whitfield to trust him. Reaching for her hand, he led her out of her apartment building to where he'd parked his car.

Ethan pushed a button for the ignition, but paused before shifting into gear. "Would you mind listening to a few Motown oldies?"

Faith shook head, staring at the man sitting inches from her. Everything about him made normal breathing difficult for her, and she couldn't fathom what it was about her date that made her feel as if he'd sucked up all of the air around her. Ethan was too close, too potent and now she knew what songwriters and poets meant when they wrote about love and its effects on one's senses.

"No, I don't mind," she said as if in a soporific trance.

Turning her head, she stared out the side window rather than look at Ethan. He'd removed his jacket, and the contours of his chest and broad shoulders were clearly defined under the black sweater molded to his upper body. She smiled when the distinctive gravelly sound of David Ruffin's voice singing lead on "It's Growing" filled the coupe.

"Motown and jazz," she said in a quiet voice. "You have an eclectic taste in music."

Maneuvering smoothly away from the curb and into the flow of traffic, Ethan concentrated on the taillights of the car in front of his. "You can't imagine how eclectic it is."

Faith turned to stare at his profile. "Are you saying you're into classical music, too?"

He nodded, smiling. "I like Ludwig, Wolfgang Amadeus and Johannes the same way teenagers are into hip-hop and R & B."

"Who's your favorite?"

"Piotr Ilyich Tchaikovsky."

Now, Faith was more than intrigued by Ethan. "I went to see *The Nutcracker Suite* at Lincoln Center one Christmas."

"Which did you enjoy more, the music or the dancers?"

"Both. What about you, Ethan?"

"I would have to say the music. One time I sat through the entire production with my eyes closed, listening and imagining what was happening onstage. I came away more awed than if I'd viewed it."

"Who exposed you to classical music?"

Ethan gave Faith a quick glance. "I come from a musical family. My parents both play the piano. They're also amateur ballroom dancers. My sisters teach music and voice at different high schools. Tonight I'm taking you to a jazz club that has been in my family for more than seventy years. I've heard relatives say that my great-uncles sold moonshine and ten-cent dinners to their customers during Prohibition and the Depression to keep the doors open. They patched a leaking roof with tin and filled the cracks in the walls with newspaper to keep out the elements during hard times, but every Friday and Saturday night the place was filled with wall-to-wall regulars who came to eat, dance and listen to live music."

"That sounds fascinating." Faith's voice was filled with awe at the same time her eyes sparkled like polished onyx. "What instruments do you play?"

"Piano, sax and occasionally the clarinet."

"Are you going to sit in tonight?"

Ethan shook his head. "No."

"Why not?"

"I asked you to come with me so we could be together. And if I sit in with the band, then that would be ignoring you."

"I told you before that I don't need you to entertain me, Ethan."

"I beg to differ with you, Faith. If I play tonight, then I would be entertaining you."

"Don't try and twist my words."

"You were the one who mentioned entertaining. How did you spend your week?" he asked smoothly, changing the topic.

Faith was grateful that Ethan had changed the subject or else she would've found herself engaged in a debate that would've probably ended with him earning his first frog point; she told him that her cousin was getting married in June and that she would become a maid of honor for the first time, therefore the Whitfields had spent the weekend with the Sanborns. He laughed softly when she told him that there'd been nonstop cooking and eating. Traffic slowed on the ramp leading to the turnpike and Ethan pushed a button to activate the navigational screen. Within seconds several alternate routes were displayed.

"Hold on," he warned, maneuvering expertly around the car in front of them once he saw an opening, and turning onto to a less-traveled road. "It's going to take us a little longer getting there, but it's worth it if we don't have to sit in bumper-to-bumper traffic."

"Do you like driving?" Her question seemed to startle him, because the seconds ticked off before he answered.

"It pays the bills."

"It pays the bills," Faith echoed. "Piloting planes also pay bills."

Ethan knew he'd walked into a trap of his own choosing with his reply. He hadn't meant for it to come out so glib, yet it was too late to take back his words. "I love flying, but I'm not as passionate about it as I used to be."

What he could not and didn't want to reveal to Faith was that he was sole owner and president of MAC Elite Car Services and MAC Executive Air Travel. He wanted her to like Ethan James McMillan, not what he represented in dollars and cents. The year before he set up the car service, he'd purchased a converted 737. His financial planner had recommended he sell two of the three brownstones and a trio of apartment buildings he'd inherited from an aunt and uncle—a pediatrician and cardiologist respectively, both of whom had had lucrative private practices. Six months before, he'd used the proceeds from the sale of the real estate to secure a loan for the thirty-six-million-dollar G 550 business jet. His decision to buy the Gulfstream was based on the age and number of miles on the 737, and Ethan knew it would be another two years before he would be forced to ground the older aircraft permanently.

"I know how you feel," Faith remarked after a comfortable silence.

Ethan's fingers tightened on the steering wheel. "You do?"

Faith's comment surprised him. The women he'd dated since his divorce were usually appalled when he disclosed that he'd given up a career as a pilot in order to become a chauffeur. What he didn't tell them was that he owned the car service *and* the private business jets with an extensive client list that included CEOs, athletes, music industry executives and those with enough money and not enough time to wait in commercial airline terminals.

"Of course. I was trained as a chef, yet I only cook when it's absolutely necessary. This past weekend was the exception because of a request for green eggs and ham. I work harder and put in many more hours decorating specialty cakes, but the results are much more rewarding."

"Will you cook for me?"

"What!"

Ethan set the cruise control and removed his foot from the gas pedal. "I know you heard me the first time, but I'll say it again. If I pay you, will you cook for me?"

"Define *cook* for me, Ethan."

"Dinner."

"When?"

"Whenever you're free."

Faith let out an audible sigh. "Lately I'm not that familiar with the word."

Reaching over, Ethan placed his hand over hers resting on her lap. "You're with me tonight."

"That's because I made time for you, Ethan."

"Are you saying I should consider myself fortunate that you made time for me?"

Faith reversed their hands, her thumb tracing the outline of the signet ring on his little finger. "No, I wouldn't say that. I'm with you tonight because I wanted to see you again."

Faith Whitfield had just gone up several more degrees on the Ethan McMillan scale of approval. It was apparent that she wasn't shy about speaking her mind or making her feelings known. He added *supremely secure* to her list of other positive attributes.

"I spent the whole week thinking about you." He smiled when he heard her soft gasp of surprise. "You're very different from other women I've known."

Recovering quickly, Faith asked, "How many have you known?"

"You're not playing fair. If you don't ask me about the women in my past, then I won't ask you about the men in your past."

"I don't have a lot of men in my past."

"Good for you."

Faith stared at Ethan in astonishment. "Why good for me?"

He exhaled a heavy sigh. "You have no idea of how difficult it is to deal with a woman nowadays, because she's usually carrying a lot of baggage from past relationships. If it's not her ex-husband, then it's baby-daddy drama."

"I have neither, so as long as we continue to see each other you won't have to concern yourself with those issues."

Ethan wanted to tell Faith that that was one of the reasons why he wanted to see her, because she was unencumbered. He'd gone out with single mothers, but hesitated getting too close to their children in the event the relationship wouldn't last. The first time it happened he was completely devastated when the mother of two young boys neglected to tell him that her children's father had been incarcerated and when paroled would come home to live with her.

"When do you think you'll be able to fit me into your very busy schedule?"

"Probably not until after Valentine's Day. It's one of the busiest times for the shop and I have two weddings on that day."

A slight frown appeared between his eyes. "How are you going to accomplish that?"

"There's your cousin's afternoon wedding at Tavern on the Green and the other will be held at a country club on Long Island later that evening. And I still haven't figured out how I'm going to get a birthday cake to Palm Beach, Florida, for a client's granddaughter's birthday party for the same day."

"Why don't you ship it overnight?"

Faith told Ethan about her telephone conversations with Tomasina Fiori. "I don't have time to fly to Palm Beach to bake a cake for her granddaughter." She didn't tell him that Tommi was at the top of her elite client list.

"How long will it take to bake and decorate the cake?"

"Probably about ten to twelve hours. Why?"

Ethan's mind worked overtime as he chose his words carefully. "I believe I'll be able to help you out."

Shifting on her seat, Faith gave him a long, penetrating look. "How?"

"I'll see if I can arrange for you to fly to Florida and—"

"No, no, no," she said in protest, cutting him off.

He put up a hand to stop her. "Stop acting like a two-year-old, Faith, and hear me out." Her jaw dropped, but no words came out. "Are you listening?"

"Yes, I am listening." There was no mistaking her annoyance with his reference to her acting like a spoiled toddler.

"I know several pilots who fly private jets between New York, Florida and California several times each week. Valentine's Day falls on a Saturday this year, so they can fly you down early Friday morning and have you back in New York either late Friday night or early Saturday morning."

Faith pondered his suggestion. She and Ranee would finish both weddings cakes by Thursday evening, so that would leave her time to go down to Florida and return before Saturday afternoon.

"That could work," she said softly.

"Of course it would work."

Faith landed a soft punch on Ethan's solid shoulder. "You don't have to sound so smug about it."

He shot her a dark look. "Why is it so difficult for you to thank me? I'm not going to ask for anything in return."

It was the second time Ethan had chastised her about not thanking him. The first was when he'd waited to drive her back to WJ's penthouse for Savanna's engagement party. "Thank you, Mr. McMillan," she drawled facetiously.

"I'm going to take back what I said about not asking for anything in return."

Faith's delicate jaw dropped slightly, her mouth opening and closing several times before she was able to say, "What are you talking about?"

"I'm going to ask that you spend the Valentine's weekend with me. Give me Sunday and Monday, and we're even."

It took a full minute before she was able to process what Ethan had just said. "You're buggin'."

"No, I'm not, Faith. I'm offering to help you out with someone I assume is a very important client, and you don't want to spend forty-eight hours with me."

"And do what, pray tell?"

"Relax, share meals and listen to music, etcetera, etcetera, etcetera."

Faith detected a hint of condescension in his voice but chose to ignore it. Ethan was right. He was presenting her with an opportunity to give all of her clients what they wanted and she was balking when he suggested she give him two days—a mere forty-eight hours.

The sound of Diana Ross and the Supremes singing "Someday We'll Be Together," coming through the speakers, and the beating of her heart held her spellbound. Were the lyrics prophetic of her future with Ethan? What were the odds that someday they would become a couple?

"Okay. I'd like very much to spend the Valentine's Day weekend with you."

Ethan's dimples winked when he flashed a grin. "Thank you, Faith."

She inclined her head. "You're welcome, Ethan. Where are we going?"

"It's a surprise. The only thing I'm going to tell you is to make certain you bring your passport and pack a swimsuit."

Faith was hard-pressed not to shout aloud. She'd been fantasizing about relaxing on a beach with a warm breeze feathering over her scantily clad body. "Thank you," she crooned laughingly, her normally throaty voice dropping an octave.

Ethan's deep chuckle joined her seductive laughter as a slender thread pulled them closer while wrapping both in invisible warmth that signaled an intense physical awareness of each other.

Chapter 9

Ethan was right. What Bessie's, named for the inimitable blues singer Bessie Smith, lacked in ambience was offset by incredible soul food, a lively crowd and a live band. The clapboard building sported a new coat of paint and a door with a security panel cutout reminiscent of those in speakeasies where the owners sold either bootleg whiskey or moonshine. Bessie's was filled to capacity. Every chair at the many round tables and those lined up along the bar was occupied.

The octet's repertoire included early jazz masters, swing and modern innovators such as Dave Brubeck, Charlie Parker and Miles Davis. Faith and Ethan shared a smile when after a short intermission they segued into smooth jazz. The guest vocalists, a talented husband-and-wife duo, sang selections made popular by Ella Fitzgerald, Billie Holliday, Al Jarreau, Diana Washington, Anita Baker, Will Downing, Sade Adu and Jonathan Butler.

Faith wasn't certain what she enjoyed more, the music or the food. She'd selected fricassee chicken, fried cabbage seasoned with pieces of smoked meat and potato salad, while Ethan ordered short ribs, macaroni and cheese and collard greens.

"How are the collards?" she asked.

Ethan picked up an extra fork, speared a small portion and extended it to her. "Taste for yourself."

Her eyebrows lifted as she chewed the tenderly cooked greens. Nodding, she smiled. "Now, that's good."

"Do you like the chicken?" He'd suggested she order the house's specialty.

Faith gave him a sidelong glance, noting the length of lashes touching Ethan's cheekbones. It wasn't fair that his lashes were longer and thicker than hers. "It's incredible. Everything's delicious. Good food, good music and—"

"And very, very good company," he interrupted in a hushed whisper.

She stared at up him through lowered lids. The flickering light from the candle on the table threw the angles of his face in sharp relief, the yellow flame firing the pinpoints of gold in his strangely colored eyes.

"You're right," she whispered, "about very good company."

Ethan inwardly railed against the restaurant's hard-and-fast rule of no dancing, because at that moment he wanted Faith in his arms, her body pressed to his so he could communicate wordlessly what he was beginning to feel for her, how she'd affected him as no other woman he'd ever met or known intimately. And if he had to truthfully ask himself whether he wanted to make love to her, then the answer would be a resounding, unequivocal *yes!*

Once he'd realized he wanted to get to know Faith Whit-field better, he knew it wasn't physical. Sex—that was something he could get from any woman, but a single interaction with Faith communicated that she wasn't just any woman, at least not one who relied on a man for her day-to-day existence.

He'd become good friends with a fellow cadet who talked incessantly about marrying her high school sweet-heart once she graduated the academy. They did marry and had remained married, but each time he spoke to her she bragged about how wonderful her married life was, which led Ethan to believe that she was continually overcompen-sating because she had to convince herself that her life was perfect. Psychologists would've termed her behavior a reaction formation, while he would've called her a liar.

However, Faith appeared to be the complete opposite. She'd talked about not wanting or *needing* a man to enter-tain her. She was independent, and she and only she deter-mined what she wanted to do next. He knew he'd pressured her to go away with him, but Ethan knew that if she truly hadn't wanted to go then she would've said so. The fact that she acquiesced was a sign that she enjoyed his company as much as he enjoyed hers.

And, more than anything else, he wanted her to have a choice, the choice whether to see or not see him and the choice to end their fragile relationship whenever she felt it had run its course.

"Amazing," he said reverently, unable to pull his gaze away from her sexy mouth.

A hint of a smile parted Faith's lips as she turned to look at the vocalists staring into each other's eyes as they sang a romantic ballad. "Yes, they are amazing."

Ethan wanted to shake Faith until she begged him to stop. Didn't she know that he was talking about her? He found it hard to believe that the woman with the incredible face and drop-dead-gorgeous body could be that self-effacing.

"I agree," he said in a tone that he doubted sounded very convincing.

"Are you working tomorrow?" Faith asked. Ethan had asked her to cook for him, and she would.

If he was surprised by her query, it wasn't evident in his expression. "No, I'm not. Why do you ask?"

"I'll cook brunch and dinner for you."

This time Ethan was hard-pressed not throw back his head and laugh out loud. Reaching for her hand, he pressed a kiss on her palm. His mouth seared a path up her arm and over her shoulder, fastening itself to the side of her exposed neck. "Bless you," he whispered close to her ear.

A wave of heat swept over her body as his rapacious mouth nibbled her neck. "Stop it, Ethan!" she said in protest. The couple at a nearby table was staring at them.

Pulling back, he stared at her. Her chest was rising and falling heavily as if she'd run a grueling race. "What's the matter, honey?"

"People are looking at us."

Ethan kissed her shoulder again. "If you don't look at them, then you won't see them looking at you. You have no idea how long it's been since I've had a home-cooked meal."

"Where do you eat?"

"I usually order takeout from a neighborhood restaurant."

Her eyebrows lifted with this disclosure. It was no wonder he was so slender. "Do you cook at all?"

He nodded. "I can heat up a can of soup or warm up leftovers in the microwave."

Faith rolled her eyes at him. "That's hardly cooking, Ethan."

"At least I'm attempting to learn," he said defensively. "I bought several cookbooks and I have a set of All-Clad cookware."

"I'm impressed."

"Damn, sweetness, can't you cut me a little slack?"

Kissing her fingertips, Faith pressed them to his mouth. "I'm sorry."

He inclined his head, smiling. "Apology graciously accepted. What's on tomorrow's menu?"

Faith angled her head, her gaze meeting and fusing with Ethan's. The look in his eyes was similar to clients who waited to see if what she'd created met their specifications and expectations. He'd admitted that he wasn't very complex, that what she saw was what she'd get. But there was something about Ethan McMillan that silently communicated that he wasn't being wholly forthright with her, and she wanted to attribute her suspicions to the number of frogs she'd dated. Well, it would pay for her to watch Ethan carefully if she were to have a relationship with him.

"I'm thinking about a Lowcountry brunch of shrimp and grits and Chinese spareribs, shrimp dumplings and stir-fry veggies for dinner. In between brunch and dinner we can go on a walking tour of the Village."

"I have a better suggestion."

"What's that?" she asked.

"Why don't you cook at my place?"

A slight frown appeared between Faith's eyes. "That would mean you coming to New York, picking me up and then driving me back only to turn around to go back to Jersey. Then there's the problem of buying what I need to cook."

Shifting on his chair, Ethan cradled her face between his palms. "That's not going to be a problem. You can spend the night with me." He held up one hand when she opened her mouth to protest his suggestion. "I have more than one bedroom, so we won't be forced to share a bed."

"Show-off," she drawled.

Shaking his head, he couldn't stop the smile crinkling the lines around his eyes. "I wasn't dissing your apartment, Faith."

"What-everrr," she drawled again.

Struggling to keep a straight face, Ethan closed his eyes for several seconds. There was one thing he could count on Faith to do, and that was make him laugh. It'd been a very long time since a woman had been able to do that.

"We can either go shopping tonight or tomorrow morning. There's a supermarket in the area that stays open 24/7, and I'm willing to bet it stocks everything you'd need. And remember I have a set of pots that need breaking in."

"I usually go to mass on Sunday."

Ethan winked at her. "I can assure you that there're a few Catholic churches in Englewood Cliffs." He paused. "What other excuse do you have for not spending the night?"

She returned his wink, then wrinkled her short nose. "Give me time. I'm certain I'll think of something."

The musical selection ended, followed by rousing applause. The band members stood up and bowed along with the vocalists. Cupping Faith's elbow, Ethan eased her off her chair. "Let's get out of here before the band takes another intermission."

"Are you trying to avoid your uncles?"

"Yes."

Reaching into the pocket of his trousers, he removed a

bill from the monogrammed clip, leaving it on the table. He signaled for the waiter at the same time he steered Faith toward the exit. "My uncles are known to strong-arm me into playing with them," he explained once they reached the parking lot.

"I wanted to hear you play. Promise me the next time we come here you'll sit in with the band."

Looping an arm around her waist, Ethan pulled Faith to his side. "I promise, sweetness."

He smiled when she went completely pliant against his length. Faith was talking about returning to North Philly with him when he'd refused to think beyond tonight. He didn't know what had come over him when he asked Faith to spend the night at his house. He just didn't want to spend three or four hours with her, then say goodbye, but days and weeks. He wanted her to see him exclusively, because the thought of her with another man made him a little crazy, kept him a little off balance.

Pressing a button on a remote device, Ethan unlocked the doors to his car. Waiting until Faith was seated and belted in, he closed the door and rounded the vehicle. The night wouldn't end when he took her back to Greenwich Village—it was about to begin.

Faith couldn't come up with an excuse why she shouldn't spend the night with Ethan by the time she returned to New York City to change her clothes and pack a bag for her overnight stay in New Jersey. They'd stopped at a twenty-four-hour supermarket that was stocked with everything she needed to prepare her Lowcountry breakfast and Chinese-themed dinner. At the last possible moment, she selected two bouquets of pale pink lilies as a centerpiece. Whenever she met her cousins for their biweekly get-togethers it was Simone who always provided the floral arrangements.

"Are we there yet?" she intoned when Ethan increased his speed along a four-lane highway.

Ethan gave her a quick glance. "Living in Manhattan has spoiled you. I bet when you grew up in Mount Vernon you didn't walk out of your house to find a supermarket, deli or greengrocer around the corner."

"No, but I didn't have to drive more than a mile to get to one."

He patted her knee covered by a pair of jeans. "We're almost there." Ten minutes later the attendant in the gatehouse waved to him as the retractable stanchions lowered, and Ethan drove through. "I'll bring in the groceries after I show you your bedroom," he told Faith when he parked inside the attached garage.

"I'll help you."

"No, you won't," he countered, "because the bags are too heavy."

Faith unbuckled her seat belt. "They wouldn't have been that heavy if you hadn't tried putting everything into three bags."

Ethan got out and came around to assist her. "I'd rather carry three bags than a dozen." Tightening his hold on her hand, he eased Faith to her feet. "Walking from the garage to the house more than twice is a waste of time."

Smiling and inching closer, Faith tilted her chin. "What's your hurry, darling? Are you trying to send me off to bed because you have a hot date with another woman?" she teased with a wide grin.

His expression stilled. "Is that what you believe? That I'd bring you here, then go off to see another woman?" She placed her hand alongside his face, but he caught her wrist, pulling it away.

Her smile faded. "Don't be so serious, Ethan. I was only teasing."

With wide eyes, Ethan stared at her as if she were a complete stranger. Didn't she know? Did she not know he *was* serious about her? He hadn't come on to her, because he wanted Faith to trust him, wanted her to believe he wasn't drawn to her because of sex. That was something he could get from a complete stranger.

He released her wrist. "But I am serious, Faith. Very, very serious when it comes to you and me."

There was a swollen silence as Faith stared at the man staring back at her. He was serious and she wasn't. She did not want a repeat of her past relationships with men whom she initially had thought would become the one with whom she would share her future.

She wanted what her parents and aunt and uncle had, she wanted what Tessa and Micah had found, what his parents shared. She wanted a man she could trust unconditionally, a man whom she would marry and bear his children and a man whom she'd grow old and spend the rest of her life with. However, she'd dated too many men, and with disappointing results.

"It's not going to work, Ethan."

His eyebrows lifted. "Why, Faith? Because you say it won't work?"

She closed her eyes and bit down on her lower lip. "It's never worked for me."

Resting his hands on her shoulders, Ethan pulled her flush against his body. "Open your eyes, sweetness." Her lashes fluttered wildly before she met his gaze. "There are no guarantees in life, but there is one thing that I'll swear to and that is I will never deliberately hurt you. And I'm serious as a heart attack when I say that I want to see you exclusively."

Faith swallowed a gasp. Ethan had suddenly turned the tables, because in the past she was the one who wanted exclusivity, a commitment. "Where were you when I was looking for exclusivity?"

Twin dimples winked at her when he smiled. "Even if we'd met before, I doubt whether we would've hit it off because you probably were involved growing your business, while I was going through changes deciding whether to give up flying."

"You're right," Faith agreed. The reason she'd dated so many men was because most of them saw her as driven, too ambitious. The exception was her pastry instructor. He'd understood her drive, and he'd also wanted to control her.

Taking her hand, Ethan led Faith up the six steps to the door that led directly into the kitchen. Within seconds of opening the door a shrieking sound rent the air. Punching in a code on the wall keypad, he deactivated the security alarm.

Faith walked into a kitchen that would meet any gourmet chef's expectations. The towering ceiling claimed a quartet of skylights, while the color of the black-and-white ceramic floor tiles was repeated in white cabinets, black appliances and granite countertops. Gleaming pots and pans were suspended from a rack over a cooking island with a stovetop grill and six burners. There were two dishwashers, two eye-level ovens, double stainless-steel sinks and another oven with a warming drawer.

She stared at the French-door-refrigerator, then turned to look at Ethan, who'd draped his jacket over the back of one of the stools pulled up under the island with a place setting for one. "You don't cook, yet you have a refrigerator with a built-in television."

He gave her a sheepish grin. "I only turn it on when I don't want to miss a game."

She rolled her eyes upward. "Don't tell me you're a football fanatic?"

"I happen to be a *fan* of football, basketball and baseball."

"What about soccer and hockey?"

"I'll watch them, too."

Faith groaned inwardly. There was no doubt Ethan would get along quite well with the men in her family. They talked and walked sports year-round. "I just want to warn you that I don't do sports."

Ethan pulled Faith into an embrace. "I'd never ask you to do something you don't want to do. I suppose I'll have to ask someone else if they want to go with me to see the Nets or Yankees."

"You have tickets to see the Yankees?"

"I thought you didn't do sports."

"I don't *play* sports, Ethan. I said nothing about becoming a spectator."

He angled his head. "I suppose I could take you whenever you're not working."

"Speaking of working, how do you get so much time off?"

Ethan sobered. "What are you talking about?"

"You're a driver, and I thought weekends were the busiest times of the week for private car services."

He lowered his head until their lips were inches apart. "I have a wonderful boss, plus I have seniority. So, whenever I want time off, I'm fortunate enough to get it. I don't believe it," he crooned without pausing to take a breath.

Faith wanted to look away, but couldn't. "What?" Her voice was barely a whisper.

"I've never kissed you."

She blinked once. "Are you asking whether you can kiss me?"

"Yes, I am." He smiled. "May I?"

Her smile matched his, bringing his gaze to linger on her parted lips. "Yes, you may."

Faith had just permitted Ethan the opening he needed to take their relationship to another level. She'd given him permission to touch her. Angling his head, he slanted his mouth over hers, caressing, tasting, sampling her sweet, sexy mouth.

Succumbing to the gentleness of his mouth, Faith pressed her lips to his. Her arms went around his waist inside his jacket, deepening the kiss as his tongue eased slowly into her mouth. Everything around them stood still as she lost herself in the soothing, healing joining.

She sank into the warmth of the man holding her close to his heart. A slow, creeping desire swirled through her body. She felt a longing that made her want to remain in Ethan's embrace until she gorged herself on his sensuality. The tantalizing smell of his cologne, the solid wall of his chest and the mastery of his tongue made her knees weak, yet somehow she found the strength to drag her lips away from his. Burying her face against his throat, Faith waited for her breathing to return to normal.

Ethan felt Faith trembling and wondered if he was moving too quickly. It was only their second date— actually the first if he didn't count their dinner at the Rainbow Room. He didn't want her to believe he'd invited her to his home in order to seduce her, because that wasn't his style. He'd become wary of women since his divorce. However, there was something about Faith Whitfield that lowered his defenses.

"Did you invite me here to seduce me?"

Easing back, he stared down at Faith with an incredulous look on his face. Had she read his mind? "That wasn't my intent," he admitted, "but after kissing you I've changed my mind."

Faith placed her fingers over his mouth. "We can't. I can't."

He pulled her hand down, smiling. "You don't have to, sweet thing. Not until you're ready."

Her gaze met his. "What if I'm never ready?"

"Then we won't. We can hang out together without having sex."

She shook her head. "I'm not that naive, Ethan. Most men, if they're normal *and* straight, won't date a woman without expecting to sleep with her."

"Do you sleep with every man you date?" Faith didn't want to tell him that she'd only had two serious relationships. Both were wonderful until she slept with them, then they became Dr. Jekyll. Their possessiveness, jealousy and controlling behavior made her life miserable. After a while she began blaming herself. What was it that turned them from princes to frogs once she opened her legs to them?

"No."

Cradling her face in his hands, Ethan dropped a kiss on her hair. "I'm not going to put any pressure on you to sleep with me. But that doesn't mean I'm going to refuse if you ask."

Faith forced a smile. "At least we know where we stand with each other."

Ethan nodded. "We toasted to trust and openness, and

that's what we'll have. Come. Let me show you to your room. I'll bring in your bag, then I'll put away the groceries."

"I'll help you with the groceries."

"That's not necessary. I know how to wash vegetables before storing them in the refrigerator."

"Don't put the shrimp in the freezer."

Looping an arm around Faith's waist, he led her out of the kitchen to the front of the house and the staircase leading to the second story. "Yes, ma'am."

"Are you also going to arrange the flowers?"

"No, ma'am. I'm a little deficient when it comes to flower arranging."

"You have to see my cousin Simone's arrangements. She can make a bouquet of weeds look like orchids."

"We all have our gifts, darling."

Faith didn't visibly react to his endearment, because Ethan had called her dessert lady, sweetness, sweet thing and now darling. Did he toss around endearments, or did he really think of her as his darling?

He led her down a carpeted hallway to a room on the right. "This is your bedroom. The bathroom is through the door on your left." Flipping a wall switch in the bedroom, light glowed from a table in a sitting area. An oversize chaise was positioned under a window covered with pale blinds in a honeycomb design.

Walking into the room, Faith stared numbly at the carefully chosen furnishings. It wasn't as much a bedroom as a bed chamber. A handsome mahogany four-poster bed, covered with pillows and goose-down quilts over a vintage linen bed skirt, invited her to sleep away the hours. The mahogany furniture was repeated in the dressing table and chair and another round table with two pull-up tapestry-covered chairs. The table was the perfect place to enjoy an early-morning or late-night cup of coffee.

"It's beautiful, Ethan."

He inclined his head. "I'm glad you like it. I'll be right back with your bag."

Faith nodded. What she'd seen of Ethan's house was exquisite, and she wondered whether he'd selected the furnishings or employed the services of a professional decorator. She was standing in the same spot when he returned with her bag. She took it from him, smiling.

"Thank you."

Staring down at her, he angled his head. "There's no clock in this room, so what time do you want to get up?"

"If I'm not up by nine, then come and get me."

Taking a step, Ethan leaned closer and kissed her cheek. "Good night, sweet thing."

A gentle smile softened Faith's mouth. "Good night." She waited until he turned and walked out of the bedroom, closing the door behind him before making her way to the bathroom. Her smile became a full grin when she spied the bathtub. Despite the lateness of the hour, she planned to fill the tub with scented bath oil and relax. She loved her apartment, but the only drawback was not having a bathtub.

Walking back into the bedroom, she hung her jacket in a closet. Three quarters of an hour later, Faith lay in the tub with a pillow cradled under her head as water swirled around her body.

I could get used to this, she mused, not opening her eyes. In fact, it was very easy to get used to Ethan McMillan. He allowed her the space she needed not to feel overwhelmed by his presence.

Even though she'd told herself that there was no room

in her busy life for romance, she wanted a romantic relationship with a man. Her eyes opened and she stared up at the ceiling. She'd dimmed the recessed lights. *He's a prince,* a voice whispered in her head.

Faith shook her head. She'd allowed her thoughts to surface. Did she think Ethan was a prince because she'd been without a man for too long? Or did she want him to be one because she missed the intimacy of sleeping with a man?

She quickly banished her thoughts. Only time would tell if Ethan was the one. And the reckoning would come when they went away for Valentine's Day weekend. Then she would know without a doubt whether she would continue to see him.

Reaching for a bath sponge, she filled it with a liberal squeeze of creamy bath wash and began soaping her throat and chest. Slowly, deliberately, she washed and rinsed her body. It was after one when she finally pulled back the quilt and slipped between crisp, scented Egyptian cotton sheets.

Faith sighed once, closed her eyes and fell into a deep, dreamless slumber.

Chapter 10

Ethan glanced at the clock on the microwave for the third time. He'd alternated watching the clock and listening for Faith's footfalls since nine o'clock. Stirring restlessly on the stool near the cooking island, he finally turned the page on the Arts and Leisure section of the Sunday *Times*.

When he'd left his bedroom earlier that morning, the door to her bedroom was closed. He'd contemplated knocking on the door, but changed his mind because she could've been in bed, in the bathroom or dressing. His relationship with her was much too new and fragile to walk in on her if she were half-dressed.

The image of Faith naked flashed through his mind, forcing him to smother a groan. Covering his face with his hands, he tried imagining the sight of her long legs, the narrowness of her waist, the firmness of her round breasts and the velvety smoothness of her sable-brown skin.

An Important Message from the Publisher

Dear Reader,

Because you've chosen to read one of our fine novels, I'd like to say "thank you"! And, as a special way to say thank you, I'm offering to send you two more Kimani Romance novels and two surprise gifts — absolutely FREE! These books will keep it real with true-to-life African American characters that turn up the heat and sizzle with passion.

Please enjoy the free books and gifts with our compliments...

Linda Gill

Publisher, Kimani Press

Peel off Seal and Place Inside...

THE EDITOR'S "THANK YOU" FREE GIFTS INCLUDE:

▶ Two NEW Kimani Romance™ Novels

▶ Two exciting surprise gifts

YES! I have placed my Editor's "thank you" Free Gifts seal in the space provided at right. Please send me 2 FREE books, and my 2 FREE Mystery Gifts. I understand that I am under no obligation to purchase anything further, as explained on the back of this card.

PLACE
FREE GIFTS
SEAL
HERE

◀ DETACH AND MAIL CARD TODAY!

168 XDL ERR5   368 XDL ERSH

FIRST NAME   LAST NAME

ADDRESS

APT.#   CITY

STATE/PROV.   ZIP/POSTAL CODE

Thank You!

(K-ROM-08)

The Reader Service — Here's How It Works:

"Good morning, Ethan. Sorry I overslept."

The object of his musings' dulcet voice came from somewhere behind him. Shifting on the stool, he stared at Faith. She looked fantastic. Her unmade face, ice-blue tank top with a pair of matching stretch pants and sock-covered feet gave her a laid-back appearance. There was something about her dressed-down look that made her more approachable. She'd tucked her cell phone into her waistband.

Rising from the stool, he closed the distance between them, leaned over and brushed a light kiss over her mouth. "Good morning." The heat from her body seeped through his T-shirt. "Hush, baby. There's no need to apologize about oversleeping. It's obvious you needed to rest."

"But I wanted to go to church early."

Cradling her face between his palms, Ethan trailed kisses along the column of her scented neck. "We have all day to go to church. The last mass is at five."

Faith braced her hands against Ethan's chest. She wanted to tell him that he was too close and that he made it difficult for her to draw a normal breath. Before making her presence known, she'd stood at the entrance to the kitchen staring at the breadth of his broad shoulders under a white T-shirt. The well-defined muscles in his back visible through the cotton fabric and the slimness of his waist in a pair of low-ride jeans made her mouth go dry, constricted her throat and had her heart pounding in her chest like booming beats from a kettle drum. If he'd turned before she was able to acknowledge him he would've known with a glance that she'd been lusting after him.

She forced a smile. "I'd like to be on my way home around that time."

Ethan lowered his hands and cradled her waist. "Spend another night with me," he crooned. "I'll take you back early tomorrow morning."

Resting her forehead on his shoulder, Faith inhaled the scent of clean laundry and the metallic fragrance of a sensual men's cologne. The man holding her to his heart had showered, but neglected to shave. The stubble on his jaw only served to enhance his good looks. The color of the emerging beard verified that his graying hair had been a sandy-brown, not dark brown or black.

She contemplated his offer. Tomorrow was Monday. Let Them Eat Cake was closed and the only thing on her schedule was decorating the first of a projected dozen wedding-theme cakes for her book.

Family members complained she worked too hard even though she paid employees to run the patisserie. She and Oliver had done all of the baking before Ranee came on board, which had left Faith with more time to contract with out-of-town clients, but now with the book project she had even less time for herself.

Cognizant of the nonstop activity and long hours she put into decorating cakes, she'd lost weight she could ill afford. Ethan was offering her a way to kick back, relax and forget about any and everything to do with baking, and she'd be a fool not to accept it.

"Okay," she said, smiling. "I'll hang out with you until tomorrow."

The words were barely off her tongue when she found herself in Ethan's arms as he swung her around. "Thank you, sweet thing."

Holding on to his neck to keep her balance, Faith smiled at him. "You're welcome. Now, please put me down." He set her on her feet. "Before we begin your cooking lessons, I'm going to put on a pot of coffee."

"I'll make the coffee."

She nodded. "I like my coffee strong."

"I realized that the night you brewed coffee for me when I'd used your apartment as a rest stop."

Her eyebrows lifted. "Was it too strong for you?"

Lowering his head, Ethan glanced down at the floor. "It was strong enough to grow hair on my chest."

"Did it?" Faith asked with a teasing grin.

He pulled up his T-shirt to reveal a flat belly and six-pack abs. "I thought I saw one the other day. Do you want to check for me?"

She wrinkled her nose. "Didn't we promise to always tell the truth?"

Ethan sobered. "Yes, we did. All right, there was no hair. But, speaking of being truthful, I want to tell you that I like you." He paused. "No. I'm not being completely honest. I more than like you."

Faith had lost count of the number of prince points Ethan had tallied to date. And, if the truth were told, she also more than *liked* him. "Then I suppose that makes two of us, Ethan, because I find myself quite fond of you."

"Fond," he repeated. "I guess I can accept that."

"You'd better, because that's all you're going to get for now."

That's all you're going to get for now. Her declaration echoed in his head as he tried to analyze what she meant by *fondness*. Did it translate into deep affection, love? Or did she feel a closeness that meant he'd become as special to her as she'd become to him? And if she was willing to parcel out her affection like drops of water, then he'd accept it, because it wasn't until he'd taken her to the Rainbow Room that he'd realized he'd been waiting ten years for a woman like Faith Whitfield. He, who'd met and known his share of women, was ready to settle down with one woman he wanted to grow old with, one with whom he would share children, one he would love for eternity.

A secret smile softened Ethan's mouth as he made his way over to a corner of the kitchen with a built-in pantry. "I put all of your nonperishables in here. The meat, fish and vegetables are in drawers in the refrigerator. The flowers are also there, too," he said as an afterthought.

Faith placed her cell phone on the countertop before she opened the refrigerator and took out what she needed to prepare brunch. Waiting until Ethan had measured coffee and water into the automatic coffeemaker, she beckoned him closer. "It's time for your first lesson."

Ethan gave her a forlorn look. "Are you going to yell at me like the chefs do on those reality shows on TV?"

Holding out her hand, she tried not to laugh. "Come, darling. I'm not going to yell at you."

Ethan crossed the kitchen and came to stand behind her. "Am I really your darling?"

Faith let several beats pass as her breath quickened and heat invaded her cheeks. She was angry at herself for her impulsiveness and for being embarrassed. She'd walked into a trap of her own making. "You throw around endearments the way you'd toss pennies into a fountain, and the first time I call you darling you want to scrutinize my feelings for you."

"I know how you feel about me."

She shivered when his moist breath feathered over the nape of her neck. "And that is?"

"You're fond of me."

"Is there something wrong with that?"

He closed his eyes for several seconds. "When I was growing up in Pennsylvania there was a neighbor's dog that I was quite fond of. Oh, and let me not forget the litter of kittens I found behind the house the year I turned ten."

"What is it you want from me?" she asked through clenched teeth. If Ethan wasn't careful he was about to get his first *ribbit.*

Ethan leaned closer, his chest molded to her back. "I don't want you to see me as a faithful dog you pat on the head whenever you pass him."

"You're hardly a *dawg,* Ethan."

"I suppose I should thank you for that." He dropped a kiss on the top of her head. "I'm ready for my lesson now."

Faith kept up a steady stream of instruction as she peeled and cleaned shrimp, peeled and chopped a clove of garlic and minced about a tablespoon of fresh parsley leaves. "Please hand me the plate with the bacon," she said to Ethan, who'd stood watching her intently.

He picked up the plate. "How do you chop that fast and not cut your fingers?"

"Practice, practice and more practice."

"Are you going to use all of the shrimp for the grits?"

"No." She gave him a sidelong glance. "I'm only going to use a few. The others are for the *bar kau.*"

"Bar who?"

"*Bar kau* are shrimp dumplings." His expression still registered bewilderment. "Have you ever had dim sum?"

Ethan nodded. "Yes."

"They're dumplings filled with minced shrimp."

"Are we going to have them as appetizers?"

"No. I'd like to serve them as a midafternoon snack. Steamed or fried, they're usually served with tea at the traditional Cantonese midmorning meal."

"Is that why you bought the green tea?" Faith had selected a small of amount of green tea leaves in the supermarket's gourmet section.

"Yes. If we're going to eat Chinese, then we should also drink Chinese."

"Speaking of drinking, the coffee's finished brewing. How do you take yours?"

"Cream, no sugar." The request was barely off her lips when her cell phone rang. Wiping her hands on a towel, she reached for the phone. The display showed Tessa's name. "Good morning," Faith said cheerfully.

"Someone woke up on the right side of the bed this morning," said a sultry voice filled with laughter. "I'm sorry about ringing you so early, but I wanted to catch you before you left for church."

"I'm going later. What's up?"

"Mama wants us to come to Mount Vernon tomorrow morning so we can select our gowns."

"What time are we meeting?"

"Early."

"How early is early, Tessa?" Smiling, Faith nodded to Ethan as he placed a large mug of coffee on the countertop in front of her. She mouthed a thank-you.

"Ten. I'll pick you up around nine."

"Hold on, Tessa." Placing her thumb over the tiny mouthpiece, she caught Ethan's stare as he took a sip of his steaming black coffee. "Can I impose on you to drive me to Mount Vernon tomorrow morning instead of into the city?"

He lowered his mug. "Of course I can take you. It's just across the river."

"I need to be there by ten."

"That's not a problem, Faith."

She removed her finger. "You don't have to pick me up," she informed Tessa. "Tell Aunt Lucy that I'll be there on time."

"Do you have a ride back to the city?"

"No."

"I'll take you back. See you *mañana, prima*."

"Tomorrow," Faith repeated.

Ending the call, she walked over to Ethan. Tilting her chin, she stared up at him through her lashes. "Are you sure you can drop me off tomorrow morning?"

Cradling her chin with his free hand, Ethan brushed a light kiss over her parted lips. "Of course I'm sure. I don't have anything scheduled until late Monday morning, so I'm all yours."

Looping her arms around his slim waist, she went on tiptoe, returning the kiss. "Thank you."

"It's the next to last house on the left," Faith told Ethan as he turned down the block leading to her aunt and uncle's home.

"Where's your parents' house?" he asked, slowing before coming to a complete stop behind a school bus with flashing red lights as several mothers stood on the sidewalk waving to their children.

"They live about six blocks from here. When I was growing up I spent as much time at my cousins' place as they did at mine. The only thing that kept us from being completely inseparable was that we attended different schools."

Ethan maneuvered into the driveway behind a Toyota Sequoia at the same time the driver-side door opened.

He shifted into Park but didn't turn off the ignition. Pressing a button, he released the trunk lock, got out, retrieved Faith's bag and came around to open the passenger-side door for her. Extending his hand, helped her out.

"Thank you for everything," he crooned in her ear. "I'd like to do it again."

Faith smiled. "So would I." She took her bag from him and turned to find Simone's puzzled gaze shifting from her to Ethan. Reaching for his hand, she urged him forward. "Come, I want you to meet my cousin."

Simone Whitfield's expression behind the lenses of a pair of oversize sunglasses changed from bewilderment to amusement when she noticed her cousin clinging possessively to the hand of the tall, slender, casually dressed man whose bearing was reminiscent of a fashion model's. It was the first time she'd seen Faith with a man who was physically her counterpart.

"Simi, I'd like you to meet Ethan McMillan. Ethan, this is my cousin, Simone Whitfield. She's the one with the magical green thumb."

Smiling, Ethan dropped Faith's hand and extended it to Simone. "It's nice meeting you, Simone."

She shook his hand, her voice temporarily locked somewhere in the back of her throat. Not only did Ethan McMillan claim an X-rated voice, but also face *and* body. Looking at him, there was no frog in the man standing in front of her.

"It's *my* pleasure to meet you," she said, her voice low and distinctively seductive. Simone, her gaze fixed on

Ethan's dimples, didn't see Faith's *Oh, no, you didn't go there with my man* look.

Ethan swung his attention back to Faith. Smiling, he gave her a soft peck on her parted lips. "I'll call you later."

Simone stared at the couple as questions crowded her head, and judging from the tender kiss, Faith's distinctive Hermès Victoria travel bag and the fact that Ethan had driven her to Mount Vernon spoke volumes. Waiting until Ethan returned to his car and backed out of the driveway, she smiled sweetly at Faith.

"I want to hear everything about the X-man," she said, looping her arm through Faith's as they climbed the porch steps of the three-story farmhouse.

Faith brow furrowed. "Who's the X-man?"

"Ethan McMillan. A man who looks and sounds like he does should come with a warning label. And, if you tell me he's racked up any *ribbits,* then I'm going to hurt you, Faith Whitfield."

The solid oak door opened suddenly and Lucinda Whitfield stood on the other side. "I thought I heard voices. Why are you two standing out here? Come on in where it's warm."

Simone gave Faith a sidelong glance as she pulled open the beveled-glass door. "We'll talk about this later," she said sotto voce.

Ethan reversed direction, heading back to New Jersey. The lingering scent of Faith's perfume filled the car. Within minutes of leaving her he'd felt her loss, and even now he continued to miss her.

He'd thought himself a fool to have invited her to spend two nights under his roof, then vacillated whether he actually wanted to drive her across the Hudson River to New York. He'd contemplated holding her captive until he uncovered just what it was about Faith Whitfield that had him craving the pastry chef like a drug addict.

If he could, he would've turned back time to prolong their time together. After they sat down to eat the incredibly delicious Lowcountry-style shrimp and grits, they'd retreated to the family room to read the Sunday *Times*. The rest of the morning and afternoon went by in a blur as he helped Faith to prepare *bar kau,* marinated bite-size spareribs and chopped the ingredients for stir-fry vegetables. After sampling fresh-brewed green tea he seriously considered giving up coffee.

They'd attended the 5:00 p.m. mass, then returned home to cook dinner together, topping off the meal with a dessert of *fraises au vin rouge,* red wine with strawberries. What he couldn't fathom was that he'd felt more like a husband spending two days with Faith than he'd felt in the eight months he'd been married to Justine.

Their relationship was easygoing, relaxed and, most important, noncompetitive or combative. Unknowingly Faith had everything he'd been looking for in every woman he'd known. What he needed to do was convince her that he wanted more than friendship; he wanted a relationship and a commitment that promised more than a few months together.

His cell phone rang as he entered the town limits for Englewood Cliffs. He recognized the ringtone for his bookkeeper. Dorie Murrow had answered his classified ad for an experienced part-time bookkeeping position when he set up MAC Executive Air Travel in a building adjacent to the livery service business. A grandmother, she had worked as a bookkeeper for an insurance broker for three decades, retired, then decided to reenter the workforce on a part-time basis.

Pressing the Bluetooth button on the dash, he said cheerfully, "Good morning, Dorie."

"It's not going to be so good, Mac, when I tell you about the call I just got from Lloyd."

A wrinkle furrowed Ethan's forehead. "What happened?"

He listened intently as Dorie told him about the harrowing cross-country flight where a corporate client and the five men accompanying him had become drunk and rowdy, endangering everyone onboard. Fortunately, Lloyd Seymour and his copilot were able to land the jet without mishap at an airfield outside LAX.

Ethan struggled to control his rising temper. As owner of the company he was responsible for the safety of his employees and their clients. "Has Lloyd agreed to the return flight?"

"No," Dorie replied. "That's why he's calling."

"Tell Lloyd to take a few days off, rest up and then come back. I'll contact Mr. King personally to let him know we no longer want or need his business. Put the file with his company's contract on my desk."

"Consider it done. Is there anything else, Mac?"

"Look for a messenger to deliver an envelope with the W-2s."

"They're here."

"Good." He glanced at the dashboard clock. "I should be there in about ten minutes."

Punching the button, Ethan ended the call. His hands tightened on the leather-wrapped steering wheel as he cursed to himself. He hadn't expected the CEO of a major pharmaceutical company and his corporate guests to become so unruly that the flight crew would consider aborting the flight. Wilson Marsh King, known as WMK in the business world, would either find another private jet for a return flight to Newark, or he and his guests would be forced to stand in line with thousands of other passengers and get a flight on a commercial carrier.

Ethan knew running his own business wouldn't be an easy task, but it was times like this when he second-guessed himself whether it was worth it. He thought of Faith's dilemma of booking two weddings and a birthday on the same day, then realized his problem with Wilson King was minor in comparison. Every MAC contract contained a termination clause. Unfortunately, this was the first time he would have to exercise it.

His annoyance had mostly subsided when he merged into traffic onto the Palisades Parkway. It had vanished completely when he maneuvered into his reserved parking space. Listening to his favorite CDs and thinking about Faith proved the perfect antidote to help him forget that he was losing a client.

Chapter 11

Faith left her overnight bag by the door, hung up her jacket in a closet off the entryway and followed Simone and Lucinda into the room the older woman referred to as her meeting room. It was here that she conferred with prospective brides and their attendants while they perused the portfolios of Lucinda-designed wedding and bridesmaids' gowns.

Petite with a rounded body and close-cropped, salt-and-pepper natural hairstyle, Lucinda Whitfield's wedding gown designs rivaled notables like Vera Wang, Amsale, Priscilla of Boston, Reem Acra and Monique Lhullier. And she'd passed her incredible talent on to her daughter Tessa.

"I don't know if you've eaten, so I put out a little something," Lucinda said, motioning to the side table with a platter of bagels, croissants and miniature pastries. The

Senseo gourmet coffee machine her husband of nearly forty years had given her as one of her Christmas gifts sat ready for brewing a single cup of coffee with the push of a button.

Simone set her oversize leather bag on the carpeted floor and shrugged out of her coat, leaving it on the back of an armchair. "All I want is coffee, so I can take a few aspirins."

Lucinda sat in her favorite chair at a round oaken table. "You need more than coffee, Simone Whitfield, if you have a headache." Her gaze shifted to her niece. "Are you going to eat something, or do you only want coffee?"

Faith smiled. "I'll have something later, Aunt Lucy." She'd eaten breakfast with Ethan.

"Sorry I'm late," said Tessa in a throaty drawl as she walked into the parlor. "Traffic was backed up on the Triborough Bridge."

"You're not late, Theresa. Simone and Faith just got here," Lucinda said.

Tessa picked up a coffee pod, inserted it into the coffeemaker, placed a cup under the spout and pushed a button. "Does anyone want a cup?"

"I'll take one," Simone volunteered. "Please make it black."

Tessa frowned at her sister. "I've never known you to drink black coffee, because you claim it stains your teeth."

Combing her wayward curls off her forehead with both hands, Simone closed her eyes. "I knew I shouldn't have had that drink last night."

"What were you drinking?" Tessa asked.

"I had a Long Island Iced Tea."

Now Faith knew why Simone hadn't taken off her sunglasses. "Where were you last night?"

Groaning, Simone opened her eyes. "Somewhere I

didn't need to be." She saw Faith and Tessa share a glance. "I wasn't with Tony," she spat out.

Lucinda opened a book filled with samples of color swatches and fabrics. "Girls, please let's get started. Remember, I only have five months to design and sew at least four gowns."

Tessa placed a saucer under a cup, handing it to Simone. "You can eliminate my gown, Mama. I've decided to wear one of the gowns I bought from you last year."

With wide eyes, Lucinda stared at her youngest daughter. "Which one did you choose?"

"The strapless silk-satin gown with the kimono-style sash. The only thing I want you to change is the color of the sash from bronze to platinum."

Simone took a deep breath after swallowing a mouthful of steaming coffee. "What's your color scheme?"

"Varying shades of gray with a robin's-egg blue."

"Elegant."

"Chic."

Faith and Lucinda had spoken in unison.

It took five hours for the Whitfield women to decide on the designs for the attendants, the size and shape of the cake, along with the filling and the wedding jewelry. Lucinda, after taking the dress measurements of her daughters and niece, retreated to her sewing room.

"Do you have time to go over what you want for your flowers?" Simone asked when Tessa glanced at her watch.

Tessa nodded. "Let's do it. I don't have to be back in the city until six."

Faith sat back, listening intently when Tessa told Simone that she wanted a bouquet of sparkling white roses and orchids tied together with the same material as her wedding gown. Using a stylus, Simone entered the details of the arrangements for Tessa's headpiece, the maid of honor's and bridesmaids' bouquets into her PDA. The list continued with the groom's, best man's and groomsmen's boutonnieres, mothers' corsages, fathers' boutonnieres and other special guests' corsages.

Simone, having removed her sunglasses and perched them atop a wealth of curly gold-tipped hair, took a breath. "You don't have to tell me now, but you should think what floral arrangements you'd want for the church pews, altar and candle holders. You also have to consider flowers for your reception—entryway, bar decorations, dining-table centerpieces, bride and groom's chair decorations, buffet table, cake and cake table and of course the powder room."

"Do you want flowers on your cake?" Faith asked. Tessa, in following through with the Asian theme, wanted a cake in four rectangular layers, each supported by three smaller squares that would be covered in white fondant and plaques featuring Chinese symbols for love, luck, happiness and prosperity. Faith had suggested to Tessa that she would cover the squares in a gunmetal-gray fondant in keeping with her wedding colors.

Tessa wrinkled her nose. "Even though some are edible, I don't want real flowers on the cake."

Faith reached for her notebook and pen. "I can make seven gum-paste cymbidium orchids. There'll be two at the corners of each layer and one on the top layer. And as soon as you give me a final headcount, I'll have my assistant make the individual cake souvenirs."

Tessa waved her hand. "Don't bother with the cake souvenirs, Faith. I know you're going to be tied up with your book project—"

Faith held up her hand, stopping Tessa. "Enough," she interrupted softly. "I have my book project under control thanks to Ranee Mason. Together we've completed twenty cakes, and if we keep to our present timetable I should have them all baked and decorated by late April or early May. That will give us more than enough time make your little souvenirs."

She would fashion the tiny cakes by trimming the edges of a sheet cake, then cutting it into squares. She and Ranee would cover each square with sugar paste and top each miniature cake with a gum paste cymbidium orchid. The cakes could be stored in airtight containers up to two weeks before the wedding.

A telephone rang, and the three women reached for their cell phones at the same time. "It's mine," Tessa said, pushing a button to answer the call. Faith shared a smile with Simone when they heard her mention Bridget Sanborn-Cohen's name. "Yes, Bridget, I'll tell Simone and Faith about it."

"Tell us about what?" Simone asked when Tessa ended the call.

Running her fingers through her short hair, Tessa dropped the phone into her handbag. "Bridget and Seth are inviting us to their place this Saturday for a little get-together. She says both of you can bring a guest."

A slight frown dotted Faith's forehead. "What's the occasion, Tessa?"

"It's nothing special. Bridget said it's going to be the first time she and Seth will entertain as a married couple. Micah told me that Bridget and Seth do a lot of entertaining on the weekends."

Tessa remembered what Micah told her—that the

activity in the two-bedroom condo on weekends had prompted him to move out and relocate to Staten Island. He eventually sold the apartment with the panoramic views of the water and the Throgs Neck Bridge to his sister and brother-in-law.

"Are you bringing your boyfriend, Faith?" Simone asked.

Tessa sat forward on her chair. "Come now, cousin, don't tell me you've been holding out on me?"

Faith couldn't stop the wave of heat burning her face and neck. "He's not my boyfriend."

Simone sucked her teeth loudly. "Yeah, right! You could've fooled me."

With her gaze going from her sister to her cousin and back again to her sister, Tessa asked, "What am I missing?"

Simone sucked her teeth again *and* rolled her eyes. "Only that Miss Prissy here shared more than a friendly kiss with her prince when he dropped her off. And, judging from the bag he took out of the trunk of his car, she'd probably spent the night with him."

Slumping against her chair's cushioned back, Tessa tented her fingers, grinning. "'Fess up, cuz."

There weren't too many things Faith hid from her cousins, because she trusted whatever she said to them would go no further. But, for a reason she couldn't fathom, she didn't want to talk about Ethan. Everything she'd shared with him was too new and too fragile to divulge.

"The only thing I'm going to say is that he hasn't shown any frog tendencies."

"What does he look like, Simone?" Tessa asked her sister.

"Scrumptious. He's tall and slender. His voice is so deep that it sounds as if it's coming from his ankles. And forget about his smile." Simone poked her cheeks with her forefingers. "The man is blessed with dimples deep enough to drown in." Like quicksilver, she sobered. "I have to admit he's the first guy I've seen Faith with who complements her beauty and style." There was a pulse beat of silence as the three women exchanged looks.

Tessa leaned forward and captured Faith's hand. "Is he good to you?"

Faith's dark eyes met a pair in clear brown with pinpoints of gold. "He's good *for* me, Tessa. It's the first time I've actually been courted by a man, and I must admit that it's a wonderful experience. Most times when guys take me out for dinner they expect me to become their dessert, or I have to spend time fighting them off because they believe it's their right to touch me without my consent."

Simone emitted an audible sigh. "Do you like him, Faith?"

She nodded. "Yes, I do. In fact, I like him a lot."

It'd been a long time since Faith had been able to admit that to anyone. She'd found herself thinking about Ethan when she least expected, and whenever they parted she missed everything about him. The topic of conversation shifted from Ethan to the men in their pasts who at one time they'd believed they wouldn't be able to live without.

Kicking off her shoes, Simone pulled her feet up under her body. "Not only did I believe that I couldn't exist without Tony but I was dumb enough to marry the lazy slug."

Tessa shook her head. "You don't have a monopoly on poor judgment. There was no way I could marry Bryce Hill because his lying ass was already married."

Faith wanted to tell her cousins that at least they weren't foolish enough to live with a man they weren't married to as she'd done with her former instructor, a man who'd been much too jealous, possessive and controlling.

"Who are you bringing with you, Simi?" she asked Simone.

"I'll ask one of the guys I bowl with on Wednesday nights."

Simone had become a member of a bowling league with Tessa, Micah and more than half a dozen police officers from his former Bronx precinct. At first she'd balked about going out at night, but after their first meeting she'd found herself looking forward to socializing with the male and female officers. She'd joined several of them the night before at a club in New Rochelle for a birthday celebration. She'd drunk only one cocktail that resulted in a pounding headache.

The conversation shifted again to Tessa's wedding plans until Lucinda came to announce that she'd prepared an early dinner. They all filed into the kitchen to eat thinly sliced lemon-herb chicken breasts, celery slaw with shrimp and a roasted corn salad. At exactly five o'clock Tessa tapped the face of her watch to let Faith know it was time to return to the city. They hugged and kissed Lucinda, then Simone, promising to see her the following week for their bimonthly Monday get-together.

"We covered a lot," Tessa said as she started up her vehicle and maneuvered out the driveway of her parents' home.

Faith nodded. "Are you sure you want a buffet reception instead of a sit-down dinner?"

It was Tessa's turn to nod. "Yes. I like the informality of a buffet because it allows everyone to mix, mingle and eat as much as they want. I don't want anyone going home hungry."

"You know right well that's not going to happen with Uncle Malcolm and Daddy cooking. Remember the food that was left over from Simi's wedding? People were taking home shopping bags."

"And there was still enough left to donate to several soup kitchens in the neighborhood," Tessa reminded Faith. "Our fathers went overboard because they were ticked off at Yolanda's mother, who wouldn't let them cater her reception when she married Vernon."

"That's because Annajean almost lost her mind when Yolie broke off her engagement to Dr. Chauncey's son to marry your brother."

"It's apparent she made the right choice because she and Vernon are still very much in love."

"Of course she made the right choice," Faith insisted. "Vernon isn't a junkie."

Tessa gave her cousin a quick glance. "What on earth are you talking about?"

"Yolie told me that she went to Terrell's office one night and caught him with a hypodermic stuck in his leg. He'd injected himself with morphine, and he was so high he hadn't realized she was even in the room. All she thought of was him being under the influence when writing prescriptions or treating his patients."

With wide eyes, Tessa shook her head. "I always wondered why he gave up practicing medicine. Do you think she reported him?"

Faith lifted her shoulders. She and Yolanda Evans had attended the same parochial school. "I don't know. But right after she married Vernon he gave up his practice and moved to the West Coast. The last I heard was that he was teaching biology at a San Diego high school."

"I'm glad my brother and Yolanda are moving back to New York. I really miss spoiling my nephews." Henry and Malcolm Whitfield's plans included closing the doors to Whitfield Caterers at the end of August to concentrate on opening an upscale bowling alley in downtown Mount Vernon the following year. Schoolteachers Vernon and Yolanda Whitfield were relocating from North Carolina to their native Westchester County to go into business with the elder Whitfields.

"Save some of that spoiling for your own little Sanborns," Faith teased.

A wave of apprehension gnawed at Tessa's confidence. "Every time Micah mentions starting a family I'm faced with what-ifs. What if I don't get pregnant? What if I'm not able to have children?"

"Stop beating up on yourself, Tessa. It wouldn't be the end of the world if you don't have a baby. Look at Rosalind. If she hadn't adopted Micah, then chances are you never would've met him. The Sanborns adopting him was a blessing, a blessing you and Micah can pass along to another child or children who're looking for a home and parents to love them."

Tessa smiled. "You always know what to say to make me snap out of it."

"That sounds good, because I have answers for everyone but myself."

"What are you talking about?"

"I've met a man who's as close to perfect as one can be, yet I've put up an emotional barrier to keep him at a distance because I don't want another failed relationship."

"That's not realistic, Faith. We're in the wedding and the happily-ever-after business, and do you think when our clients exchange vows they believe their union isn't going to last? No," Tessa said, answering her own question. "I knew Micah exactly one week before I did something I'd never done with any other man. I slept with him. Did I feel uncomfortable? No. Did I experience guilt? No again. I did it because I wanted and needed him at that time. If you want and need Ethan, then you're going to have to trust him and trust your own instincts. You've admitted that he's good for you. Let go and let him be good *to* you," she said in a quiet voice. Tessa paused, waiting for a response from her cousin. "Are you in love with Ethan?"

Tessa's query rendered Faith mute for several seconds. She knew she wasn't in love with Ethan, but that didn't mean she wasn't falling in love with him. "I don't think so."

"If he is everything you say he is, then give yourselves a chance to find out whether you could have a relationship, or even a future, together."

Faith emitted a nervous laugh. "Let us get used to having a relationship before you start talking about a future."

"Remember Simone and I always said you'd be the first one to get married."

"Well, Simi beat both of us to the altar."

"Anthony Kendrick doesn't count," Tessa countered. "He and Simone dated longer than they were married."

"What a waste."

"I suppose my sister had to go through what she did with Tony so she could recognize an unadulterated certified bum."

Laughter bubbled up from Faith's throat and spilled over as her features became more animated. "What's worse on a scale of one to ten—a bum or a frog?"

Tessa's laughter joined her cousin's. "From what you've told me about the men you've dated, I'd have to say they're running neck and neck."

The cousins laughed hysterically about the boys with whom they'd grown up, dated and had given their hearts and innocence to. Fifty-five minutes after leaving Mount

Vernon, Tessa dropped Faith off in front of her Greenwich Village apartment house, then continued on to Brooklyn.

Faith walked into her building, retrieved her mail, made her way up three flights to her apartment. Once inside she stripped off her clothes and headed for the bathroom. After a leisurely shower, she slipped into a pair of sweatpants and pulled on a T-shirt; she checked her voice mail, grateful that there were no messages. Not having to return calls meant she could relax and catch up on paperwork for her bakeshop. She had to do the biweekly payroll and sign quarterly payroll-related tax returns her accountant had mailed to her at the patisserie.

She planned to go into Let Them Eat Cake early tomorrow morning to bake and hopefully decorate one more wedding-theme cake. Then she would download the digital photos and type the recipes and decorating instructions. If they kept to their present schedule, then Faith projected that she and Ranee would be able to decorate at least forty cakes before Valentine's Day. A smile tilted the corners of her mouth. There was no doubt she would be able meet Peter Demetrious's deadline.

When she'd asked Tessa about a wedding photographer she said she'd asked Peter to do still photos of her ceremony and reception, while also obtaining the services of a videographer. Peter hadn't committed but promised Tessa that if he could shift his schedule, then he would be honored to photograph her very special day.

Spending most of the day planning Tessa's wedding reminded Faith of the two Valentine's Day weddings and Tomasina Fiori's granddaughter's birthday party. She had to talk to Ethan about her flight schedule to Palm Beach before committing to Tommi's request. She also wanted to ask him to come with her to Bridget's house on Saturday.

Two hours later she reached for the cordless phone and walked over to the window seat and sat down. Crossing her legs in a yoga position, she dialed his number. She smiled when his sensual voice came through the earpiece. Simone was right. His voice was definitely X-rated.

"How are you, Ethan?"

"Much better now that I hear your voice."

"Is something wrong?"

"No, it isn't," he said much too quickly. "How can something be wrong when I'm talking to the most beautiful woman in New York?"

Her smile widened. "Are you flirting with me, Ethan McMillan?"

"I'm trying to. You have to let me know whether I'm succeeding."

"You are."

"Good."

"I called to ask you to arrange a flight for me to go to Palm Beach, and also if you can get off Saturday night."

"Consider Florida a done deal. As soon as I contact the pilot, I'll let you know the time of your departure and arrival. What's going on Saturday?"

"I'm invited to a dinner party, and I'd like you to come with me as my guest. And if you're able to get Sunday off I'd like for us to..." Her words stopped when she realized what she was prepared to ask him.

"You want us to do what?" Ethan asked after a pregnant pause.

Faith felt as if she'd just come down with a severe case of foot-in-mouth. She inhaled, held her breath, then let it out slowly. "I'd like to spend time with you so we can talk about *us*."

There was a swollen pause on Ethan's end. "What's up, Faith?"

"What are you talking about?"

"Are you planning to hand me my walking papers?"

"No! No, Ethan," she repeated in a softer tone. "I just need to clear up a few things when it comes to our relationship."

"I didn't know we had a relationship," he countered.

"Well, we do," she insisted.

There came another pause. "In that case I'll make certain to ask my boss for the weekend off."

Faith was certain he heard her sigh of relief. "Thank you."

"No, Faith. I should be the one thanking you."

"I'll call you toward the end of the week to give you the particulars for Saturday."

"And I'll call you before the end of the week," Ethan countered. "I'd love to talk longer but I have another call coming through and I have to take it. Good night, darling."

"Good..." What she wanted to say trailed off when she heard the silence that indicated he'd switched over to his other caller.

Depressing a button, she placed the receiver on the cushioned seat. She willed her mind blank as she stared through the slight opening in the window shutters. What she didn't want to do was read more into Ethan's calling her darling. But she knew they'd reached the point where their relationship had to be resolved.

Faith had to make up her mind whether she wanted to continue to date Ethan after their Caribbean jaunt, or break it off before she found herself in too deep.

Her feelings for him intensified each time she heard his voice over the phone, and grew whenever they were together. She worked the long hours, pushing herself to the brink of exhaustion because when she went to bed—alone—it was to sleep and not dream about the man she wanted to make love to her. She'd encountered prolonged periods in the past where she hadn't slept with a man, but right now she wanted to be anything but celibate.

Faith knew she was a passionate woman because her two serious relationships had proven that. What she didn't know was how much longer she could continue to date Ethan and not ask him to make love to her.

Chapter 12

The weekend came, and it wasn't until the stationer Faith used for the bakeshop's marketing products dropped off the colorful banner she'd requested informing her customers to place their personalized Valentine's Day orders before the tenth that she realized January had come and gone. And it was only during the first two weeks in February the days of operation for Let Them Eat Cake went from five to six.

The past week she'd established the habit of rising early and going into the shop before dawn. Most nights she didn't leave until after nine, eating just enough to keep her energy level up, and when she returned home it was to take a quick shower and fall into bed.

Faith was grateful for Saturday for two reasons: going to the Cohens' reassured her that she wouldn't spend the night at the bakeshop and that she would get to see Ethan again. As promised, he'd called to give her her flight schedule for Palm Beach. He'd arranged for a driver to take her to Teterboro Airport Friday morning for a 6:00 a.m. flight, and her return flight was scheduled for ten that evening. He'd also confirmed their getaway weekend where they would spend forty-eight hours together somewhere in the Caribbean, and no matter how much she begged and pleaded with him to tell her where they were going he wouldn't relent. She'd hung up on him, fuming. Ethan had earned his first *ribbit* for being obstinate.

She left Let Them Eat Cake at three to unwind before she readied herself to go to Bridget and Seth's dinner party. Faith walked into her apartment and placed a box filled with an assortment of brownies she planned to take to the Cohens' on the countertop, hung up her coat and kicked off her leather clogs. She headed for the bed, knowing a couple of hours of sleep would offset the fatigue that had come crashing over her like the pounding surf washing up on a beach.

The telephone rang and she smothered an expletive. Reaching for the cordless instrument, she recognized Tessa's number on the display. "Hello, Tessa. What's up?"

"I'm calling about tonight's gathering. Bridget just called to cancel because Seth's grandmother was admitted to the hospital this afternoon."

"Is it serious?"

"They've been told it's a mild heart attack. The problem is that it's not her first one, so they're going to keep her and run further tests. Even though she's eighty-eight she's still feisty."

Faith smiled. "Good for her. If you talk to Bridget, tell her I'll light a candle for Seth's grandmother."

"I'm sure they'll appreciate that. I was really looking forward to meeting your Ethan, but I suppose that'll have to wait for another time."

She wanted to tell her cousin that he wasn't *hers* to claim as her own. "There'll be another time," she said instead. Faith chatted with Tessa for five minutes more, then rang off. Retrieving her handbag, she took out her cell phone and punched in the programmed number to Ethan's cell phone. He answered after the third ring, his deep voice coming through the earpiece.

"Yes?"

A slight frown creased her forehead with his brusque greeting. "Did I catch you at a bad time?"

"Yes…no."

Her frown deepened. "Either it's yes or no, Ethan."

"No, Faith. I didn't mean to bark at you. Please accept my apology."

"Apology accepted." She disclosed the details of Tessa's telephone call. "We don't have to get together this weekend if you don't want to."

"But I do, Faith. What if I pick you up around five? I'll call you when I get into the city."

"Make it six and you have a deal."

"Six it is. I'll see you later, baby."

Ethan hung up before she could say goodbye. She *had* caught him at an inopportune time because he'd ended the call abruptly. Was he having problems with his boss because of his requests not to work weekends, or with some of the other drivers who also may have wanted weekends off to spend time with their friends or families?

Setting the tiny phone on the bedside table, Faith

reached for a throw at the foot of the bed and spread it out over the comforter. She set her clock for five, then lay down to take a nap.

Faith, pushing a button, answered the intercom when the downstairs bell chimed throughout the apartment. "Who is it?"

"Ethan."

"Don't bother to come up. I'm on my way down."

Releasing the button, she unlocked the door, leaving it slightly ajar. She put on her coat, gathered her keys, the box of brownies and overnight bag. Flicking off the light switch, she locked the door.

Ethan was waiting for her on the second-floor landing. Easing the bag from Faith's loose grip, he looped his free arm around her waist and pressed a kiss to her fragrant, curly hair. "I decided to meet you halfway." His gaze lingered on her face with the subtle colors that highlighted her dark eyes and lush mouth.

"You look very nice."

Faith was helpless to stop the rush of heat suffusing her face, and it wasn't the first time she was thankful for her darker complexion because it prevented Ethan from seeing her blush like a gauche schoolgirl. But it wasn't the first time she reminded herself that she wasn't a girl but a thirty-year-old woman, who, where men were concerned, hadn't always chosen wisely.

She'd become an astute businesswoman, had established a reputation as an up-and-coming cake designer and she was solvent. Yet none of that mattered whenever she and Ethan shared the same space. Tessa had asked her if she was in love with Ethan, and she'd been truthful with her. Now, after seeing Ethan again, she could acknowledge that she was falling in love with him. But as much as she wanted to share a bed with him, she was just as apprehensive as before, because that would change everything.

Faith realized her vacillation was predicated on the idea that if she did permit him to make love with her he would become like all of the other men who saw her as someone they could dominate and control. And she'd lost count of the number of times she'd questioned herself as to what type of vibes she gave off to make them change from nice guy into *gangsta* the moment their relationship went from platonic to intimate.

She'd admitted to Tessa that Ethan McMillan was good for her, but she also wanted him to be good *to* her.

They walked four blocks to where Ethan had found a parking space. "You're rather quiet tonight," he remarked, activating the remote device that unlocked the doors.

"I've been thinking," Faith said.

"What about?"

She waited while he opened the passenger-side door for her. "Us."

Ethan reached for Faith's arm. "If you don't mind, I'd rather talk about it later."

She met his unwavering stare in the glow of an overhead streetlight. "I don't mean to come off sounding selfish, but I've had a helluva day, and *if* whatever you want to talk about is going to end with us at each other's throats then I'd rather not talk about it tonight."

Faith nodded. "Okay." What she's suspected earlier was exacerbated by his admission to having a "helluva day." She sat down, buckled her seat belt and waited for Ethan to get in beside her. "May I ask you one question?"

He inserted the electronic key into its slot before pushing the ignition button to start the car. "Yes."

Shifting on the leather seat, Faith turned to stare at him. "Are you having problems with your job because you're seeing me on the weekends?"

Ethan struggled not to laugh. When he told Faith that he had a wonderful boss he was referring to himself. Some of his employees saw him as a hard taskmaster, but the fact was that he was a fair and realistic manager. Earlier that morning he had to suspend one of his drivers because the man had come to work smelling of alcohol. It had been his second infraction. There was no way he could risk injury and/or a lawsuit because of an alcohol-related accident. Faith had called him when he'd ordered the man to check into a substance-abuse program or face the loss of continued employment.

"No, I'm not," he said as he maneuvered away from the curb and into the flow of traffic. "Whatever problems I have have nothing to do with you."

"That's good to hear," she said softly.

"Is it?"

"Yes. I'd never permit a man to interfere with what I've worked so hard to make a success."

Ethan's eyebrows shot up. "Are you saying there's no room in your life for love and happily ever after?"

"No, Ethan. That's not what I'm saying. I've sacrificed a lot to stay afloat and grow my business. When I first opened Let Them Eat Cake I was so far in the red that I thought I wasn't going to survive the first year. My accountant told me it would take at least three years to show even a small profit because of the location. Rents in Manhattan are exorbitant and a West Village location is almost prohibitive."

"Are you still in the red?"

"No, only because the fees I charge as a cake decorator for Signature Bridals I've invested in the patisserie. Then there're all my other private clients like Tommi Fiori who make up more than three-quarters of my income."

"Is the bakeshop breaking even?"

"It's now showing a small profit."

"What's the percentage?" Ethan asked.

"It's about ten percent."

Ethan gave Faith a sidelong glance. "A ten percent profit margin is very risky. What if there's a prolonged drought in the Midwest and the price of flour skyrockets? The same can be said for sugar. Within a matter of months your ten percent margin can drop to where it's not realistic to keep the doors open. And then there's the matter of rent. What if the owner of the building decides to sell it and the new owner either doubles your rent or wants you out because he can renovate the entire building and turn it into co-op apartments?"

A frown caused vertical lines to appear between her eyes. "I'm aware of the risks."

"Yet you continue to take them."

"That's what business is all about, Ethan. It's about taking risks and I've become the ultimate risk taker."

"But you don't have to, darling," Ethan argued in a quiet tone. "You're working hard, not smart. You have your private clients and I'm certain your involvement with Signature Bridals keeps you busy. And there's no doubt when your coffee-table book on cakes is published you'll become a celebrity. Why kill yourself with the bakeshop?"

Faith couldn't help smiling. "You sound like my cousin Tessa."

"She sounds like a very smart woman. Have you considered selling it?"

Faith stared at Ethan as if she'd never seen him before. It was the second time that week someone had broached the topic of her selling the shop. "Have you been spying on me?"

"No. Why would you ask me that?"

"One of my employees said the same thing. She said that if and when I'm ready to sell, then she wanted to put in the first bid. I sell the shop, then what, Ethan? Where do I bake sheet cakes? Definitely not in the oven in my apartment," she said answering her own question. "I'm going to need an industrial oven."

"Do you own or lease your apartment?"

"I rent it," Faith confirmed.

"When does your lease expire?"

"I have another year."

"Can you sublet it?"

Faith nodded. "Yes." She had a sublet clause in her lease. "Why?"

"Sell your shop and buy a loft or brownstone with the proceeds. Then have the space configured so that you can it use for your business and personal use. Meanwhile, you can sublet your apartment with a twenty-five percent markup to cover what may become unforeseen incidentals. For example, if you're paying two grand a month, then you can put an extra five hundred in your pocket every month."

Shifting on her seat, Faith stared at Ethan's distinctive profile, her expression registering surprise and admiration. "You sound like quite the entrepreneur."

"I had a good teacher. WJ is an astute businessman, and everything I know I learned from him." What Ethan didn't tell Faith was that it was his cousin who'd encouraged him to go into the transportation business. "Think of my suggestion that you sell your shop, because all of the makeup in the world can't camouflage the dark circles under your beautiful eyes. And you're thinner now than you were a week ago."

A soft gasp escaped Faith. "If you have a problem with my looks, then maybe we shouldn't see each other."

"I don't have a problem with your looks, Faith. You've heard me say more than once that you're beautiful."

"Then what is it you want?" she snapped, not bothering to temper her acerbic tone.

His dimples flashed when he smiled. "Right now I want Faith Whitfield."

Emotions that she didn't want to acknowledge warred within her with Ethan's statement. "But you do have me, Ethan. Am I not here with you?"

He shook his head. "Yes, you are, but what you've shown me is the haughty, rigid businesswoman who takes herself much too seriously. I want the Faith who's not afraid to throw back her head and laugh without censoring herself. The Faith who's willing to throw caution to the wind where she can frolic butt-ass-naked in the rain." Ethan smiled when she gasped for the second time within a matter of minutes.

Faith crossed her arms over her chest. The heat in her face had nothing to do with her being embarrassed about his reference to being naked. How dare he refer to her as haughty. If he wanted haughty, then he should meet her mother.

He rested a hand over her denim-covered knee as the light from the dashboard glinted off the signet ring on his right hand. "There's no need to pout, darling."

"Don't 'darling' me, Ethan."

"Are you saying you're *not* my darling?"

"Yes, I am," she drawled sarcastically.

Ethan wanted to tell Faith that she *was* his darling and so much more, but didn't want to engage in a diatribe that would challenge his fragile relationship with her. The woman sitting beside him had no idea how much she affected him. Her gorgeous face and beautiful body occupied his thoughts when he was awake or asleep. Everything about her invaded his dreams until he woke up in a sweat with a certain part of his body throbbing for release.

Slowing, he stopped for a red light, leaned to his right and pressed his mouth to her smooth cheek. "I'm sorry I called you haughty."

Faith turned and stared out the side window. "No, you're not."

"Yes, I am."

He attempted to kiss her again, but Faith swatted at him. "Stop it."

The light changed and the vehicle shot forward in a burst of speed. "Stop what, Faith? You have no idea what I go through counting the days when I'll get to see you again, how agonizing it's become for me to get a restful night's sleep because I dream of making love to you. And if I were granted one wish it would be to fast-forward to February fourteenth where I could have you all to myself for two whole days."

Faith closed her eyes as she replayed his passionate revelation in her head. Had he read her mind? She opened them but refused to look at Ethan. "What we have isn't that one-sided, Ethan. I know what you're feeling because I'm going through the same thing." A pregnant silence swelled inside the vehicle as the slip-slap of tires on the roadway kept pace with their measured breathing.

"I'm going to ask you one more time, Faith, and I want the truth. Are you my darling?"

Ethan's query was so soft Faith thought she'd imagined it. Pulling her lower lip between her teeth, she nodded. "Yes," she finally admitted, the single word resembling a sob.

There came a beat. Ethan rested his arm over the back of her seat. "You are the first woman I've ever known that's the complete package. I find you aloof, but to me that's an integral component of your appeal, along with your beauty and intelligence. Whether you know it or not you're a siren, a temptress. You've got my nose so wide-open that a semi could drive right up to my brain. You, Faith Whitfield, have become my sweetest temptation."

In one quick second their gazes met and held. Leaning to her left, Faith pushed a button on the dashboard. The haunting, moaning sound of a sax filled the car. She didn't want to talk because what she was experiencing at that moment could not be verbalized. She willed the tears filling her eyes not to fall, but failed. Reaching for the hand draped over the back of her seat, she brought it to her mouth and kissed his fingers as moisture dotted his skin. Ethan emitted a ragged sigh but didn't take his eyes off the roadway.

The remainder of the trip from Manhattan to New Jersey was accomplished in complete silence until they reached the city limits for Hackensack. Ethan activated the Bluetooth device and within minutes was connected to an Italian restaurant. He ordered entrées and salads as if he'd memorized the menu.

"I'll pick it up in about twenty minutes."

Disconnecting the call, Ethan stared at Faith staring back at him, complete surprise freezing her delicate features. "No cooking this weekend, and that's an order. I'm going to make certain you get some sleep."

She couldn't stop a hint of a smile finding its way across her lips. "Yes, sir," she countered, saluting him.

Faith sat on the rug, across a low table from Ethan, her legs tucked under her body. He'd started a fire in the fireplace in the family room, lit dozens of candles, tuned a radio to a station featuring classical music and set the table with the food he'd ordered from his favorite Englewood Cliffs restaurant. She swallowed a mouthful of spaghetti tossed with an incredibly delicious pesto sauce before touching a napkin to the corners of her mouth. The pasta was the perfect complement to veal scallops in a butter sauce flavored with lemon and capers.

Picking up a bottle of rosé, Ethan refilled his wineglass, then added a small amount to Faith's. He flashed a dimpled grin. "Are you ready for dessert?"

Pressing her palms to her flat stomach, she shook her head. "I can't eat another morsel."

"Why don't you go to bed? I'll clean up here."

"Are you sure you don't want help?"

Rising to his feet, Ethan circled the table and sat next to her, his left hand cradling the back of her head at the same time his right arm went around her back. Deliberately, as if in slow motion, he eased her up from the floor.

His head lowered until their mouths were inches apart. "You have to learn how to relax."

She closed her eyes against his intense stare. "I know how to relax."

"Your body's very tense."

Faith opened her eyes. She wanted to tell Ethan that her

tenseness came from him being too close, that she found it difficult to draw a normal breath. She felt an intangible strength coming from him, seeping into her where her apprehension as to whether she could risk becoming involved with a man vanished like a wisp of smoke.

In Ethan James McMillan she'd discovered a man she'd learned to respect and trust more than the others she'd known. Whenever they were together she hadn't had to concern herself with countering unsolicited advances as she had in the past. Most times she hadn't progressed beyond the one-date rule when she found herself sparring with her dates because they hadn't respected her enough not to kiss or touch her without her permission.

At first she'd thought his rigid self-control was a result of his military training, but then realized it probably was a combination of upbringing, moral and ethical fortitude.

"I'll be all right after a leisurely bath."

Ethan brushed a light kiss over her lips. "I'll tuck you into bed after you finish with your bath."

"I'll try and wait up for you."

He smiled at her as he would a child. "Thank you." Ethan had promised to tuck her in when it was her bath, bed, body and life he wanted to share. He wanted Faith Whitfield so much that he feared blurting out how much he needed her. And his need surpassed any emotional or physical craving he'd ever known. He wasn't certain when he'd fallen in love with Faith, but knew what he felt for her went beyond reason or comprehension.

Wrapping her arms around his neck, Faith pulled Ethan's head down and she kissed him. Her lips caressed his until they parted. She swallowed his breath as their tongues met in a slow, heated joining that sent shockwaves throughout her body.

Ethan's hands slipped down the length of Faith's back, cupping her hips as he pressed his heated groin to her body. A turbulent rising desire held him in a stranglehold that rendered him light-headed. He had to stop, he had to get away from Faith or embarrass himself when he spilled his passion like a bumbling adolescent in his first sexual encounter.

His hands came up and he cradled her face between his palms, breaking off the kiss. "Go take your bath," Ethan whispered hoarsely. "Please." He was pleading with Faith and didn't care if she knew it.

A shy smile softened her mouth. "Okay."

Ethan managed to nod as he watched Faith turn and walk out of the dimly lit room. Ten minutes later he'd cleared away the remains of their dinner, adjusted the fire-place screen and extinguished the candles.

Chapter 13

Ethan walked out of his bedroom, down a hallway and into the guest bedroom suite. The door was open, and as he stepped inside he noticed the lamps on the bedside tables were on the lowest setting, casting long and short shadows throughout the space.

His gaze swept over the made-up bed, and he went completely still. Faith wasn't in bed, so he assumed she was still in the bathroom. He turned to leave, then spied her on the chaise in the sitting area.

Placing one foot deliberately in front of the other, Ethan approached the woman whose very presence kept his emotions in a constant state of turmoil. He valued their fragile friendship, but at that moment it wasn't friendship he sought from Faith. That he could get from any woman. What he wanted from the woman with whom he'd found himself totally enthralled was something deeper—a closeness that could only be achieved through the intimate act where they would cease to be separate.

What he wanted more than to have Faith love him as he loved her was for her to learn to trust him. The night he'd taken her to the Rainbow Room and they'd made a toast to trust, he'd known that a man had hurt her—deeply.

I want trust. I want to be able to trust you. Ethan didn't know why, but he was able to recall her plea as if it'd been etched in his brain. And there was no doubt she'd loved whomever she'd given her heart to because she was still hurting.

Had he been her first love? Had she given him her innocence? Or was what she'd shared with him a once-in-a-lifetime love? The questions haunted Ethan, and he feared the answers would be a resounding *yes!*

He'd married Justine, believing they would spend the rest of their lives together, but in the end he'd had to walk away or lose himself completely. He'd suggested going to marriage counseling, but she refused, saying she didn't need someone telling her what to do, that she knew how to be a wife.

His ex-wife's mood swings, inconsolable crying jags and her penchant for throwing objects, some that'd missed him by mere inches, had become the bane of his existence. Her volatile behavior forced him to accept assignments overseas, and in the end it was he who'd filed for a divorce, citing irreconcilable differences. Justine didn't contest his decision and within eight months of exchanging vows it was over.

Moving closer, Ethan stared down at Faith sprawled gracefully on the chintz-covered chaise. A hint of a smile found its way over his features as he stared at the delicate white cotton nightgown trimmed in pale blue lace with tiny pearl buttons dotting a pleated bodice. His heated gaze inched slowly from her exposed neckline to her long, smooth legs. His smile widened when he saw the sexy red polish on her pedicured toes. It was obvious that Faith did take time out for pampering. His smile faded when her eyes opened and she stared up at him.

"I almost fell asleep waiting for you."

Folding his lanky body down beside her, Ethan leaned over and pressed a kiss to her eyelids. "Why didn't you get into bed?"

"I was waiting for you to tuck me in."

Shifting slightly, he gathered her in his arms, scooping her up and coming to his feet. The heat from her scantily clad body burned Ethan's through the T-shirt and sweatpants he'd slipped into after taking a quick shower. He carried her effortlessly to the bed.

"Not here," Faith said in protest.

Ethan went still at the same time sucking in a lungful of breath, holding it until he felt the band of tightness constricting his chest. "Where?" he asked, hoping his silent prayer would be answered. Since coming face-to-face with Faith Whitfield, he'd lost count of the number of times he'd fantasized sharing a bed with her.

"I'll give you one guess," Faith teased with a sensual smile.

Shock and surprise froze Ethan's features. "You know what this means, don't you?" Faith nodded. "There's no turning back once we sleep together." She nodded again. He held her steady gaze. "I'm in this relationship for the duration, Faith."

Seconds ticked off as the deafening silence rose to a crescendo. "So am I."

Faith was tired of the pretense, the denial, of fighting

her feelings for the man holding her to his heart. She'd been wrestling with issues of trust that bogged her down so much that she'd forgotten to live and grasp the happiness that was right in front of her. Work had become a balm providing a barrier against a loneliness she hadn't wanted to acknowledge.

Looping her arms around Ethan's strong neck, she rested her head on his shoulder, feeling his heat, inhaling his distinctive masculine scent. *I love him.* The three words assailed her with the velocity of a rocket launching toward the heavens.

She'd held him at bay, not touching or kissing him whenever the urge was so strong as to make her feel as if she were coming out of her skin. She'd worked herself into an exhaustive state so as not to be reminded of the strong passions within her. The closest she'd come to succumbing was when she'd kissed Ethan in the family room. It was she who'd initiated the kiss, slipped her tongue into his mouth, and the evidence of his arousal had signaled they both were close to yielding to a desire that had to be resolved.

Inwardly, she was able to reconcile her love for Ethan when she still wasn't able to put the insecurities of her past to rest. It'd been she who was always the first to profess her love, and the result had made her a victim to men who'd used her love for control and domination.

She smiled. Her love for Ethan would remain her secret, until he proved to her that he wouldn't use it to change her into someone she either couldn't or wouldn't become.

Ethan carried Faith into his bedroom and placed her on his bed, his body following hers onto the firm mattress. The glow from the recessed light in the space between the bedroom and adjoining bathroom provided the only source of illumination as he tried to make out her expression. He sat up, supporting his back against the headboard, and then eased Faith up to straddle his thighs.

Was she ready for him and what they were about to share? He was certain he was more sexually experienced than she was, but would that be enough to bring her to climax?

The questions kept coming, bombarding Ethan relentlessly. Why, he mused, did it matter so much with Faith when it'd never been that way with other women? He'd slept with them and did what was necessary for them both to achieve physical satisfaction. But he knew the answer before the questions formed in his mind. It mattered because she was different, and not only had he fallen in love with her, but he also loved her enough to offer his protection as her husband and as the father to any of their potential children. The notion of fathering a child shocked him.

Cradling her face between his palms, he brushed a light kiss over her parted lips. "There's something you need to know."

Faith stared at the shadowy face inches from her own. "What's that?"

There came a beat, the sound of their heavy, measured breathing breaking the fragile silence. "I love you."

The emotion in the deep voice elicited a rush of tears she was helpless to hold in check. They overflowed and trickled down her cheeks. They landed on Ethan's hands when he undid the tiny pearl buttons on her nightgown. Faith bit down on her lower lip when the bodice parted and he touched her. His fingers closed over one breast, squeezing gently before cradling the other. Without warning, a rush of heat and moisture bathed her core, leaving the area pulsing and ready for his complete possession.

Ethan let his senses take over as he registered the quickened cadence of Faith's breathing, the twitching muscles under his hands as he covered her small, firm breasts. She let out a soulful moan when his mouth replaced his hands. He suckled her at the same time he slid his hands under the narrow straps holding up the nightgown, pushing them off her shoulders and down her arms, the delicate fabric pooling around her narrow waist.

Faith grasped her lover's head, holding him fast as she buried her face in his close-cropped hair. He was making her feel things she'd forgotten, suppressed emotions she believed she would never experience again. Love and lust merged in a turbulent passion that made it impossible for her not to move. A spark of desire cut a swath from her breasts to the area between her legs as she rocked back and forth over the rising erection under her hips.

Ethan pulled a nipple into his mouth, teeth nipping gently before shifting his attention to the other breast. He'd managed to temper his desire for the woman sharing his bed because he wanted to offer a passion that would make Faith forget every man she'd ever known. Forget them because he wanted to become the last man in her life.

Rising several inches off Ethan's lap, Faith struggled not to let out the screams building up in the back of her throat. She squeezed her thighs together in an attempt to stem the increasing pulsing sensations.

"Oh, no!" she gasped.

Ethan released her breast with a soft popping sound. His head came up and he tried to make out Faith's expression. "What's the matter, baby?" There was no mistaking the concern in his query.

Struggling not to climax, Faith gulped in a lungful of air. "Do it now, Ethan. Please."

She was begging him to make love to her, but it was of no import because she wanted Ethan in the most intimate way possible. She, who'd looked for and treasured foreplay, wanted no part of it now because her lust was akin to a craving that had to be assuaged or she'd lose herself in an abyss of longing that would go on forever.

Letting his senses take over, Ethan registered the quickened pace of Faith's breathing, the rocking sensations of her hips against his erection and the moans that alternated with sighs that signaled she was as ready for him as he was for her.

His hands went to the nightgown around her waist, pulling it up and over Faith's head. His T-shirt followed; he eased her off his lap, then removed his sweatpants and briefs.

He felt Faith's gaze following him as he leaned over and removed a condom from the drawer of the bedside table, and with steady hands he ripped open the packet and slipped the latex over his erection. The rising scent of desire mingling with the sensual feminine perfume wafted in his nostrils as he eased Faith down to the mattress. Parting her legs with his hand, Ethan positioned his rigid flesh at the entrance to her femininity.

Burying his face between her neck and shoulder, he breathed a kiss on the fragrant flesh. "Stop me if I hurt you."

"Don't talk, Ethan. Just do it."

"Yes, ma'am," he whispered in her ear.

Faith closed her eyes. She'd ordered him not to talk when she wanted to tell him to shut the hell up and make love to her because she wanted and needed to feel the desire and passion that made her wholly woman. She pulled her lower lip between her teeth when Ethan slowly eased his sex into her body. He hesitated before he pushed inside her, inch by inch. A shared sigh came when he was fully sheathed, their bodies fused in a joining that made them one.

Her lips quivered as long-forgotten passions swirled throughout her, calling to mind what she'd been missing for a very long time. Ethan's slow, gentle lovemaking temporarily swept away her fears, doubts, as she surrendered to the passion holding her captive. The fire at the top of her thighs flared to life with the quickened thrusts, awakening a response so deep that their coming together had become an act of complete possession.

What had begun as soft whimpers escalated to moans of erotic pleasure before erupting into cries of pure delight when Faith surrendered to the ecstasy. Rising up off the mattress, she went completely still, then collapsed, her heart pounding uncontrollably as a passion she'd never experienced held her suspended for several seconds before freeing her in an awesome climax that left her crying and struggling for her next breath.

Making love with Faith elicited more than sexual desire for Ethan. Their lovemaking signaled a new beginning, a chance for both to love again. Her heat, smell, the silken feel of her skin and her erotic moans shattered his control. He fastened his mouth to Faith's and breathed in the last of her passion as he released his own inside the latex protecting her. His tongue plunged into her mouth over and over as the moment of shared ecstasy quieted.

They lay together, limbs entwined. Ethan didn't want to move but he had to get up and discard the condom. He pressed light kisses along the column of her long neck. "I'll be right back."

A hint of a smile softened Faith's lips. "I'll be waiting for you to tuck me in."

He returned her smile. "Isn't that what put us in this compromising position?"

"Are you complaining?"

Ethan ran the tip of his tongue over her parted lips. "No."

"I'm glad because I really like making love to you."

"And I you," he countered, easing away from the warm moistness of her tight body. "Don't move."

Faith wanted to tell Ethan that she wouldn't be able to move even if her very life depended upon it. Never had she experienced such an incredible sense of fulfillment as she did now.

"Don't you dare get up," Ethan whispered in Faith's ear as she moved to get out of bed.

Faith went completely still. She'd been awake for a while, waiting for sunrise, but hadn't gotten out of bed because she didn't want to wake Ethan. "I have to get up," she whispered back.

"Why?"

"Why?" she repeated, her voice rising slightly. "I've been lying here for the longest time trying not to wake you up. For your information, Ethan McMillan, I have to go to the bathroom."

"Oh."

Rolling over, she glared at him in the shadowy light coming through the window blinds. "Oh. Is that all you have to say? Where did you think I was going?"

"I thought you were going to get up and start cooking."

A low, sultry laugh escaped her. "Didn't you order me not to cook this weekend, darling?"

Ethan smiled. "Yes, I did. Somehow I didn't think you'd be so obedient."

A shiver of annoyance swept over Faith before she forced herself to relax. "Just how are you using that word? If you expect me to become a pushover, then you can forget about a relationship of long duration because I'm out of here."

Moving quickly, Ethan straddled her body, not permitting her to move. "I stand corrected, darling. I meant agreeable."

"That's better. Now, either you let me up or I'm going to embarrass myself and ruin your mattress." He shifted off her, slipped out of bed, then reached for Faith and picked her up. "I can walk," she said in protest as he walked out of the bedroom and headed in the direction of her bedroom.

"Can't you relax enough to let me become your knight in shining armor this weekend?"

"Yes," she said, laughing. "But I much prefer a prince to a knight."

"Aren't knights more gallant than royals?"

Faith rested her head on his solid shoulder. "Not in my fairy tale."

"Now I'm intrigued. You're going to have to tell me about your fairy tale."

"I will, but not now."

"When, darling?"

She knew it was time to tell Ethan about the men in her past, but she didn't want to ruin their brief time together talking about the mistakes she'd made when choosing badly. "I'll tell you about it after I've drunk one too many during our Valentine's Day tryst."

"I'll be certain to remind you in case you forget," Ethan said as he lowered Faith until her bare feet touched the cool white blocks of the stone flooring. Not waiting, he turned and left her to her morning ablutions as he retreated to do the same. He'd wanted her to share his shower, but that would come later.

He'd waited a long time for a woman like Faith Whitfield to come into his life, and the moment he realized he'd fallen in love with her, he also realized that some things in life were worth waiting for.

True to his word, Ethan wouldn't permit Faith anywhere near the kitchen except to sit down and eat. He prepared breakfast—a Greek omelet made with spinach and feta cheese, freshly squeezed orange juice and the most delicious homemade flaky biscuits shipped frozen by Northern California Galaxy Desserts. Breakfast became a leisurely affair when they read the Sunday *Times,* cleaned up the kitchen, then crawled back into bed together. Both dozed off to sleep, not waking again until late afternoon when they had to rush to make it to church for the last service.

"I'm going to drop you off at home before I go and pick up dinner," Ethan informed Faith as he maneuvered out of the church's parking lot.

"Why don't I go with you?" she asked.

"I have to wait for a call telling me that it's ready."

"What did you order?"

Ethan's dimples deepened when he smiled. "It's a surprise."

Crossing her arms over her chest, Faith exhaled a heavy breath. "Be like that."

"I'm immune to pouting, so you can give it up."

She cut her eyes at him. "I can think of another way of punishing you."

It was a full minute before Ethan realized what she was

alluding to. "O—kay," he drawled. "If you want to play dirty, then I've got something for you."

Faith became suddenly alert. "What?"

"Withhold the goodies and you'll find out."

"What are you talking about, Ethan?"

"I'm talking about you refusing to sleep with me, sweetheart."

She felt like screaming, because she'd thought he was different from the other men who believed sex was the glue that cemented a relationship. "It's not about sex, Ethan, and it will never be about sex. I'd continue to date you even if we never shared a bed."

"And I you," Ethan countered.

Faith sat staring out the windshield as the man with whom she'd fallen in love decelerated and turned off on the road leading to his subdivision. She was confused by his admission that he was willing to date her without the added benefit of sharing a bed.

"But for how long?" she asked.

"I can't answer that question. There's the saying that some things in life are worth waiting for, and *you* fall into that category."

Pinpoints of heat stung her cheeks with his compliment. "Thank you."

"I should be the one thanking you, because you make it very easy to love you."

Faith closed her eyes. "Don't spoil what we have with declarations of love."

"What are you afraid of, Faith? Don't you feel as if you have a right to have a man love you?"

"It's not that at all, Ethan. Past experience has taught me that relationships based on love don't work for me."

"You want one based on sex?" There was no mistaking the thread of shock and confusion in his query.

Faith shook her head. "No, Ethan. What I want is a relationship based on trust. To me trust supersedes love. Anyone can profess to love someone or something, and still inflict hurt and lasting pain, but trust must be earned."

"Do you trust me, darling?"

Faith shared a glance with Ethan as he activated a remote device raising the barrier at the gatehouse. "Yes."

An expression of satisfaction filled Ethan's eyes as he waved to the man in the gatehouse. He drove a short distance and pulled into the driveway alongside his town house. Within seconds of shifting into Park his cell phone rang. He answered the call, ending it quickly. Rising slightly off his seat, he reached into the pocket of his slacks for a set of keys, handing them to Faith.

"Go on in, sweetheart, and wait for me. I'll be back in about fifteen minutes."

Faith took the keys, slipped out of the car and made her way to the front door. She unlocked it and walked in. Ethan hadn't bothered to turn on the alarm. After hanging up her coat in a closet off the entryway, she strolled through the living room and formal dining room and into the kitchen, silently admiring the house that still had the smell of newness.

The two-bedroom, two-story structure provided the perfect getaway for comfortable living and relaxation. There were only eight homes in the private enclave, half containing two-bedroom suites and the other three-bedroom suites with formal living and dining rooms, gourmet kitchens, family rooms, multiple full and half baths. Ethan had decorated his home in an eclectic mix of contemporary and the strong geometric shapes reminiscent of Frank Lloyd Wright's style that combined the essence of nature-inspired forms with rhythms, colors and structures. When she'd remarked on the house's tidiness he'd admitted that he had a cleaning service come in once a week.

There still were many things about Ethan that remained a mystery, but Faith had reconciled that she didn't need to know *that* much about the man with whom she was sleeping. Her priority was how he related to her whenever they were together. There was no doubt they could engage in a relationship without the angst she usually encountered whenever a man sought to micromanage her life, as long as he respected her boundaries.

Ethan walked into the kitchen cradling one large shopping bag to his chest while gripping the handles of another. "Honey, I'm home," he announced in his best Ricky Ricardo imitation.

Faith glanced up from setting the table with china and silver. "How was your day?" she asked, playing along with him.

Resting the bags on the granite countertop, Ethan slipped out of his jacket and left it on the back of a tall stool. "It's wonderful, but I thought I told you that you weren't to work this weekend."

She adjusted the water goblets at each place setting. "I'm only setting the table, Ethan."

"That's working," he countered.

"All I've done is eat, sleep and bathe."

"And don't forget making love," he reminded her with a wide grin.

Wrinkling her nose, she tapped her forehead with the heel of her hand. "Now, how could I forget that?"

Moving closer, Ethan pulled Faith into a close embrace. "It's apparent it wasn't that memorable if you forgot."

Resting her hands on his chest over a black silk and wool-blend sweater, Faith kissed his warm, brown throat. He felt and smelled so good. "It could be I have a problem with short-term memory and require remediation."

"How many lessons do you think you're going to need?" he said teasingly.

She felt his fingers tighten on her waist. "If you're on your B game, then it'll take many more lessons, but if you elect to bring your A game then perhaps five, maybe six."

A crooked smile tilted the corner of his mobile mouth at the same time he shook his head. "Either I'm getting old, or I'm out of practice."

Faith emitted a delicate snort. "I don't think so."

Going on tiptoe, she anchored her arms under his shoulders, brushing her mouth over his. He increased the pressure until her lips parted. The kiss deepened, their tongues meeting, tasting and exploring what the other had to offer. A slumbering desire came to life, and she felt as if she were being devoured—whole. Everything going on around her and the man holding her to his heart ceased to exist as she lost herself in the moment.

What she wanted to tell Ethan was that he was the only man who'd brought her to climax during their first physical encounter. If he was out of practice, then she didn't want to think of him being in top form, and one thing for certain was that he wasn't too old to make love to a woman.

Ethan's hands moved from Faith's waist to her hips, cupping the flesh and permitting her to feel his hardening sex. He wanted her more than he'd ever wanted any woman he'd encountered. Struggling against the need to take her in the kitchen, on the floor or countertop, Ethan took a step backward to put a modicum of space between them.

Breathing heavily, he stared over her head. "If you don't stop kissing me like that then I'm going to be the only one eating tonight."

Faith caught his meaning immediately, the veiled threat eliciting a pulsing and rush of wetness at the apex of her thighs and leaving her as aroused as he. "Whatever you have in those bags smells wonderful," she said, hoping Ethan hadn't registered the breathless quality in her voice.

Ethan didn't want to talk about food. He wanted Faith in his bed with him inside her body; even when they'd gotten into bed earlier that day he'd wanted to make love to her but managed to suppress the need to take her again. What he didn't want was for her to believe that all he wanted from her was her body. The only thing she'd asked from him was trust and it was something he would give her.

"I decided that we could have a private tailgate party."

Faith folded her hands on her hips. "Did you bring beer?"

Ethan shook his head. He'd never acquired a taste for the brew, and rarely kept it in the house. He made an exception when entertaining family and friends. "I'd like something a little stronger than beer."

"What do you want?"

"Can you handle a Manhattan?"

She flashed a saucy moue. "The question should be, can you?"

"You'll just have to wait and see."

"How do you like yours?"

"Is there a difference?" Ethan asked.

Faith smiled, nodding. "Yes. It can be dry or sweet."

Staring at the woman with whom he'd fallen in love, Ethan gave her a lingering glance. It was apparent that she was as versed in mixing cocktails as she was cooking and baking. "I don't like sweet drinks, so I have to assume I've always had it dry."

"Do you want me to put the food on the table while you make the drinks?"

He shook his head. "I want you to sit and relax."

Faith crossed her arms under her breasts. "I feel so helpless sitting around doing absolutely nothing."

Ethan stared at Faith, knowing he was fighting a losing battle. "Okay, sweets. You can make the drinks."

Grinning broadly, Faith put her arms around his neck and kissed his cheek. "Thank you, darling."

He splayed a hand over her slim hips. "You're most welcome, darling."

Faith busied herself, making two trips as she selected the ingredients she needed from the well-stocked bar in a corner of the living room and carried bottles of Canadian whiskey, sweet and dry vermouth and bitters into the kitchen; she filled a shaker with ice, then added whiskey, dry vermouth and a dash of bitters, stirring and straining the chilled liquid into a delicate martini glass.

Ethan removed more than half a dozen decorative Chinese takeout containers from the bags and placed them on the table. Crossing the kitchen, he peered over Faith's shoulder as she slipped into the role of mixologist. "Hey, now, you really made it look nice."

"What's a dry Manhattan without an olive and a sliver of lemon peel?"

"But you knotted the lemon."

She rolled her eyes at him over her shoulder. "It's supposed to be knotted. It's all in the presentation, Ethan."

"Where's yours?"

"Slow down, partner. I'm going to make one but I like mine sweet." She handed him his drink, watching intently as he took a sip. "How do you like it?"

A slow smile spread over his handsome face. "It's real nice. As soon as you fix yours we'll sit down to eat."

Faith substituted sweet vermouth for the dry and a maraschino cherry for the olive, and, walking slowly, carried her cocktail to the table where Ethan had pulled out a chair for her. She sat down and blew him a kiss when he rounded the table to sit opposite her.

The private tailgate party had become a gastronomical feast. He'd ordered small bite-size pieces of barbecue spareribs, crisp spicy chicken chunks, piquant shrimp and thinly sliced beef roasted on bamboo skewers, guacamole, deviled eggs stuffed with pimentos, a peppery cole slaw and carrot salad. She sampled a little of each while taking sips of her sweet and decidedly lethal cocktail.

Ethan stared at Faith over the rim of his glass. "Why hasn't some man made you his wife?"

Faith stared back at him through her lashes. "Why? Are you putting in a bid?"

His deadpan expression didn't change. "Maybe I am."

A hint of a smile touched her mouth as she shook her head at his cryptic response. "Sorry, but I've been there, done that."

"I thought you said you'd never been married."

"I haven't, but I did come close once," she admitted. "I lived with a man who'd proposed marriage, but I couldn't bring myself to accept because I realized my life as I wanted it wouldn't have been my own."

Reaching across the table, Ethan held her hand, gently tightening his grip when she attempted to pull away. "What happened?"

She shook her head. "I really don't want to talk about it now."

He released her hand, successfully concealing his disappointment behind a polite smile. Faith didn't want to talk, while he wanted to tell her that he was tired of dating and sleeping with women because that was what they'd expected him to do; he wanted to get married again, and this time get it right. He wanted to father children with Faith as their mother; and he wanted her to be the last woman in his life.

Picking up his glass, he drained the contents. He motioned to her half-filled glass. "Do you want another one?"

"No, thank you. I'm good."

You're good, while I'm not, Ethan thought as he rose to his feet and made his way to the counter to make another drink. Perhaps if he drank enough of the potent cocktails, then he could temporarily forget about Faith and her reluctance to let him share a corner of her life.

His mantra was to be happy, patient and positive, but it was patience that had become a challenge because of Faith's reluctance to let him get close to her.

Chapter 14

Ethan took a sip of his cocktail, grimacing. Although he'd used the same ingredients as Faith, it didn't taste the same. "I need your help," he said, crossing the kitchen and extending the glass to her. "Take a sip and tell me what I did wrong."

Faith took a small amount of the liquid into her mouth, held it for several seconds and then swallowed it. She wrinkled her nose. "Yuck! You put in too much bitters."

Bowing gracefully from the waist, Ethan pressed his hands to his chest in supplication. "I will never attempt to mix another drink while in your presence."

"Please bring me some ice," she ordered him softly.

"Where did you learn to mix drinks?" he asked as he activated the ice feature on the refrigerator door.

"My father taught me." She reached for a clean glass from an overhead rack and gave Ethan a sidelong glance when he moved next to her at the cooking island. "My father and uncle own a catering business and I learned to mix drinks before I was the legal drinking age."

"Did you sample what you'd mixed?"

She shook her head. "No. There was a strict rule in my house about underage drinking and smoking. Dad used a grading system similar to wine tasters. He has a very discerning palate, and one sip was enough to let him know whether I passed or failed."

Looping an arm around her waist, Ethan watched intently as the woman with whom he'd found himself entranced quickly and expertly mixed a dry Manhattan. "Is there anything you don't do well?"

"I don't do commitment well."

His grip on her body tightened. "It's usually guys who are reluctant to commit."

Faith smiled. "Well, guys aren't the only ones who wish to remain unencumbered." She handed him the glass, watching as he sampled her concoction, his eyebrows lifting in surprise. Seeing Ethan up close under the track lights revealed a light sprinkling of freckles over the bridge of his nose that made him appear suddenly boyish.

But there was nothing boyish about a thirty-eight-year-old man who'd been trained to fly military fighter jets. More important, he hadn't made love to her like a gauche boy but like a man who knew exactly what to do to bring a woman pleasure and ultimate sexual satisfaction.

And she'd done to Ethan what she'd sworn she would never do: not be open with him. He'd admitted that he loved her, while she was unable to tell him that she also loved him. However, past experience revealed that the moment she told a man she loved him, their relationship became one of possession and control. She would continue to date Ethan, sleep with him but not reveal what lay in her heart until she was certain she could trust him completely. The sherry-colored eyes watching her darkened as Ethan lowered his head and brushed his mouth over hers, the smell of whiskey on his breath heady and aromatic.

"You taste good," she crooned in a sultry tone.

Raising the glass, Ethan put it to her lips. "Take a sip." He stared intently as she swallowed. "Nice isn't it?"

First there was an iciness followed by heat spreading throughout her chest. Nodding, Faith smiled. She'd mixed the perfect dry Manhattan. "It's nice and smooth. Hanging around you may get me to change my preference from sweet to dry."

The heat moved lower, settling in her belly and still lower to the area between her legs. Her arms circled Ethan's trim waist at the same time her hands searched under his sweater to his warm flesh, fingertips feathering over his pectorals.

"What are you doing?" he gasped, his breath quickening with a rising desire he was helpless to control.

Moving closer, Faith pressed her breasts to his bared chest. "I'm feeling you up."

Ethan set down the martini glass and gripped her shoulders. Without warning, her mouth replaced her hand when she flicked her tongue over his chest, and he jumped as if branded by hot metal.

"Faith—don't!" He'd bellowed her name as a rush of blood hardened his sex. Ethan knew he was going to embarrass himself the moment her hand cupped his erection, squeezing gently. Reciprocating, his hand slipped between her legs and cupped her mound. Her gasp of surprise reverberated throughout the space.

He wasn't aware of the runaway beating of his heart slamming against his ribs, shaking knees or how close he was to ejaculating when he swept Faith up in his arms and walked in the direction of his bedroom.

Time stood still for Faith and Ethan. Gazes locked, passion racing out of control, they tore off their clothes and reached for each other. What had begun as teasing became an unrestrained coupling that ended quickly in an explosive ecstasy that left them both trembling uncontrollably.

Ethan barely had time to protect Faith from an unplanned pregnancy before she straddled him. This coming together was hers to dictate and control, and he surrendered all that he was and had to her.

Faith melted against Ethan's moist chest and gritted her teeth tightly to keep from blurting out that she'd fallen in love with him. That would remain her secret—for now.

"Please stop in front of the next house," Faith said to the taxi driver as she pushed a bill through the slot in the Plexiglas partition. She'd contemplated canceling the Monday-night get-together with her cousins, but Tessa wanted her to see what she'd chosen as her wedding stationery.

The warm feeling of making love and being in love still lingered. Ethan had driven her back to New York earlier that morning with a promise of taking her to a small Harlem jazz club Wednesday evening. Her first impulse was to decline his invitation because she wanted to work late, but she changed her mind. Everyone, including her parents, complained that she worked much too hard, didn't eat enough and didn't know how to relax and enjoy the fruits of her labor. Tessa's pronouncement of *Don't forget that you pay people to run Let Them Eat Cake* came back in vivid clarity whenever she pushed herself to the point of exhaustion. Not only had she told Ethan that she would go with him, but she also invited him to spend the night at her apartment.

There was no doubt Ethan was good to and for her. She was more relaxed, had gained some of the weight she'd lost, and jump-started her hormones to a state where she found herself craving him at the most inopportune times. However, what was more important, she trusted him, had fallen in love with him, a love not based on a physical need but an emotional desire to give and receive all that she was and could have with that special man.

Faith paid the fare on the taxi meter, got out and walked up the stairs to Tessa's Brooklyn Heights town house with a shiny brass plate engraved with Signature Bridals affixed to the wall of the three-story structure. Within seconds of ringing the bell, the solid oak door with stained-glass panels opened, and she went completely still because she hadn't expected to see Micah Sanborn. Their bimonthly Mondays had only been girls-only gatherings.

Micah kissed Faith's cheek. "I was just leaving," he said softly as a way of explaining his presence.

She rested a hand on the sleeve of his tailored dark blue, pinstriped suit jacket. He looked larger, more imposing in the business suit. "It's always good seeing you, Micah."

He winked at her, smiling and flashing his straight white teeth in a smooth dark brown face. "Same here, Faith." Micah gave her a mock salute. "Don't work too hard."

"I won't," she countered, walking into the entryway and closing the door behind her cousin's fiancé. Faith hung up her coat on the coat tree in the foyer illuminated with wall sconces and an Art Deco–inspired ceiling fixture. She glanced at the large, exquisite bouquet of fresh flowers in a glass vase with a creamy, whitewashed, leafy metal overlay; she recognized the arrangement as Simone's signature. The flowers were a pink parfait bouquet of frilly lsianthus, fragrant carnations, velvety roses and double-petaled Angelique tulips.

"I'm here!" Faith announced as she made her way into the kitchen and put the box from Let Them Eat Cake into the refrigerator. Mouthwatering smells reminded her that she'd shared breakfast with Ethan but hadn't stopped to eat lunch. "Micah let me in," she explained when Tessa gave her a questioning look.

Simone turned from tossing a salad to smile at her cousin. She'd swept her long curly hair up into a ponytail. "Hey."

Faith returned her smile. "Hi. The flowers are incredible."

Simone and Tessa exchanged a knowing glance. "I told you she would mention the flowers because they're pink," the floral designer quipped. She extended her hand to her sister. "Now, pay up, Tessa."

Faith shook her head. "I can't believe you guys were placing wagers on what I'd say. How much did you win, Simi?" she asked, walking into the half bath off the kitchen.

"A dollar."

She stuck her head out of the bathroom. "Damn! A dollar! I thought I'd be worth more than that."

"You are," Simone said, "but I didn't want to overtax Tessa's bank account because of her wedding."

"Yeah, right," Faith drawled. "Tessa has more money than both of us combined."

Tessa flashed a grimace. "I plead the Fifth."

Faith washed and dried her hands and returned to the kitchen. "What's on the menu, Tessa?"

"We're having surf and turf, loaded baked potatoes and Caesar salad."

"Good, because I'm hungry."

"What did you bring for dessert?" Simone asked.

"Tiramisu."

"Oh, damn!" Tessa moaned.

"Ditto!" Simone shouted.

The sisters had made it known years ago that tiramisu was their favorite dessert. "Is there anything you want me to do?" Faith asked Tessa, who'd uncovered a large pot of boiling water.

"No. I've everything under control. As soon as I boil the lobster tails, I'll broil them along with the steaks. How do you like your steak?" A platter held three two-inch-thick cuts of filet mignon covered with black, green and red cracked peppercorns.

"Medium well."

Twenty minutes later, the three women sat down at the table to eat. Baked potatoes with a crisp outer skin dusted with sea salt and filled with crisp crumbled bacon, fresh green onion and melted crumbled blue cheese, perfectly broiled lobster tails, seared grilled steaks in a peppercorn-mustard sauce and an accompanying salad set the stage for another meeting of Whitfield women.

The topics segued from their clients to the guest list for the Whitfield-Sanborn nuptials. Tessa delayed serving coffee and dessert as she showed Faith her wedding stationery. She'd chosen an elegant invitation, superbly crafted with vellum wrappings and extraordinary gray and robin's-egg-blue ribbons that matched her color scheme.

Faith ran a fingertip over the delicate ribbons. "I love them. What did Micah say?"

Tessa closed her clear brown, gold-flecked eyes for several seconds. "He hasn't been much help."

Reaching across the table, Faith placed her hand over Tessa's. "What's going on, cuz?"

"He's been no help to me. Whenever I ask him about something, he says 'Whatever you want.' Or 'Whatever you think is best.' Why wouldn't I ask him a question or solicit his input if I didn't want to include him about a decision that affects both of us?"

Faith shook her head. "Consider yourself blessed, Tessa, because I remember you telling me about the fiancé who wouldn't let his fiancée make a move or decision without consulting with him first. There was no doubt the man was a control freak. Can you imagine what kind of marriage you would have if Micah micromanaged your very existence? You're going to be the bride and the consummate wedding planner, so why would he interfere in something he knows nothing about? All you should concern yourself with is making certain he shows up at the appointed time to make you his wife."

"Preach, girl," Simone whispered softly.

A rush of color darkened Tessa's face. "So, you think I overreacted when I told Micah to think hard and long about whether he truly wants to marry me."

"No, you didn't," Faith whispered, shaking her head in shock.

"Yes, I did," Tessa shot back angrily.

"When did you tell him this, Tessa?" Simone asked.

"Last night."

"Is that why he was here when I got here?" Simone continued, questioning her sister. Tessa nodded. "And what did he say?"

Tessa flushed again. "I can't repeat it."

"I hope he tore you a new one," Simone mumbled under her breath.

Faith sucked her teeth. "I hear you, Simi. If your silly sister lets him go, then I'm certain there are hundreds or maybe even thousands of other sisters ready to snap him up. Haven't we spent the past ten years bitchin' and moanin' about not being able to find a good black man? And we weren't talking about marriage, but a relationship that's based on honesty and trust. Simone married an educated bum, while I've dated more losers than I can shake a stick at. And please don't forget the one who you warned me not to move in with and eventually became my jailer. This is not to say you haven't dealt with your share of zeros, but now you have someone who's the real deal, Tessa. Please, don't blow it by becoming a Bridezilla."

Pushing back her chair, Simone stood up. "You tell her, Faith. Maybe she'll listen to you because she thinks her sister is just blowing smoke when I tell her to get a grip. If she doesn't want Micah, then I'll take him. That way we can keep him in the family."

Tessa's eyes widened as she stared at Simone as if she was a stranger. "You'd go after *my* man?"

Faith wagged a finger at Tessa. "If you break off the engagement, then he's not *your* man. What's it going to be? Are you or are you not getting married?"

There came a pregnant pause before Tessa said softly, "Yes, I'm going to marry Micah."

Forcing a plastic smile, Faith met Tessa's stare. "You only get one time to act a fool, because the next time you'll find yourself looking for a new maid of honor."

"Same here," Simone said as she filled a coffee carafe with water. "Not only will you need another bridesmaid, but you'll also have to search for another floral designer."

Tessa glared at her cousin, then her sister. "You know y'all ain't right."

"Neither are you," Faith countered, "when you've co-ordinated enough weddings to avoid the wedding catastrophe pitfalls."

"But it's different because I'm the one getting married. You'll know what I'm talking about when it comes time for you to get married, Faith."

She shook her head. "Remember, I'm the most level-headed of this generation of Whitefield women. I've never given into histrionics or temper tantrums."

"That's because you have ice water in your veins instead of blood," Simone said as she measured coffee beans in a grinder.

"Whatever," Faith drawled sarcastically.

Tessa stood and began clearing the table. "Are you still seeing—what's his name?"

"Ethan McMillan," said Simone, supplying his name.

Heat flared in Faith's cheeks. "Yes. We're still dating."

Simone snapped her fingers as she made a circle. "Good for you. By the way, does he have a brother?"

"Unfortunately, he doesn't."

"Bummer," she mumbled.

Tessa placed dishes and silver in one of the double stain-less-steel sinks. "I thought you were getting along with one of the guys in our bowling league."

Simone shook her head slowly. "We went out to dinner two weeks ago, and all he talked about was his ex-wife. It's apparent he's still in love with her. I'm not looking to get married again, but I'm not about to compete with an ex for a man's attention."

"That's because you're spoiled and vain," Tessa said, teasing her sister.

Resting her hands on her hips, Simone stared at Tessa through a long fringe of lashes. "Not! You're talking to the wrong Whitfield when it comes to vanity. It's Aunt Edie and Faith who were the models."

"That's only because you weren't tall enough," Faith said in defense of herself and her mother. It was Simone who'd attracted all of the boys, and in later years men. But she was oblivious to all of them because of she'd given her heart to Anthony Kendrick.

The topic changed again, this time to their fathers' new business venture. The Mount Vernon zoning board had approved the site where Malcolm and Henry Whitfield planned to open an upscale bi-level bowling alley with a game room for those under eighteen and a jazz club for anyone twenty-three and older.

The identical twin brothers were scheduled to close down and sell the catering hall and surrounding property to a developer before the end of the year. The developer planned to raze the two-story Revival Regency-style mansion with stone-colored brick, a bowed entry and portico constructed on sloping lawns that overlooked an English garden and a pond filled with water lilies and a family of magnificent, graceful swans. The brothers projected their new enterprise would be up and running in time for them to celebrate their sixtieth birthday.

* * *

Faith thought about her own life and what she would probably be doing at sixty, when she sat beside Simone as she drove her to Manhattan. Would she still own a patisserie? Would she still bake wedding cakes? Would she be married, have children or even grandchildren?

"You're kinda quiet," Simone remarked as she maneuvered off the Brooklyn Bridge.

"I've been thinking, Simi."

"What about?"

"My life."

"Your life is wonderful, Faith. You've fulfilled all of your wishes. You're a pastry chef, you're writing a cookbook and you're dating a man who isn't a frog. What else could you possibly want?"

"I don't know, Simi."

Simone had asked Faith the same question she'd asked herself since Ethan's declaration of love. He'd admitted to loving her, whereas none of the men with whom she'd had what she thought of as a relationship of long duration had ever uttered the three dreaded words. She'd heard "I like you," "I'm fond of you" but never "I love you." One had even told her that he adored her, yet he'd cheated on her.

She was used to the adoring looks and the empty words and promises that slipped out in the throes of passion. What Faith had to ask herself was whether she'd become so jaded that she was unable to believe that a man could truly love her. She'd told Ethan that she trusted him, when in reality it was only a half-truth.

What she feared most was that everything she'd shared with Ethan McMillan had happened much too quickly from their initial encounter. Was it because she'd lowered her defenses to let him become a part of her life, or was it because she wanted to prove that vanity and impulsiveness had led her to choose unwisely.

"Something tells me that Ethan will become the last man in your life."

Simone's sultry voice pulled Faith from her mental examination. "That's because you're probably tired of hearing me complain about the men I've dated."

Simone tapped her horn lightly as she maneuvered around a slow-moving sedan driven by an elderly man. "The guys you've gone out with once, I don't consider dates."

She stared at her cousin's delicate profile. "What are they?"

"Horrific encounters of the most awful kind."

Faith laughed. "Even though we may not see eye to eye on a lot of things, this is one time I have to agree with you, Simone."

"Our not seeing eye to eye started when I announced my engagement to Tony, and it was obvious you saw things in him I refused to accept."

"I must admit that Tony fooled me, too, when you first started seeing him. At least then he held down a job."

Simone emitted an unladylike snort. "That was the first and the last time he had a steady nine-to-five of any duration. Even though I loved him, I got tired of his excuses, praying that if he loved me enough he would change."

"You shouldn't want him to change, Simi, no more than you should change to please him. In any relationship we should be willing to accept what's presented or walk away. I don't want to change Ethan, but I also don't want him to try to change me. I've accepted who I am, and it's up to him to take me as I am. I've lost count of the number of times I've been called a 'stuck-up bitch,' but I'd rather be that than become a doormat for a man."

"I wish I could be more like you and Tessa," Simone said wistfully. "Tessa said she'd never go out with a man twice if he didn't open the door for her, or walked three or four steps ahead of her. I used to tell her that she was too picky, but she'd get on me saying that why should she accept anything less than what Daddy did for Mama."

"She's right. Our fathers treat our mothers like queens, and as daughters of queens shouldn't Whitfield princesses be afforded the same respect?"

"Hell, yeah!" Simone said loudly, smiling. Signaling, she turned down the block leading to Faith's apartment building. Putting the vehicle into Park, she leaned to her right and hugged her cousin. "Love you, Faith."

Faith hugged and kissed Simone's soft cheek. "Love you back."

"The next meeting will be at my place."

Pulling back, Faith stared at the luminous hazel eyes staring back at her. "I'll come early and help you cook."

Simone's smile was dazzling. "Thanks."

"Drive carefully, Simi." She'd warned her because there was a time when Simone, unbeknownst to her family, would drag race with the boys in their neighborhood.

"I will." She waited for Faith to get out and unlock the front door to her apartment building before executing a perfect three-quarter turn on the narrow street and took off with a burst of speed that left other drivers and pedestrians staring slack-jawed at her.

Chapter 15

Ethan stood in the middle of an open space in the first-floor apartment of a brownstone building along a street in East Harlem with a contractor who'd gone over the architect's plans for the three-story structure. He'd sold all of the properties he'd inherited from his aunt and uncle, but had elected to keep one as collateral. And because the building had been abandoned for years, it would have to undergo a complete renovation.

The contractor pointed to the plans spread out on a board supported by two sawhorses. "Are you certain you want this floor completely open?"

Ethan nodded. "I'm quite certain. Back here," he said, pointing to an area labeled with CL and BR, "I want a wall of closets, two full bathrooms and one half bath. And, speaking of walls—they all should be made of brick."

The stocky, ruddy-faced man with a shock of iron-gray

hair nodded as he jotted down the specifications for what his client wanted for the grand century-old residence. It wasn't often that he worked for someone who was as hands-on as Ethan McMillan. He respected the man because he knew exactly what he wanted and was willing to pay for his expertise. Ethan had hired him to put in an industrial kitchen that included walk-in refrigerator and freezer, industrial dishwashers, granite workstations and counters, ceramic floors, a dozen wall ovens, stove-top ranges, hoods and grills all bearing the top-of-line Viking label.

Ethan checked his watch. He'd told Faith he would pick her up at her place at seven, and it was now six-thirty. Extending his hand, he smiled at the contractor. "Thank you, Mr. Janus, for rearranging your schedule to meet with me."

Christos Janus's large hand closed on Ethan's in a viselike grip. "No problem, Mr. McMillan. I will order the materials, and as soon as my men finish up on the job they're working on, we'll start here."

Ethan waited until the contractor locked and secured the building, then made his way to the garage where he'd parked his car. He hadn't spoken to Faith since dropping her off early Monday morning at the patisserie. Tuesday he'd copiloted the Gulfstream V SP to London for a group of European-based musicians and piloted the return flight earlier that morning. It wasn't until he sat in the cockpit awaiting the signal to take off that he realized how much he missed flying. Soaring thousands of feet above the ground in the business jet with its EVS and all the comforts of a living room had become a heady experience. The "Enhanced Vision System," an infrared camera that showed an image of the view in front of the camera on a display, was a sophisticated feature that permitted the aircraft to land in lower visibility conditions than a non-EVS-equipped aircraft. Lloyd Seymour, his Air Force Academy roommate, had brought the G550 in for a smooth landing on a private airstrip despite the thick fog blanketing the London countryside.

Arriving at the garage, he handed his ticket to the parking attendant, paid the fee, then took another glance at his watch. Reaching into the breast pocket of his jacket, he retrieved his cell phone and punched in Faith's number. The seconds ticked off. New York City was undergoing a thaw, and the streets were teeming with people taking advantage of the summerlike temperatures before winter returned with a vengeance to remind everyone that spring was officially six weeks away.

"Hey, sweetness," he crooned when he heard her dulcet greeting. "I'm running a little late."

"So am I. I just walked through the door, and I still have to shower and change my clothes."

"If you want, we don't have to go out tonight. I could pick up something and we can eat in."

"Will you please, Ethan."

He went completely still. "Are you all right, Faith?"

"I'm okay. I'm just a little tired."

A frown formed between his eyes. "Tired or exhausted?"

"Just a little tired."

"What do you want to eat?"

"Surprise me, darling."

Ethan felt his pulse quicken with Faith's endearment. He loved her, loved her more than he'd loved any woman, and they'd shared that love in the most intimate way possible. She'd willingly come to his bed, yet that wasn't enough. He wanted her in his life—forever.

"How about Thai?"

"It sounds good."

"I'll see you in about an hour." He smiled when her tinkling laughter came through the earpiece.

"I'll be here."

Ethan ended the call at the same time the parking attendant maneuvered down the ramp with his car. He gave the man a tip, slipped behind the wheel and headed downtown.

Faith heard the deep baritone through the speaker on the intercom and pressed the button to release the lock on the downstairs outer door. She unlocked and opened the door to her apartment and waited for Ethan, her heart beating a runaway rhythm when she saw him coming up the staircase with a shopping bag and leather carry-on bag in each hand.

An inviting smile parted her lips when their gazes met. She opening the door wider. "Hi."

Lowering his head, Ethan pressed a kiss to the side of her neck. She smelled wonderful. His gaze swept over her damp, curly hair, bare face and down to a white body-hugging tank top, black leggings and matching ballet-type shoes.

"Hi." He walked into her apartment to find it dark. The only illumination was dozens of votive candles on every flat surface, creating an atmosphere that was enchanting and mysterious.

Taking the shopping bag from his loose grip, Faith placed it on the floor next to the countertop. "I thought because the weather is so nice that we'd dine under the stars."

"I thought we were eating in." Ethan slipped out of his jacket and hung it on the coat tree.

"We are. Look out the window."

He crossed the space and peered out the tall, narrow

windows that were usually concealed behind wooden shutters. A smile crinkled the lines around his eyes. Faith had covered the fire escape with a blanket and large throw pillows, while three candles flickered behind glass chimneys.

"I think I'm going to enjoy sleepovers at your place."

Faith glanced at Ethan over her shoulder. "I suppose you'll be all right until you start feeling claustrophobic." Her apartment would fit inside his house at least three times.

"I happen to like your apartment, Faith." He walked over to her. "Do you need me to help you with anything?"

"I believe I have everything under control." She took out a large plastic container filled with prawn soup, then another with shrimp and a green leafy vegetable and third one with rice vermicelli and chives. She smiled. He'd bought a six-pack of a popular Asian beer.

Ethan kissed the nape of her neck. "I'm going to wash up."

While Ethan retreated to the bathroom, Faith filled bowls with the spicy South Asian dishes. He returned in time to help her carry the food outside where they sat cross-legged on the pillows, eating, drinking and listening to music coming out of the open windows of a neighboring apartment.

Ethan placed his chopsticks across the edge of a bowl and lay down, cradling his head on folded arms. Millions of stars dotted the clear winter sky. "What do you say we spend the night out here?"

Faith rolled her eyes at him. "I say no."

"Haven't you ever slept under the stars?"

"No."

"You don't know what you're missing." Extending his hand, he beckoned her. "Come lie down next to me, darling."

Moving closer, Faith lay down next to Ethan and rested

her head on his shoulder. His aftershave was a tropical combination of lime, lemon and mandarin with a blend of coriander, nutmeg and clove. "That's all right. I won't miss what I've never had."

Ethan looped an arm around her shoulders, pulling her closer. "What are you thinking about?" he asked after a long, comfortable silence.

She shifted, pressing her face against the softness of his sweater. "I can't believe we've known each other a month."

"Why can't you believe it?"

"It seems so much longer."

Ethan closed his eyes. "Yes, it does." He felt closer to her than he had in the eight months he was married to Justine.

"Please don't change on me." Faith's entreaty came out as a soulful plea.

He opened his eyes and peered down at her. "What are you talking about?"

Faith told Ethan everything about the two men who'd impacted her life to make her wary of entering into a relationship with a man. "It was only after I'd broken off with Joel that I realized that becoming involved with a man with whom you share a career wasn't in either of our best interests. At the time I was modeling. The call for black male models wasn't as great as it was for females, and whenever he wasn't picked for a show or layout his dark moods escalated until I was afraid to be around him. I always felt as if I had to walk on eggshells around him. It all ended when I left modeling to enroll in culinary school.

"I've made some not-so-good decisions in my life, but moving in with Lars tops the list. As my teacher he was perfect, but after I graduated we started seeing each other. I suppose I had stars in my eyes because he is an award-winning chef and teacher and the fact that he was older and worldlier than I made me heady."

"How much older was he than you?" Ethan asked.

"Fifteen years. He asked me to live with him after we dated for six months, and I agreed. As a couple we presented the perfect host and hostess when entertaining. And because Lars was much more experienced than I when it came to sex, he again became my teacher. What I didn't understand was that he refused to allow me to initiate sex. Night after night I had to suppress my urges because I didn't want him to think of me as an oversexed nymph."

Ethan's fingers tightened on the tender flesh of her upper arm. "Did he call you that?"

Faith nodded. "Yes. He became more contentious, accusing me of having affairs with other men. The final straw was when he began stalking me in the hope that he'd catch me with another man. One day I'd had enough and contacted a real estate agent to find me an apartment. She showed me this one, and I gave her a check on the spot. I waited for Lars to go to Malatya, Turkey, for the international arts and apricot festival and I moved out."

"Did you ever see him again?"

"I saw him about a year later at a dinner party for a Danish diplomat. He was there with a much younger woman. When he stared at me I thought I saw fear in his eyes, fear that I would tell his date about his bizarre behavior. It never came to that because he left before dinner was served."

"So, you think because you had two bad experiences that I—"

"Bad experiences with men that I'd slept with," Faith said, interrupting Ethan.

Ethan sat up, bringing Faith up with him. "You believe because you slept with two idiots that any man you sleep with will turn into a maniac?"

She nodded again. "I can only go on past experience, Ethan."

"Your model boyfriend was nothing more than an insecure playboy, while your sugar daddy was a jealous control freak."

Faith's eyes narrowed. "Lars wasn't my sugar daddy."

"I'm not going to debate adjectives and nouns, but the problem was that he was much too old for you, Faith. To him you would always be the student and he the mentor, believing he knew what was best for you." Ethan cradled her face between his hands. "I won't try to change you, because I don't want you to change. I love you just the way you are."

Shifting, Faith straddled his lap, her arms going around his neck. She felt the steady, strong beats of Ethan's heart against her breasts. "And I love you just the way you are," she whispered in his ear. "I didn't want to love you. In fact, I didn't even want to like you."

Ethan savored the shared moment of knowing Faith loved him as he loved her, and for the first time in a very long time he felt an overwhelming feeling of peace—that all was right in his world. "Let me make you happy, darling."

She snuggled closer. "I am happy, Ethan."

"That's not what I'm talking about."

Easing back, Faith tried to make out his expression in the shadowy darkness. "What aren't you saying?"

The seconds ticked by as Ethan formed his words carefully. He didn't want to frighten Faith, but he also didn't want to lose her if he put too much pressure on her—only because she'd openly admitted that she didn't do commitment well. He'd tired of the dating scene, sleeping with women whose names and faces he forgot once he left their beds and he was lonely.

"I want us to see each other exclusively."

Faith stared at him as if he'd lost his mind. "Isn't that what we're doing? Perhaps I shouldn't ask that, because I don't know if you're seeing another woman."

"I'm not seeing anyone else."

"And neither am I." There was a tone of annoyance in her voice.

Ethan nodded, smiling. "Good."

"Is that it?"

His smile faded. "Should there be something else?"

"No," Faith said much too quickly. As long as he didn't ask her to live with him, then she was amenable to their current relationship. She'd sworn a solemn oath that she would never live with another man unless they were married. Moving off his lap, she stood up. "I'm going inside to clean up."

Ethan rose in one fluid motion. "Don't bother. I'll clean up."

Reaching for his hand, she threaded her fingers through his. "We'll do it together now that we're officially a couple."

The deep chuckle starting in his chest bubbled over into full laughter. "Whether you realized it or not, we became a couple on our first date."

"Oh, no. You didn't go there, Ethan James McMillan. You were *that* certain that I would go out with you again?"

"No."

"Then why are you talking trash?"

He gave her a wide smile, dimples winking attractively. "I just wanted to know how much I could get away with."

She returned his smile. "Not much, mister."

"Damn, sweetness, can't you cut me some slack?"

"I'll think about it."

"Don't think too long," Ethan said to Faith's back as she leaned over to pick up the pillows.

He gathered the bowls, took them into the apartment, then returned to the fire escape to extinguish the candles and pick up the blanket. Meanwhile, Faith had turned on the floor lamp and loaded the dishwasher.

"What else do you need me to do?"

Straightening, she glanced around. "Please close and lock the windows. One time I left them open and I had a stray cat for company until the landlord sent someone over to trap it."

Ethan closed and locked the windows before drawing the shutters for complete privacy. "What do you do in the summer when it gets too hot in here?"

"I have a window unit I put in every summer."

"Where is it?"

"It's down in the basement. All of the tenants kick in a fee to have their portable air conditioners stored there until it's time to put them in the windows."

"Do you ever have a problem not getting enough heat?"

Faith shook her head. "No. I've always had heat."

Ethan walked forward and pulled her gently into his embrace. "What time are you getting up in the morning?"

Tilting her head, she visually examined the face looming above hers. "Because I have a houseguest, I decided to go in later."

The beginning of a smile tipped the corners of his mouth. "How late is later?"

She'd decided to take the morning off because she

wouldn't see Ethan again until February fourteenth when they were scheduled to fly to the Caribbean.

"How does noon sound to you?"

"It sounds wonderful," Ethan crooned as his head came down to take her mouth in a passionate kiss that sucked the oxygen from her lungs. "We still haven't had dessert."

Faith wasn't given time to respond to this cryptic statement as she found herself in his arms and being carried to the bed. He swept back the white comforter and placed her gently onto the mattress.

Time stood still as she watched Ethan through lowered lids as he reached into the pocket of his slacks to remove a condom and placed it on the pillow bedside her head. Slowly, deliberately, he pulled his sweater up and over his head. The lingering light from sputtering candles turned his upper body into a statue of aged bronze. She couldn't see his eyes, but felt the heat of his gaze as he unbuckled the belt around his slender waist. One by one the garments came off—shoes, socks, slacks and briefs—until he stood before her gloriously naked and fully aroused.

She closed her eyes when he moved over her, her fingers catching and tightening in the crisp linen. He undressed her, his breathing deepening with every piece of clothing until she was as naked as him.

"Breathe, Faith."

The tightness in her chest eased as she let out her breath, unaware she'd been holding it since the brush of his heavy sex touched her bared thighs. A mysterious smile softened her mouth as she extended her arms. "Take me *now*." Tonight there would be no foreplay.

The husky timbre of her softly spoken command swept over Ethan like the heat from a jet taking off from a carrier.

The roar of the engine and the intense heat never failed to suck the air from his brain and lungs.

He complied, lowering himself over her prone body. Her smell, the velvet softness of her body threatened to swallow him whole. He'd been lost for more years than he wanted to remember, but with Faith he'd come home. She was his refuge, safe haven and a place where he wanted to live forever. His lips took hers gently, nibbling at the corners. His teeth closed over her full lower lip, suckling and drawing it into his mouth.

Whenever she lay with Ethan, Faith felt both primal and refined. With him she could let go of her inhibitions to give her lover all of herself while experiencing the essence of why she'd been born female to his male.

Wrapping her arms around his back, she arched, silently communicating the need for him to fill her with his hardness. She didn't have to wait. Ethan slipped the condom down his erection and pushed into her hot, moist, throbbing body, both of them sighing in satisfaction as they ceased to exist as separate entities.

Passion exploded with the velocity of a backdraft, and without warning they climaxed simultaneously, the aftermath leaving them shaking uncontrollably. Ethan's broad shoulders rose and fell heavily with each breath it took for him to fill his lungs with much-needed oxygen. Whispering endearments in Faith's hair, he closed his eyes. It'd ended too quickly. He'd wanted dessert to become a long, drawn-out affair where he could savor and relive their joining even when separated by time and distance.

It pained Ethan that he had to leave her. He'd assumed the responsibility of driving a flying-phobic head of sales for a toy company to Miami for a sales convention. He would've given the task to several of his other drivers, but all were booked solid with other clients.

Faith felt the weight bearing down on her, but she was too spent to protest. "Dessert was wonderful, my darling."

Ethan smiled. "I need seconds."

"Can you wait until later?"

He chuckled softly. "I can, but only if you promise to give me more."

"I promise."

Those were the last two words Faith muttered as sleep overtook her. She never knew when Ethan withdrew from her, got out of the bed to discard the condom, turned off the floor lamp or returned to pull the sheet up over her moist body.

He gathered her in his arms and shifted her slight body until his groin was pressed to the roundness of her bottom. It was when the last votive flickered and went out that he closed his eyes and joined her in sleep.

Chapter 16

Ethan walked into his Miami Beach hotel penthouse suite, flopping down fully clothed on the king-size bed. The drive from New York to Miami was uneventful. Upon his client's request on the drive southward they'd stayed over in Wilmington, North Carolina. If it'd been up to Ethan he would've attempted to make the fifteen-hundred-mile drive in a day and a half instead of two.

He still had another two days in Miami before heading back to New York. Although the toy company executive had reserved a room for Ethan in one of the finest hotels on the beach with spectacular views of Biscayne Bay, he was bored *and* he missed Faith. The bright lights from the upscale restaurants and nightclubs were not enough to pull him out of his funk. Reaching for his cell phone, he punched in the numbers for Faith's cell. It wasn't quite ten o'clock and he hoped that she hadn't retired for bed. It rang twice before she answered.

"Let Them Eat Cake, Faith Whitfield speaking."

"I'd like to order one kiss, two hugs, three wild, passionate—"

"Oh, no you didn't," she said, laughing and cutting him off.

"Yes, I did. How are you?"

"I'm good. How are you, Ethan?"

"Bored as hell."

"Surely you jest," she teased. "There's nothing boring about Miami and you know it. Why aren't you out clubbing instead of calling me?"

"I don't want to go to a club."

"Whenever I'm in Miami I party until I drop, then shop and max out my cards."

"I did do some shopping today."

"Good for you. But you need to go out and enjoy yourself, Ethan. Take in some of the sights in South Beach."

"Not this trip. Maybe the next time I come down you'll come with me."

"It'll have to be later in the year."

Ethan smiled. Faith, who'd admitted she wasn't good at commitment, was seeing their relationship as one that would continue beyond a few months. "I'm going to hold you to that promise."

Her soft laugh came through the tiny earpiece. "I promise only if you promise to go out and take advantage of a mini working holiday."

"Okay, sweetness. I promise to go to a jazz club tomorrow night."

"Good for you. I'm going to have to hang up because I

have to get up early tomorrow morning and pack for Palm Beach and our Caribbean getaway. Don't call me tomorrow night because I'm going to be in the shop most of the night decorating your cousin's cake. And when I get back from Palm Beach I'm going to be up late putting the finishing touches on another wedding cake for the fourteenth."

"What are trying to do, Faith? Kill yourself?"

"Excuse me! But I do have a business to run."

Ethan closed his eyes. It was obvious she'd taken umbrage to his statement. "That's true, darling," he said, hoping to placate her, "but you can't run yourself into the ground."

"Have you forgotten that I have an assistant?"

"No, I haven't."

"What are you afraid of, Ethan? That I'll be too tired to service you once we get to the Caribbean?"

White-hot rage raced through Ethan, rendering him speechless for several seconds. "I'm going to forget I heard that remark, because one thing you're not to me and that is a sex object. If I don't talk to you tomorrow, then I'll pick you up Saturday night around ten."

"I'll be ready."

The line went dead and he knew Faith had ended the call abruptly. "I'm not trying to control your life," he whispered, depressing a button on his cell. All he wanted to do was love and protect Faith. He admired her independence and her drive for success, but not at the risk of burning out.

He'd cautioned Faith because at one time in his life someone had warned him that he was putting in too many hours flying. It'd taken the sage advice of William Raymond to make him reassess his life.

WJ had pulled him aside at a family reunion and read him the riot act. His cousin wasn't afraid to say what other family members had been whispering about. The months following his split with Justine, he was rarely home more than three days a month, because he'd accepted assignments none of the other pilots wanted. When new air routes to former Communist-bloc countries opened up he was the first one to accept.

William Raymond had asked him point-blank if he had a death wish because he'd lost more than twenty pounds, his eyes appeared sunken in his head and he'd become almost monosyllabic. His cousin said if he was going to work that hard for a commercial airline, then he should be in business for himself.

Self-made millionaire WJ sat him down and outlined how he should set up a ground transportation company. After conferring with a financial planner, Ethan sold the properties willed him by his aunt and uncle, and a year later the former U.S. Air Force fighter pilot added private air transport to his car service.

Do not mix business with pleasure, a quiet voice whispered. As long as he and Faith didn't discuss business their relationship was smooth and problem free, but whenever he attempted to advise her about Let Them Eat Cake or Signature Bridals she balked and came at him like a charging bull.

Faith had promised him that she would accompany him to Miami later in the year, and he promised himself that he would never broach the topic of her business with her again unless she solicited his input or advice.

Ethan moved off the bed and made his way into one of the two bathrooms to shower. Instead of sitting, listening to music or people watching he'd spend the night in a hotel room—alone. And there was no doubt he would spend the remainder of his time in the colorful, pulsating South Florida city the same as this night.

Friday morning a driver arrived at Faith's apartment before six, stored her luggage in the trunk of the Lincoln Town Car and headed up the Westside Highway and across the Lincoln Tunnel for New Jersey. A sleek corporate jet sat on a private airstrip at the Teterboro Airport, awaiting her arrival. Within minutes the copilot scanned her driver's license through an electronic device and led her up the steps into a jet that was as luxurious as a living room. She wasn't the only passenger onboard the aircraft. A couple reclined in seats that converted into beds. Both appeared to be asleep.

"Good morning, Miss Whitfield. Welcome aboard," greeted a petite blond flight attendant wearing a navy-blue pantsuit with a white blouse and blue-and-white-striped scarf tied around her neck. "I'm Jourdan, and I'm here to make certain your flight will be a pleasant one. As soon as we reach cruising speed you will be offered breakfast. You'll find a menu on your seat. Please circle the items you want, and our onboard chef will accommodate you."

Faith returned the woman's open, friendly smile. "Thank you."

She silently thanked Ethan for making the arrangements for her flight to Palm Beach. It was the first time that she didn't have to stand in line at overcrowded terminals to check in and struggle with her own luggage. She'd packed two bags, one with a change of clothes and the other with the supplies she needed to bake and decorate a fairy-tale castle cake. Faith planned to fill the turrets on the towers with sweets that were certain to delight not only the party girl but also her guests. The cake had to be made a day in advance to allow the sugar paste to dry. Taking a seat, she secured her seat belt and waited for takeoff.

Fourteen hours after touching down at the Palm Beach Airport, the jet carrying Faith came in for a smooth landing back at the Teterboro Airport. Two limos were parked behind a condoned-off area awaiting the jet's arrival. As soon as the flight attendant opened the door and the steps were lowered, the cars maneuvered close to the aircraft. The doors opened and shock upon shock slapped at Faith when she recognized the man getting out of one of the Town Cars and striding purposefully toward her.

Fatigue and apprehension about seeing Ethan again vanished completely as she rushed forward and flung herself against his chest, her arms going around his neck. Ignoring the stares coming from the jet's crew, she kissed every inch of his face before fastening her mouth to his in a heated kiss that melted the vestiges of resistance toward the man to whom she'd given her heart.

Cradling his lean face between her hands, she smiled up at him. "Don't tell me that you're my driver?"

His dimples winked at her. "It's me in the flesh." His fingers circled her delicate wrists, bringing her arms down to her sides, and he led her over to the car. He held the door open while she slipped into the front passenger's seat. "I have to get your luggage."

Ethan returned to the aircraft where the crew unloaded her bags. Lloyd Seymour gave his boss and friend a wide grin. "She's gorgeous, Mac."

He nodded. "Thanks for bringing her back safe."

"No problem. We'll see you tomorrow night."

Ethan nodded again. "You bet."

Lloyd, the copilot and flight attendant were scheduled to fly down to the Caribbean Saturday night with their respective spouses for two days before returning to the States Monday evening. Ethan had instructed his office manager not to book any flights for the Valentine's Day weekend so as to give his employees time to celebrate the holiday with their loved ones.

Picking up Faith's carryon and a large bag, he made his way back to the car and stored them in the trunk.

Faith gave Ethan a sidelong glance when he got in beside her. "I hope you weren't embarrassed that I kissed you."

Angling his head, Ethan smiled as he started up the car. "You've got to be kidding. I'd love to be greeted like that every single day."

She didn't want to read more into Ethan's statement than necessary. Did he want to see her every day? Did she want to be with him every day? "When did you get back?"

Shifting into gear, he maneuvered away from the airstrip. "I got here an hour before you touched down."

Faith rested a hand on his shoulder. "You must be exhausted."

"I'll get some rest after I drop you off."

"You're not going back to New Jersey tonight, are you?"

Ethan exhaled a long sigh as he concentrated on the road in front of him. "No. I'm going to stay in the city with WJ."

"Are you in the wedding party?"

"No."

Faith kept up a steady stream of conversation during the drive to Manhattan, entertaining Ethan with the process it took to create the fairy-tale castle for a ten-year-old girl obsessed with princes, princesses, unicorns and magical castles.

Ethan double-parked in front of Let Them Eat Cake, waited with Faith as she unlocked the door, leaving only when she activated the alarm and locked the door behind her. He hadn't wanted her to remain in the shop alone, but swallowed his protest because he didn't want to do or say anything to challenge their fragile truce.

Faith walked to the rear of the bakeshop and turned on the light. Her gaze went to the chalkboard filled with Ranee's neat print: "Prendergast—2/14—completed 4 heart shapes and covered with royal icing. Need ribbons and roses to complete. Courier called to confirm pickup and delivery to Tavern on the Green and Lake Success, Long Island."

"Thank you, Ranee," she said aloud, although there was no one around to hear her.

If she hadn't hired the talented apprentice, there was no way she would've been able to complete two wedding cakes scheduled for the same day. And, if it hadn't been for Ethan, she never would've been able to accommodate Tomasina Fiori's granddaughter's fairy-tale birthday cake.

Operating totally on adrenaline, Faith changed into a pair of loose-fitting pants, tunic top and leather clogs, washed her hands, then gathered the materials she needed to make four realistic-looking ribbons with bows and more than a dozen pressure-piping white and pink royal-icing roses.

Music blared from a radio, the station playing everything from pop to hip-hop as Faith concentrated intently on piping the flowers onto nonstick baking paper before drying them under a special lamp. When dry, she removed them from the paper with a palette knife and attached them to the cake. The process was painstakingly slow, but her reputation as the consummate cake designer for Signature Bridals was always in the forefront. Whether fashioning flowers by hand or utilizing a piping bag, the results were nearly indistinguishable except by the most discerning professional pastry chef.

Faith met Oliver Rollins at the front door as he walked in. His white eyebrows lifted. "When did you get back?"

She offered him a tired smile. "I got in around midnight. I'm going home to get some sleep before I have to assemble the two wedding cakes."

"Good luck."

"You, too," Faith said over her shoulder.

Let Them Eat Cake was scheduled to open two hours earlier than normal to accommodate the bakeshop's regular customers and the many special orders for Valentine's Day. She'd instructed Ranee to close at four o'clock instead of six not only to give the behind-the-counter employees time off to prepare for their own special Valentines, but because they'd worked nearly twice their regularly scheduled hours. Faith had also left envelopes with Ranee filled with a cash bonus for each of the workers. The generous tip William Raymond gave her for his daughter's engagement party she'd passed along to her loyal and hardworking employees.

She turned up the collar on her jacket to ward off the frigid air coming off the Hudson River. The above-average temperatures plummeted to below freezing, reminding everyone in the northeast that winter wasn't willing to release its hold on the region.

Faith made it home, retrieved her mail from the boxes in the building's vestibule, then slowly climbed the staircase to her apartment. Moving as if she were an automaton, she managed to brush her teeth and take a quick shower, but not before turning off her cell and house phones and setting the alarm clock. She climbed into bed and was asleep within seconds of her head touching the firm pillow.

Chapter 17

Ethan walked into the solarium in his cousin's penthouse and met his mother's startled gaze. He'd changed out of his suit and into a pair of lightweight tan slacks with a coffee-brown silk, short-sleeved shirt. A pair of sandals had replaced his imported slip-ons.

His cousin's wedding was spectacular. The bride was radiant in a satin organza gown that flattered her full, shapely figure, and the groom was staid and handsome in a tailored tuxedo; the parents of the bride and groom were elegant and smiled while exchanging high-fives once their son and daughter were announced as husband and wife.

Despite her father's celebrity status, Savanna and Roland had invited only fifty guests, and one-third of the fifty were family members. William Raymond III, who'd come to New York with the elder McMillans, managed to keep a low profile. Ethan noticed immediately that his godson had changed. He was more reserved and had seemingly matured during the short time since he'd gone to live in Pennsylvania. Savanna and Roland were spending their wedding night at the Waldorf-Astoria before flying to Maui the following morning for a two-week honeymoon in the Pacific.

Cora McMillan covered her son's hand with her own when he rested his lightly on her shoulder. "Where are you going dressed like that?" she asked softly.

Leaning closer, Ethan pressed a kiss to her short silver hair. The only thing he'd inherited from his father was his height and slender body. Everything else, including his coloring, eyes and dimples were Cora's.

"I'm taking off a few days to hang out in the Dominican Republic."

"Good for you." Cora squeezed his fingers. "WJ says that you work too hard."

Ethan shot his cousin a withering glare. "He's a fine one to talk." He kissed his mother again. "I'll call you after I get back."

"Will we see you for Easter?"

"Sure. Tell Dad I'll call him sometime next week. I'd like to discuss something with him."

Norman McMillan was behind closed doors with WJ in the latter's office, no doubt discussing Billy's adjustment to a new college. Cora and Norman planned to spend the rest of the weekend in New York City before driving back to Cresson, Pennsylvania. His sisters and brothers-in-law had come in for the wedding and reception, but elected not to stay over because they'd left their young children with babysitters.

Ethan left the solarium and took the elevator to the underground parking garage to pick up the Town Car he'd driven to and from Florida. He would leave it at the airport where one of his drivers would pick it up to have it serviced by the Mac Elite Travel mechanics.

Starting up the car, he adjusted the heat. The outside temperature read a chilly sixteen degrees when the week before the mercury was seventy-six. Right now, all Ethan wanted was to soak up the tropical heat with Faith. He didn't want to think about anything to do with his employees or his business. He activated the Bluetooth feature on his cell phone and dialed the number to Faith's apartment. She answered on the first ring.

"If you're calling to cancel, then I'm going to hurt you, Ethan McMillan."

He laughed. "Why would I cancel, sweetheart?"

"I don't know. You've been rather moody lately."

"If I'm moody, then it's your fault."

"What did I do?"

"It's what you haven't done." Faith had become an itch, one that lay so deep beneath his skin he was unable to scratch it. Ethan wanted her at the most inopportune times, and that annoyed him because he'd never permitted a woman to get to him to the point where all of his waking hours were spent thinking of her.

"Do you care to explain yourself?"

"I don't think I can. I'll have to show you."

"Where are you, Ethan?"

He paused, peering through the window at the street signs. "I'm about half a mile from your place."

"I'll be downstairs waiting for you."

"Don't bother. I'll come up and get you."

"Don't come up, because New York's finest are blitzing the neighborhood with parking tickets. Hang up, darling. I'll be downstairs when you get here."

He ended the call, and when he maneuvered onto Patchin Place he saw Faith standing at the curb in front of her building holding on to a single piece of luggage. He pulled up alongside a parked car, released the trunk and got out.

Eyes wide, Faith stared at Ethan as he rounded the car. "Where's your coat?"

He closed his mouth over hers briefly, took her bag, helped her into the vehicle and shut the door. After storing her bag in the trunk with his, he slipped behind the wheel. "It's at home. The jet will be waiting for us by the time we get to the airfield, and a car will be waiting for us whenever we get back."

"Okay, Superman," she mumbled under her breath.

"I heard that, Faith Whitfield."

I meant for you to hear it, Faith thought.

Ethan gave Faith a quick glance. "What's the matter, sweets? No comeback?"

Wrinkling her nose, she shook her head. "Sorry, handsome. I intend to enjoy the next two days, and that means no fighting."

"We don't fight, Faith."

"What do we do, Ethan?"

"Disagree."

Shifting on her seat, she rested her head on Ethan's shoulder. "For the next forty-eight hours I don't even want us to disagree about anything. What I do want is to go to sleep with you beside me, wake up with you beside me and get to know more about you in the most intimate way conceivable."

Laughter rumbled in Ethan's chest. "Why does your agenda match my agenda?"

Faith's soft laugh joined his rich chuckle. "It's because officially we're a couple."

"You're right. We are a couple."

It's because officially we're a couple. Faith's pronouncement played over and over in Ethan's head as he stared through the windshield. Commitment-shy Faith Whitfield had agreed to date him exclusively, yet he wanted more.

He wanted more than weekend sleepovers and nightly telephone calls, wanted to go to sleep beside Faith and wake up with her not for two days but forever, and he wanted to give her all of Ethan James McMillan, whatever he had, with her as his wife and the mother of their children.

Faith's second experience as a passenger in a private jet was vastly different from her first. This aircraft was newer, sleek and state-of-the-art. The seats were configured to recline into queen-size beds, showers were installed in the bathrooms and flat-screen televisions were mounted throughout the cabin. She was greeted warmly by the same flight crew from her Florida trip; however, with a passenger manifest of twelve, an additional flight attendant was added.

Seated and buckled in, she shared a smile with Ethan. "You're spoiling me."

His eyebrows lifted as an overhead light fired the gold in his eyes. "Why would you say that?"

"I can't even imagine taking a commercial flight now after taking off from private airstrips, not standing in line to go through security checkpoints, eating gourmet meals prepared by an onboard chef and having access to bathrooms with showers."

"It's not what you know, but who you know."

"Come again?"

"The people I drive for also own the corporate jets, so

the perks include a seat or two if the aircraft isn't filled to capacity."

"I like those perks. By the way, you never told me where we're going."

"I didn't?" Ethan's expression was one of shocked innocence. "I thought I told you we were going to Punta Cana in the Dominican Republic."

Faith rolled her eyes at Ethan, then clamped her jaw tightly. She'd promised herself she wouldn't argue or disagree with him for the next two days, and she wouldn't. He knew right well he hadn't told her but that was all right. She was going to spend the weekend away from the cold in tropical magnificence with a man who'd changed her and her life forever.

The flight to the Caribbean island was just short of a bacchanal. Latin-infused beats flowed from speakers like in a Miami nightclub, champagne flowed like water to wash down smoked oysters, caviar on tiny crackers, sushi, countless varieties of deviled eggs along with steak tartar. Once the seat-belt light was extinguished a few of the passengers danced in the aisle. The Gulfstream Aerospace Corporation G550 had become a flying club. The only thing missing was a glittering disco ball.

Faith didn't remember much after the jet landed at the airport in Punta Cana around two in the morning; they were required to fill out a form and pay a nominal fee to enter the country. A driver drove her and Ethan to a house in the mountain region while the other passengers boarded a small bus to take them to Natura Park, an eco-friendly resort frequented by European tourists.

Ethan shook Faith gently when the driver parked under an overgrowth of mango trees. "Wake up, darling. We're here."

She came awake with a start, looking around her in the blackness of the night. Ethan had opened the door on her side of the Land Rover. "Where are we?"

Reaching over, he unbuckled her seat belt. "Let's go."

Before she could react he swept her off the seat and carried her up a slight incline to what looked like a house constructed entirely of bamboo, with a sloping roof covered with palm leaves. Dim light filtered through the shuttered windows. Ethan opened the door to an open space where an enormous four-poster mahogany bed draped in mosquito netting was the single room's focal point.

Carrying Faith as if she were a child, he crossed the room and placed her gently on the bed. "Don't move. I'll be right back."

She managed to affect a lopsided grin. "I can't move." And she couldn't even if her very life depended upon it. Her head was spinning from one too many glasses of champagne mixing with the rich food and now the heat: Faith knew she had to get out of her jeans and sweater before she fainted.

Pushing herself into a sitting position, she unsnapped her jeans and eased them down her hips. She kicked off her running shoes and socks, took off her jeans and then the sweater, leaving her clad in a lacy brown and ecru-trimmed bra and matching bikini panty. A layer of moisture covered her body, settling between her breasts. Intoxicated or not, she had to get out of bed and shower.

Ethan returned, closing and locking the door behind him as she slipped off the bed. "I need to get my toiletries so I can shower." Her voice appeared unnaturally loud, the place being so quiet that sound carried easily in the open space.

A table lamp, dimmed to its lowest setting, cast shadows over a towering mahogany armoire, a round table with two pull-up chairs in the same material and a rattan love seat and chair covered with plump cushions in a tropical motif.

"We'll shower together. That way we'll save water."

Reaching down, Ethan grasped the handles to Faith's carry-on and walked toward her. It was if he were seeing the perfection of her slender body for the first time. His gaze moved slowly from her narrow feet, long, shapely legs, slender, toned thighs and hips, slender waist he could span with both hands, and up to a pair of small, firm breasts rising and falling above the delicate lace of a push-up bra.

He set down her bag next to her feet, then ran the back of his hand over her cheek. His free arm went around her waist, pulling her against his chest. Slowly, deliberately he lowered his head and breathed a kiss over her slightly parted lips. When a soft moan escaped her he took full possession of her mouth, tasting the lingering essence of champagne on her lips and tongue.

Both had overindulged, but that was the reason they'd come to the island that was to become their private Garden of Eden to gorge on nature, tropical food and drink. Ethan had openly confessed to Faith that he loved her, and for the next forty-eight hours he would communicate without words that although officially they were a couple, he wanted them to become one in the legal sense. His fingers deftly undid the clasp on the back of her bra and he slipped the straps off her shoulders. It fell silently to the cool stone floor.

Faith felt hot, then cold and then hot again. She gasped when Ethan's hand moved over her belly and under the elastic band of her panties. Within seconds he'd become a sculptor, touching, caressing a priceless piece he'd fashioned for his eyes only.

Anchoring her arms under his shoulders, she held on to

him because she didn't trust her trembling legs to support her quaking body. His fingers were gentle as he parted the folds concealing her sex and moved his thumb up and down, around and around over the swollen bud of flesh that never failed to bring her maximum pleasure.

"Oh…oh…" Her moans trailed off as a spasm gripped her so violently that she was rendered speechless.

Ethan withdrew his hand. Wrapping his arms around Faith's waist, he lifted her and made his way to the bed. She was burning up and he was on fire!

Parting the netting, he placed Faith on the mattress and moved over, his gaze never leaving her face as he undressed, tearing the buttons on his shirt from their fastenings in his haste to lie with her. Once naked, he placed a hand under her hips and eased her panties down her legs. Faith raised her arms to welcome him into her embrace, but Ethan didn't want to make love to her in the conventional missionary position. Tonight he would take from her what he'd wanted to do the first time they'd shared a bed.

Smiling, he moved closer, his hands caressing her thighs. Then, without warning, he grasped the backs of her knees and anchored her legs over his shoulders as he moved lower and pushed his face against her mound.

"No, Ethan!" she screamed.

Yes, Faith! He couldn't tell her that he intended to make her his possession in the most intimate way imaginable because his tongue was busy tasting the essence of her femininity, the taste and smell of her etched in his brain for an eternity.

Never had Faith felt so helpless, powerless. Not only was her lover assaulting her body but also her mind with his uninhibited lovemaking. She couldn't move, couldn't extract his rapacious tongue as it moved in varying rhythms that alternated from a deep, exploratory plundering to a gentle flicking. Unable to take the sensual assault, she arched and gave in to the erotic pleasure that carried her to heights she'd never known. Her breath came in long, surrendering moans as her body shuddered uncontrollably until it stilled, as a lingering ecstasy continued to eddy through her middle like ripples across a pond.

Ethan's smile was that of supreme male triumph as he lowered Faith's legs and moved up to kiss her. "Now we can take that shower."

Her lips still quivering from unspoken passion, Faith closed her eyes and pulled his lower lip between her teeth. "You're going to pay for that," she gasped.

Nuzzling her neck, he pressed a kiss under her ear. "How, baby?"

"What if I go down on you without giving you fair warning?"

He kissed her again. "What you won't get is a complaint from me." Sitting up, he pulled her up with him. "Let's take a shower, then try to get some sleep."

Faith didn't have to wait long to make good on her promise to pay Ethan back for his unexpected and unorthodox lovemaking. The shower was an enclosed outdoor structure made of closely packed stalks of bamboo rising six feet above the stone floor with a thatched roof of palm leaves. After brushing their teeth at a sink in an alcove equipped with a commode and indoor-type plumbing, they stepped into the shower and turned on the lukewarm water.

The nocturnal sounds coming from the nearby jungle, the heat, humidity and the ribbons of light filtering through the slats on the shutters from the lamps on the bedside tables had become so ethereal that Faith hadn't wanted to believe she was a part of the primordial setting.

She and Ethan became children again, splashing soap and water until she slid down the length of his lean, hard body and took his sex into her mouth. The motion was so quick and unexpected that Ethan cried aloud, the sound floating up and startling birds nesting in the many trees above them.

Faith was relentless, not letting him go until he forcibly pushed her back and entered her with a swiftness that left both screaming. Miraculously, sanity returned in time for Ethan to pull out before he spilled his release inside her. They stood together, shaking from the aftermath of what could've happened if he ejaculated inside her. They washed again, this time without the former child play, dried their bodies and went to bed.

Ethan fell asleep right away, but Morpheus wasn't as kind to Faith. She lay in the darkness, listening to the soft snores of the man pressed to her back while berating herself for what could've happened if Ethan hadn't pulled out in time. They'd picked her most fertile time of the month to engage in risky sex.

Faith had said that she wanted children, but she wanted to be married first. The decision to have a child would not only be hers but also her husband's. Once she returned to the States she would see about going back on the Pill. Her gynecologist had suggested she come off the contraceptive if she wasn't having sex. Well, now she was having sex and she wanted to protect herself from an unplanned pregnancy.

Chapter 18

Ethan woke to the distinctive smell of brewing coffee. Cradling his head on folded arms, he stared through the sheer netting, watching Faith set the table. It was apparent she'd discovered the utility kitchen concealed behind a wall of louvered doors.

"What time is it?"

Faith turned and smiled at him across the room. "It's after one."

Pushing into a sitting position, he continued to stare at Faith. She wore a white halter top with a pair of loose-fitting drawstring cotton pants that rode low on her hips. Her hair was now long enough to curl sensuously on the nape of her neck. Swinging his legs over the side of the bed, Ethan left it and walked on bare feet to close the distance between them.

Faith put up a hand. "Don't come any closer."

A perplexed expression crossed his face. "What's wrong?"

"Don't you dare come to the table without your clothes."

Ethan glanced down as if to check whether he was actually nude. "I wasn't going to sit."

Resting her hands on her hips, Faith glared at him. "What are you doing?"

"All I want is to give my girlfriend a kiss." She lowered her gaze when he leaned over and kissed her cheek. "Do you know what you sound like?"

She shook her head. "No. What do I sound like?"

Smiling, he gave her bottom a gentle pat. "A wife." Turning on his heels, Ethan didn't see Faith's delicate jaw drop at his rejoinder.

Faith screwed up her face. "A wife," she whispered under her breath. "I don't think so."

The chatter of birds calling out to one another woke her from her slumber, while Ethan lay next to her soundly asleep. She managed to get out of bed, shower and get dressed without waking him. A brief stroll outdoors revealed the existence of a larger house about five hundred feet from the one where she and Ethan were staying.

The views from the mountaintop with streams from twin waterfalls, lush vegetation, towering palm trees, pale sand and the clear blue-green waters of the Caribbean set the stage for a spectacular retreat. She'd found the kitchen with a sink, stove-top range, microwave and a well-stocked refrigerator behind a wall of sliding louvered doors.

Faith had finished chopping the ingredients for an omelet she would pair with *salchicha y plátanos maduros*—sausage and fried sweet bananas—when Ethan returned, wearing a tank top, walking shorts and sandals.

He bowed from the waist. "Do I pass inspection?"

Smiling, she tilted her head as he kissed her. "You look great." He'd showered but hadn't bothered to shave. "Even though it's a day late, I have something to give you for Valentine's Day."

"I have something for you, too." Ethan went to his luggage and took out a small colorful shopping bag. "Happy belated Valentine's, baby."

She took the bag and handed him two small packages wrapped in silver-and-black-striped paper with a black satin bow. "Happy Valentine's, darling." Sitting at the table, Faith reached into the bag and removed one of two gifts from Ethan. She opened the larger of the two to find a bottle of her favorite perfume. "How did you know I wear Valentino?"

Ethan gave her a smug smile. "Good detective work." He made certain to look at the bottle when she'd stayed over at his house.

She peeled the paper off the second gift, then opened the box to reveal a Cartier love bracelet in eighteen-carat white gold with diamonds. He'd had it engraved with the date and his initials. A tiny screwdriver lay beside the bracelet.

She didn't know what to make of Ethan's exquisite gift. The love collection, designed by the legendary jewelry house, symbolized the powerful and indestructible tie that binds two beings together, but she didn't know whether she wanted that type of commitment from Ethan because of the short time they'd known each other. Her hand trembled noticeably when she picked up the circle of gold and held out her left hand.

"Please put it on."

Ethan slid the bracelet over her wrist and closed it, using

the screwdriver. He placed the screwdriver in her hand and closed her fingers over it. "You hold on to it, because I know how you said you don't do commitment well."

She flashed a shy smile. "That's something I'm going to have to work on."

Resting his forehead against hers, he kissed the end of her nose. "Take your time, sweets." Pulling back, he picked up his gift from Faith and ripped off the sophisticated paper and bow. "Wow!" She'd given him a pair of gold cuff links that were an exact match for his signet ring. "They're exquisite."

Faith traced the engraved monogram on the ring on his right pinky. "You never take off your ring, so I had to rely on my memory when it came to the lettering for your initials." The block-letter design was bold and masculine.

Twisting the ring off his finger, Ethan slipped it over Faith's ring finger on her left hand. It was too big. He removed it and placed it on each of her slender fingers until it slid down her thumb without falling off.

"What size are your fingers?"

"I have unusually skinny fingers."

"The size, Faith?"

"My ring finger is a five."

"Mine is twice that size."

She placed her hand over his. "That's because you have a large hand and very long fingers. Thank you for the bracelet. It's beyond beautiful."

Ethan cradled the back of her head, his fingers playing in her curly hair. "Its beauty doesn't begin to compare to yours."

"Open the other one," Faith urged softly. Her smile widened into a full grin when he cradled a Limoges porcelain frog-prince box on his palm. The artfully hand-made figurine was painted by the most famous maker of French porcelain.

"How many frogs have you kissed, darling?"

"Too many to count," she countered. "So far you haven't earned any *ribbit* points."

An attractive blush darkened his handsome face. "I suppose I should consider myself lucky."

"Ethan," Faith said after a comfortable silence.

"What is it, baby?"

"We can't do what we did last night in the shower."

He sat up straighter. "What are you talking about?"

Faith met his steady gaze. "We can't make love again without protection. I don't want to get pregnant."

He recoiled as if she'd slapped him. "I pulled out in time."

"I know you did, but I don't want to take that risk again. When we get back to the States I'm going on the Pill."

A full minute passed before Ethan asked, "Do you want children?"

Faith saw the heartrending tenderness of the gaze of the man she loved beyond reason. "Of course I want children, Ethan. It's just that I'd rather be married before I start a family."

"Marry me, Faith."

"Stop playing, Ethan," she drawled, smiling.

His expression stilled and grew serious. "I'm not playing. I want you to marry me."

Faith shook her head. "No, no, no."

"Why?"

"Why?" she repeated. "We've known each other six weeks, and that's hardly enough time on which to base a marriage."

"What does time have to do with love?"

"Nothing."

"Exactly," Ethan confirmed.

Faith thought of her parents, who'd married after knowing each other two months and had recently celebrated their thirty-fifth wedding anniversary. The difference was that Edith knew she was going to marry Henry Whitfield within minutes of being introduced to him. However, it was different with her because even though Faith knew there was something different, special about Ethan she hadn't consciously thought of marrying him.

"Do you find me so repulsive that you'd never consider marrying me?"

Her mouth opened, but no words came out. "Is that what you believe?" Faith asked when she finally recovered.

He picked up the frog-prince figurine. "You must see me a frog."

"A frog prince," she insisted.

"A frog by any other name is still a frog." A pregnant silence ensued as Ethan and Faith stared at each other. "Believe it or not, I knew I wanted to marry you the moment you told me your name."

Faith's eyes widened with Ethan's passionate confession. He'd repeated verbatim the same thing her mother had said about her father. But, she wondered, could she hope her marriage to Ethan would mirror her parents'? Could she become his wife, bear his children and look forward to growing old together?

And it wasn't as if she didn't love Ethan, because she did. She'd told and shown him in and out of bed. He was sensitive, well-spoken, generous and a passionate and considerate lover, but could she trust him not to stifle her creative, independent spirit? She'd been raised to become an independent black woman in control of her own destiny and as a Whitfield woman she was expected to continue the tradition of the others who'd gone before her.

A hint of a smile played at the corners of Ethan's mouth when he sensed Faith's indecision. Placing his hand over hers, he squeezed her fingers. "What's bothering you, darling?"

Faith closed her eyes. "I do love you—"

"And I you," he said, stopping her words.

She opened her eyes. "Please don't interrupt me, Ethan, or I'll lose my nerve."

Ethan nodded. Her indecision had changed to vulnerability. "I promise not to say anything."

"I don't know what it is, but I seem to attract men who want to change or mold me into something or someone who suits their needs or personality. Most complained that I'm too ambitious, that I work too much, that they never saw me when it was convenient for them. Then there were the ones I refused to sleep with and to them I'd become a 'stuck-up bitch.' I've had men who've asked me to lend them money once they found out that I had my own business, and then there were others who wanted to move in with me because they liked the fact that I lived in the West Village. I am who I am and I don't want to change. Not for you, Ethan, not for any man. I've accepted who you are and what you do, and I don't want you to change not even for me."

Rising to his feet, Ethan pulled Faith up with him and cradled her head in his hands. "I don't want you to change, because then I wouldn't recognize the woman to whom I've given every single piece of myself. I'm only going to ask three things from you."

Easing back in his loose embrace, Faith stared up at Ethan staring back at her. "What are they?"

"Have my babies. Take my name and wear my ring."

A rush of tears filled her eyes and overflowed. Going on tiptoe, she brushed her mouth over Ethan's as he lowered his hands and picked her up. There was no need for words. Her lips communicated silently that she would marry him, change her name and have his children.

"When do you want to marry?" she asked tearfully.

Ethan swallowed the lump in his throat as a wave of emotion rendered him temporarily speechless. He hadn't lied to Faith when he admitted to giving her all of himself, and what she hadn't known and would never know was that he'd changed in order to gain her confidence, win her love and capture her heart. Interacting with her had tested his manhood and his patience.

"On our way back to the States we can fly to Vegas and get married."

"We can't get married in Las Vegas."

He heard the desperation in Faith's voice and the distress marring her beautiful face. "Why not, darling?"

"I'm a Whitfield."

Ethan smiled. "True. But you'll also become a McMillan."

"That's not what I'm talking about, Ethan. The Whitfields are in the wedding business, and it would be very bad for business if a Whitfield has a Vegas wedding."

"We can have a civil ceremony in Vegas and follow that with a church wedding with our friends and families in attendance."

There were many more questions Faith wanted to ask Ethan, but the enormity of what she'd agreed to overwhelmed her. A fist of fear squeezed her heart and she prayed that she wasn't about to make the most grievous mistake of her life.

What are you doing? Have you gone and lost what's left of your mind? Don't do it! Do you realize that you don't know this man, yet you've committed to becoming his wife?

The questions continued to assault Faith right up to the moment she was to exchange vows with Ethan McMillan. Suddenly she felt totally alone, even though the minister and his wife, who would serve as a witness to their nuptials, were in attendance. She jumped slightly when Ethan reached for her ice-cold fingers, bringing them to his mouth and dropping a kiss on the Ritani setting platinum solitaire engagement ring with two carats of a round brilliant-cut center diamond and channel-set diamonds between the prongs and micro pave diamonds on the prongs.

The Ethan she'd thought she knew had vanished, replaced by a stranger who'd begun revealing tiny pieces of what made him the man he was. The Punta Cana property was William Raymond's Caribbean hideaway and Ethan always stayed in the guesthouse when visiting the island.

Her uneasiness escalated when it wasn't Captain Lloyd Seymour who piloted the G550 to Vegas, but her husband-to-be. She rounded on him within seconds of walking into their hotel suite. Ethan managed to calm her down long enough to explain that he was president and sole owner of MAC Elite Car Services and MAC Executive Air Travel.

A numbed silence followed. His disclosure explained everything: his luxury home in an exclusive North New Jersey enclave, the one-hundred-thousand-plus sticker price on his car and the elegant cut of his tailored wardrobe. Ethan McMillan had played her—big-time!

She'd wanted to call a carrier to reserve a flight back to New York but her love for him overrode her anger at him for letting her believe he was a chauffeur. In the past she'd gone out with men she didn't particularly like because she'd tired of spending weekends home alone. She'd moved in with Lars because she was attracted to his maturity and worldliness.

Ethan was different, a throwback to her father's generation where men were raised to be gentlemen. Faith had spent years kissing frogs in the hope she would finally encounter a prince. And she'd found her prince in Ethan McMillan, and there was no way she was going to let him go.

"Darling?"

The sound of Ethan's deep voice shattered her reverie. Her gaze lingered on his close-cropped hair before moving to the stark-white shirt, dark blue tie and faint pinstriped gray suit. A mysterious smile touched her lush mouth.

"Yes?"

"Are you ready?"

Her smile widened. "I've never been more ready." And she was ready to marry Ethan and more than ready to share her life and future with him. Easing her hand from his grip, she held on to her bouquet of pink roses and tulips and smiled at the minister.

Ethan couldn't take his gaze off his bride, unable to believe that within minutes he would belong to her, and she to him, that their lives and their futures would be inexorably entwined. The delicate flowers in her boutique matched the silk slip dress flowing around her long legs.

He returned his attention to the minister. "Do you,

Ethan, take Faith to be your wife, to love, honor and cherish from this day forth?"

Ethan nodded. "Yes, I do."

The minister nodded to Faith. "Do you, Faith, take Ethan to be your husband, to love, honor and cherish from this day forth?"

Faith shared a smile with Ethan. "I do."

Reaching into the breast pocket of his jacket, he removed a plain platinum band and slipped it onto Faith's finger. "With this ring, I thee wed, as a symbol of a love that has neither beginning nor end."

Faith slipped a matching band off her thumb and onto his ring finger. "With this ring, I thee wed, as a symbol of strength, enduring love and trust." She blocked out everything going on around her until she felt the cool firmness of her husband's lips on hers. Pinpoints of hot tears pricked the backs of her eyelids.

The former Faith Vinna Whitfield was now Mrs. Faith V. Whitfield-McMillan.

"No more, Ethan," Faith said in protest as he lifted the bottle of champagne in an attempt to refill her glass. She'd drunk more champagne in the past few days than she had in all her life. It hadn't mattered that it was her favorite wine, but she did want to remember the events of her wedding night.

"What are you smiling about?" Ethan asked when she pressed her back to the mound of pillows cradling her shoulders.

After their wedding at the very popular The Little Church of the West they'd returned to their hotel suite and ordered dinner with a bottle of premium champagne. Ethan had suggested a Grand Canyon wedding where a helicopter would fly them over the Hoover Dam, Lake Mead and Fortification Hill—an extinct volcano—and take their vows at a landing below the rim of the Grand Canyon at four thousand feet above the Colorado River, but Faith flatly refused.

Faith's smile grew wider. "I can't believe I'm going to have not one but two wedding nights."

"We can have more than two whenever we decide to renew our vows."

"Speaking of renewing vows, my parents renewed theirs last November for their thirty-fifth wedding anniversary."

Ethan placed his half-filled flute on the table on his side of the bed. "My folks have yours beat by a few years. My parents celebrated their fortieth last year. By the time we celebrate our fortieth I'll be seventy-eight and you a mere seventy."

Sliding down off the pillows, Faith pressed her face to her husband's flat, hard belly. "Do you think we'll still be able to make love at that age?"

Running his fingers through her hair, Ethan smiled. "I hope we will, because I pray I'll never tire of making love to you."

Faith breathed in his body's natural scent and the lingering scent of soap on his bare skin. "I think I'm going to wait to go back on the Pill."

Ethan's fingers stilled, shock stopping the breath in his lungs. "Are you sure?" His query came out in a whisper.

"Very sure," she whispered back. And Faith was as certain about having a baby—Ethan's baby—as she'd been about anything in her life. All of her wishes had come true. She'd become a chef, she had a book deal and she'd married a prince.

They'd discussed their living arrangements and agreed to stay in Greenwich Village during the week and in New Jersey on the weekends. Once she sold the patisserie and set up a professional kitchen where she could cater to her private clients and Bridal Signatures, then she'd give up her apartment and relocate to Englewood Cliffs.

"You don't want to wait before we start a family?" Ethan could've bitten off his tongue the instant the query came out, but he wanted to be certain that Faith wanted what he wanted.

"No. Besides, you're graying at an alarming rate, and I don't want our son or daughter teased when other kids mistake you for their grandpa."

"Oh, hell no," he drawled. "You didn't call me grandpa."

Faith didn't have time to react when Ethan flipped her effortlessly onto her back and straddled her. Within seconds her nightgown lay on the carpet and he parted her legs. His hand moved up between her thighs to find her slick and wet. She was as ready for him as he was for her.

Ethan pushed into his bride's tight, hot, pulsing flesh as a deep groan came from the back of his throat. He felt as if he'd waited an eternity to experience flesh against flesh, and this time he wouldn't be forced to pull out before releasing his passion inside her. He alternated quickening and slowing in order to prolong bringing them to climax.

Faith bit down on her lower lip to stop the moans of ecstasy from slipping through her lips as the involuntary pulsing took her higher and higher until her muscles clenched in a violent spasm of explosive pleasure that made her feel as if she'd stepped outside of her own body.

As she lay drowning in floodtide of pure pleasure,

Ethan's climax overlapped hers, his growl of satisfaction and heavy breathing keeping pace with the beating of her runaway pulse. His body melted into hers where they'd become one—in the literal and figurative sense.

Chapter 19

Faith sat in the kitchen in what was now her Englewood Cliffs house, listening to the voice-mail message. She'd called her parents twice before, but each time got the recorded message. Exasperated, she punched in Simone's number, sighing in relief when she heard her husky greeting.

"Hey, Faith. What's up?"

"I've been trying to reach my parents, but I just get their voice mail."

"They went away."

"Where, Simi?"

"Our dads surprised our moms with a seven-day Windjammer cruise for Valentine's Day."

Faith couldn't stop the smile spreading across her face. "Where did they go?"

"They mentioned touring the British Virgin Islands and also the French West Indies."

"Good for them."

"What did you do for Valentine's Day?"

Taking a deep breath, Faith let it out slowly. "I got married." The scream that came through the earpiece nearly shattered her eardrum.

"I don't believe it! You married your prince?"

"Yes."

"Oh, I'm so happy for you, Faith. When am I going to see you and Ethan?"

"I was hoping to come over Sunday, but I guess we'll wait until our folks get back."

"I'm supposed to pick them up at the airport Saturday afternoon. I'll have something at my house on Sunday instead of Monday."

"Are you cooking?" Faith teased.

"Very funny, Faith—whatever your new name is."

"It's Whitfield-McMillan."

"Good for you. You kept your name."

She'd decided to hyphenate her last name as much for retaining her identity as for professional reasons. "Do you want me to bring a dish?"

"No. I'll order food from El Sabor." The restaurant was renowned for serving the best Caribbean food in West-chester County.

"Now you're talking. We'll see you Sunday. What time should we come?"

"Three. We'll have an early dinner. After that we'll sit around and talk."

Faith hung up without bothering to ask Ethan whether he'd be available Sunday to meet her family since as the boss he didn't have to request time off from work. The man she'd married was nothing short of an enigma. He'd admitted that he never would've considered going into the transport business if it hadn't been for WJ, who'd put up the collateral for the loans for Ethan to purchase three Town Cars for his car service. She made another call, this one to Tessa, whose reaction was similar to Simone's. Instead of screaming, she cried—sobbing loudly until Faith rang off. She was still sitting on the stool at the cooking island when Ethan walked in carrying a monogrammed leather bag.

"I'm ready," he said, smiling.

Hopping off the stool, Faith approached her husband, arms outstretched. He dropped the bag and she went into his embrace. They stood in the middle of the kitchen, silently communicating their love for each other. Then, as if on cue, they pulled apart. They'd become a couple—officially and legally—in and out of bed.

Ethan swung into the circular driveway behind two vehicles, coming to a complete stop behind a car that was the same make, model and color as the one he drove. "Someone has excellent taste in cars."

Faith gave him a sidelong glance. "That's my father's Benz. The Lincoln belongs to my uncle Malcolm. It looks as if we got here before Tessa and Micah."

"It looks as if my father-in-law and I have something in common."

"What's that?"

"We both love you."

Unbuckling her seat belt, Faith felt a warm glow flow through her. She hadn't been married a week, and every day she discovered something new about the man to whom she'd pledged her future. He admitted to praying before taking off and landing an aircraft, worked out several times a week at the gated community's on-site health spa and didn't eat organ food. And she didn't think she would ever get used to him declaring his love for her.

"My family's going to love you, Ethan."

"We'll see," he said skeptically as he got out and came around to help her out. The lightly falling snow that'd begun at daybreak had intensified, blanketing roadways, lawns and rooftops. Ethan smiled at Faith as she tilted her head and stuck out her tongue to catch the falling flakes. He found the gesture both childishly endearing and ardently provocative. The vivid image of what her rapacious tongue had reduced him to their first night together in Punta Cana would stay with him forever.

Light blazed from the front windows of the white and navy-blue-trimmed two-story farmhouse-style structure. A wreath of dried lavender encircled a heavy brass door knocker shaped like a lion's head.

Mounting the three steps that led to an expansive wrap-around porch, Faith rang the doorbell. The door opened and on the other side stood Simone Whitfield with a wealth of gold-tipped hair floating around her face and shoulders, grinning broadly. Light from a table lamp in the entryway fired the brilliant green in her large hazel eyes.

Her arms went around her cousin's neck as she pulled Faith's head down to kiss her cheek. "Congratulations!"

"Simi, please stop. You're strangling me."

Simone released her, seemingly embarrassed when she saw Ethan staring at her. "Sorry about that." She extended her arms to her cousin's new husband, and wasn't disappointed when he stepped forward to hug her. "Welcome to the family."

Smiling, dimples winking attractively, Ethan returned the kiss she'd pressed to his jaw. "Thank you, Simone."

The doorbell chimed melodiously throughout the house. "Either that's Tessa or the food," Simone said as went to answer the door. "Go on back. Everyone's in the kitchen," she said over her shoulder.

Faith extended her hand to Ethan. "Give me your jacket and I'll hang it up." He was casually dressed in a pair of gray flannel slacks, matching pullover cashmere sweater and black suede wingtips. Ethan had wanted to wear a suit to meet her parents for the first time, but she told him family get-togethers were always informal. Events held at the catering hall were the only exception.

She hung her coat and his jacket in a closet, then reached for his hand and led him through the living room, down a hallway and into the kitchen. Faith saw her father as he rose slowly to his feet, a slow smile parting his lips until it was a full grin. His normally tawny-brown face was several shades darker as the result of his recent Caribbean cruise.

"Hi, baby girl," Henry Whitfield said, reaching for his daughter and forcing her to let go of her husband's hand. Wrapping his arms around her waist, he lifted Faith off her feet, kissing her forehead as he'd done when she was a little girl. "Congratulations, princess."

Faith met her father's misty-eyed gaze. It wasn't often she saw Henry Whitfield get emotional, but it was apparent her becoming a married woman had him fighting back tears. She kissed his smooth sun-browned cheek.

"Thank you, Daddy." Her arms tightened around his neck. "I'm not going back on my promise to let you walk me down the aisle to give me away in marriage."

"Thanks, princess," Henry whispered, setting her on

her feet. He stared at her back as she went over to her mother and aunt, extending her left hand to show them her wedding rings. He turned his attention to Ethan. What he saw he liked, and it was apparent his daughter had chosen well. Extending his hand, he smiled. "Henry Whitfield."

Ethan took his hand, feeling the strength in the older man's handshake when he tightened his grip. He found Henry elegant and imposing. Tall and broad-shouldered, the middle-aged man claimed a solid body that confirmed he was in peak condition. Close-cropped curly salt-and-pepper hair, brilliant hazel eyes and a trimmed mustache and goatee made for a very arresting face.

"I'm honored, sir. Ethan McMillan."

Henry's eyes narrowed. "Are you military, son?"

Ethan cast his gaze downward. "I was."

"Which branch?" Malcolm asked.

Turning slightly, Ethan stared at Henry's identical twin brother. It was nearly impossible to tell them apart. "The Air Force."

Smiling, Malcolm angled his head. "Well, well, well. What do we have here? My niece has married herself a flyboy."

"That she did," Ethan confirmed, his tone filled with supreme confidence.

Lucinda and Edith Whitfield exchanged amused glances. It was apparent their husbands were going to have Ethan McMillan run the Whitfield gauntlet before giving him their seal of approval. Simone's ex-husband had failed miserably, but that hadn't stopped her from marrying Anthony Kendrick. However, within seconds of Ethan McMillan walking into the kitchen with Faith they'd given each other a barely perceptible thumbs-up sign.

Malcolm stood up and offered Ethan his hand. "Malcolm."

His dark eyebrows lifted slightly when he felt the grip of fingers on his hand. "What can you fly?" he asked.

Realization dawned, and Ethan wanted to kick himself for falling into the Whitfield brothers' trap. Although he and Faith were legally married, her father and uncle felt compelled to put him through an inquisition. Crossing his arms over his chest, he stared at Henry, then Malcolm.

"I've flown an F-15 Eagle, an F-16 Fighting Falcon, an F-22 Raptor, a Gulfstream C-37A, and as of late a Gulfstream G550 business jet." Ethan was hard-pressed not to laugh when the brothers' eyes widened in shock. "Even though the F-16's official name is Fighting Falcon, we *flyboys* call it the 'Viper,' after the *Battlestar Galactica* starfighter."

"Which one is the best?" Henry asked.

Faith rolled her eyes at her father. "Daddy, please."

"All your husband has to do is answer the question, princess."

"I didn't bring him here for you to interrogate him."

Henry trained his gaze on Ethan. "Can you answer the question, or is it classified?"

"I'm not privy to what is classified because I'm no longer in the military. But, to answer your question as to what's the best, it would all depend on the mission. If flying a reconnaissance mission, then it would have to be the F-22. It's a stealth air superiority fighter."

Edith rose gracefully to her feet. It was time to end the non-sensical chatter about fighter jets. "Faith's right, Henry." She cut her eyes at her husband when a frown creased his smooth forehead. "Ethan didn't come here to discuss the specs of military aircraft, but to meet her family." Closing the distance between her and her new son-in-law, she kissed his clean-shaven cheek. "Please call me Edith. Welcome to the family."

Ethan hugged and kissed his mother-in-law. He knew exactly what his wife would look like in another twenty-five years, because Faith was an exact replica of her stunningly beautiful mother.

"Thank you, Edith."

Lucinda moved off her stool at the cooking island and extended her arms. "And I'm your Aunt Lucinda."

Ethan hugged the petite woman. "It's nice meeting you…" His words trailed off when Simone walked into the kitchen.

"The caterers are setting up the food in the dining room." She smiled at Ethan. "I hope you've met everyone?" He nodded. "Good. After we sit down to eat we'll discuss your and my cousin's wedding. You are going to have a real wedding, aren't you?" Simone asked when Faith and Ethan exchanged a glance.

"Do you think I'm going miss out becoming a Signature bride?"

Edith reached for her daughter's hand and pressed a kiss to her fingers. "We have a lot of planning to do."

The doorbell rang again. "That must be Tessa and Micah," Simone announced.

Ethan was introduced to Tessa Whitfield and her fiancé, Micah Sanborn, wondering if Micah had gone through what he'd just experienced with the bookend Whitfield brothers, and how he had fared. What Henry and Malcolm failed to realize was that he'd been tested to the limits of breaking as a cadet and then again in flight school. He'd flown into battle with enemy aircraft rockets missing his jet fighter aircraft by mere inches and he hadn't veered from his intended target.

It didn't matter what the Whitfields felt or thought about him, because the fact remained that Faith was legally his wife.

* * *

Faith walked from the bakeshop to her apartment building, enjoying the lingering warmth of the setting sun. Springtime in New York City was her favorite time of the year, and in another two weeks she would exchange vows in the church where she'd been baptized, made her first communion and confirmation. Friends and family members had received wedding invitations with a proviso that in lieu of gifts, donations be sent to the United Negro College Fund. Despite the request, gifts and envelopes were beginning to pile up in a spare room at her parents' home.

Ethan had called her to let her know that he wanted to take her out to dinner before going to New Jersey to start the weekend a day earlier than usual. Her first impulse was to decline his offer, but she changed her mind because she needed a change of pace from the frenetic activity that made up her days and nights. Living in Manhattan during the week proved advantageous because it gave her time to decorate cakes for her book project. Peter Demetrious had e-mailed her that he was coming to New York at the beginning of the week for ten days and wanted to photograph as many cakes as possible. She'd returned his e-mail to let him know that he could set up a·shoot for her cakes, because, with Ranee's assistance, she was six weeks ahead of her June thirtieth deadline.

Faith met Ethan's family for the first time at Easter, bonding with his sisters, brothers-in-law and their rambunctious young children who took delight in calling her Aunt Faith. Her reunion with Billy Raymond was strained at first until he asked to see her alone where he apologized for his less-than-polite behavior during their initial encounter.

Ethan regaled her with stories about his grandfather,

James Ethan Macmillan, who'd worked as a coal miner for one of the most infamous coalmine companies in Marshall County, West Virginia. Instead of being paid in currency, the owners paid their employees in script that was only honored at the company store. After a series of mine explosions James Macmillan met secretly with union organizers to address the mines' hazardous conditions. The mine bosses discovered his clandestine meetings and hired goons to beat him senseless. James recovered, found one of his attackers and retaliated in kind, escaping under the cover of night to Pennsylvania. Once there he changed his surname from Macmillan to McMillan. However, family members referred to him as Mac rather than Mick, and the tradition continued with Ethan.

If she and Ethan were to have a son, Faith wondered whether he would be called Mac, too. She didn't consciously think about a baby until her menses revealed she would have to wait another month. Realistically she knew she wouldn't be able to handle being pregnant while preparing for her own wedding and spending long hours on her feet decorating cakes. In the past two months she and Ethan had gambled with making a baby. Their efforts hadn't borne fruit. But now she wasn't as certain. Her period was late, and when she'd gotten out of bed earlier that morning the room spun dizzily before her feet touched the floor.

I'll wait another week before taking a home pregnancy test just to be certain, Faith mused as she climbed the staircase to the apartment.

Ethan sat across the table from his wife in the upscale restaurant on the second floor of a brownstone off East Harlem's Fifth Avenue. The venue featured live jazz on

Friday and Saturday and various gospel groups for Sunday brunch. He wasn't certain whether it was the flattering glow from the candle, her lightly made-up face or her longer curly hair that framed her face, but Faith's beauty was surreal.

He pointed to the goblet of fizzy water at her place setting. "Are you certain you don't want something stronger than water?"

Faith smiled, nodding. "Very certain. Anything alcoholic is certain to put me to sleep, and what kind of company would I be if I fell asleep on my incredibly charming dining partner?" What she didn't tell her husband was that she suspected she was carrying his child, because if there was one thing she could count on it was her menses. It always came on time.

Attractive lines fanned out around Ethan's eyes when he returned her smile. "Who have you been hanging out with?"

Her smile faded. "What are you talking about?"

"I've never known you to talk trash."

She flashed an attractive moue. "I can't compliment my husband?"

"Of course. But you usually aren't that generous when it comes to compliments."

"Don't play yourself, Ethan McMillan. Didn't I pay you a compliment last night?"

"Yeah, you did, but in the throes of passion."

Faith's cheeks burned in remembrance. "You're not supposed to mention *that*."

"Why not?"

With downcast eyes she said, "What goes on in the bedroom stays in the bedroom." Whatever Ethan was going to say was preempted by their waiter bringing their entrées.

They spent the next ninety minutes dining on succulent plank-grilled salmon, rosemary-encrusted chicken, stir-fry vegetables, rice pilaf and live music from a talented quintet. They left the restaurant to find the sidewalks were teeming with people. New Yorkers were out taking advantage of the longer days and warmer temperatures.

"Where are we going?" Faith asked when they began walking in the opposite direction from where Ethan had parked his car.

"I want to show you something."

"What?"

"It's a surprise."

She glanced up at his distinctive profile, trying to gauge his mood. "Aren't you going to give me a hint?"

"Nope."

"Be like that," she intoned in the same manner as when she was a child and couldn't get her way with her cousins.

Ethan chuckled softly. He'd taken Faith to Harlem to eat for two reasons: to unwind and enjoy good food and music at one of his favorite restaurants and to see the renovated space that was to be his wedding gift to her.

"We're almost there," he said as he led her around the corner.

All Faith saw was an immaculate, tree-lined block with brownstones lining both sides of the street. "I hope you've noticed that I'm wearing heels that aren't made for walking."

"But of course I noticed, and probably half the Harlem male population also noticed." Faith wore a black linen wrap dress with a pair of black patent-leather pumps, and he'd noticed the surreptitious male glances directed at her during their stroll from the garage to the restaurant.

"Very funny, Ethan," Faith drawled.

He stopped in front of a brownstone halfway down the block. Wooden boards covered the windows of the second and third floors. Reaching into a pocket of his slacks, he removed a key and led her up the stairs to the entrance.

Faith pulled back. "What are you doing?"

"It's okay," Ethan tried reassuring her. "Before I show you what's behind this door I want you to put the patisserie up for sale."

"What!" The single word exploded from her mouth. "And why would I want to do that?" she asked. There was no mistaking the thread of hardness in her voice.

"You'll see."

"See what, Ethan?"

"Patience, baby," he crooned as he unlocked the front door, then deactivated the security system he'd had installed to protect against break-ins. He flipped a wall switch, and naked bulbs hanging from ceiling fixtures illuminated an area covered with dust and wood shavings.

Faith followed Ethan down a broad hallway with unfinished cement floors. A curving staircase, sans banister and railing, led to the upper level. Her annoyance escalated until he unlocked a pair of carved mahogany doors and they slid open as if mounted on glass. Recessed and track lighting lit up the yawning space like bright sunlight. Her shock was evident when her mouth formed an *O*, but no words came out. What Ethan wanted to show her was an industrial kitchen that rivaled those in cooking schools.

"I wanted to wait until after our church wedding to show it to you, but thought if you saw it now you'd want to unload Let Them Eat Cake as quickly as possible."

Eyes narrowing, she rounded on him. "You did all of

this without consulting me? You never asked me whether I wanted to sell my bakeshop. You just assumed I would because you believe it would be in my best interest."

"But we talked about it, Faith."

"We didn't talk about it, Ethan. You mentioned it as a suggestion, but I never agreed." She was practically screaming at him, but at that moment she didn't care.

"Didn't you say your assistant had mentioned buying you out?"

"That's all she did. She said that *if* and when I'm ready to sell she wanted to put in the first bid." A rush of hot tears filled her eyes, and Faith closed her eyes to keep Ethan from seeing them. "I really appreciate your trying to look out for me, but what I can't abide is you making decisions for me." She opened eyes that were shimmering with tears. "All I've ever asked from you is trust and honesty, and it appears you're incapable of that."

Ethan struggled to keep his temper in check. All he wanted was to love and protect his wife, and right now she was making it hard as hell to do that. Instead of selling off his last Harlem property, he'd kept it with the intent of using a portion of it for his wife's business, and instead of embracing his generous offer she'd thrown it back in his face. He'd instructed the contractor to renovate the third floor into spacious units he would sell at the prevailing rates for the gentrified neighborhood. The second floor would be converted to living space he planned to share with Faith and the children he hoped to have with her.

"I've never deceived you, Faith."

"No, you haven't. You just keep secrets." Her voice was softer, almost conciliatory.

Smiling, he took a step. "Is that so bad when the outcome is a good surprise?"

"How would you feel if I kept secrets from you?"

Cradling her face between his large hands, he dropped a kiss on the end of her nose. "Are you keeping secrets from me?"

Her penetrating gaze met and fused with his. Faith thought of the possibility that a new life was growing inside her, but it was only that—a possibility. "No."

"Good," Ethan whispered as he covered her mouth with his. "Because from this day forward I promise never to hide anything from you again."

Wrapping her arms around his waist inside his jacket, Faith pressed her breasts to his chest. "You'd better not or I'll be forced to pay you back."

Ethan smiled, remembering the last time she'd promised to repay him for putting his face between her legs. "It's been a while since you've punished me," he teased.

Faith traced the outline of his mouth with the tip of her tongue. "Maybe if I've gotten over my snit by the time we get home I'll think about obliging you."

Dimples caressed his lean cheeks with his broad grin. "You promise?"

Affecting her best diva attitude, Faith rolled her eyes while sucking her teeth. "No."

Throwing back his head, Ethan laughed until his sides hurt. He was still laughing when he led his wife around the brick-walled, stainless-steel kitchen that provided everything she'd need as the cake designer for Signature Bridals. After locking up, he told her about his plan for the property, leaving nothing out.

Looping her arm through his, Faith fell in step with her

husband. "Maybe we should think about living in Harlem full-time. It's not as if we won't have enough room if we have more than one child."

"That's a thought. There's no doubt we're going to outgrow the house in Jersey after a while."

"How many bedrooms do you want on the second floor?"

"At least four or even five. We're going to need at least two guest bedrooms."

"And I'd like a small ballroom for dinner parties," Faith suggested.

"If you want the ballroom, then I should reconsider keeping the entire building."

"But you'll lose money by not putting it on the market."

Ethan lifted a broad shoulder under his jacket. "It doesn't really matter."

"Yes, it does matter, Ethan. What if I give you the proceeds from the sale of Let Them Eat Cake?"

He shook his head. "No, baby. I'm not going to take your money."

She stopped in the middle of the block, causing several pedestrians to bump into her and Ethan. She ignored the cutting glances and mumbled curses. "Since when did it become your money and my money? Are we not married, Ethan?"

"The last time I checked we were."

"Then that settles it. We'll use the proceeds to renovate the third floor for entertaining. I'd like to put in a glass ceiling for a solarium. Simone can suggest the plants and flowers to go into it."

Ethan half listened to Faith go on about what she wanted for the brownstone property. He would agree to anything she wanted because he loved her just that much.

And he loved her enough to marry her not once but twice before they celebrated their first wedding anniversary. What troubled him was which anniversary would they celebrate—the first or second? Just to be safe and not incur Faith's wrath he would be prepared to celebrate both.

Chapter 20

"Something old, something new, something borrowed and something blue," Faith whispered as she stared at her reflection in the full-length mirror in her childhood bedroom.

The Cartier bracelet Ethan had given her for Valentine's Day was old; her white halter satin gown and matching shoes were new; she'd borrowed the single cascade of diamond earrings from her mother and she'd tucked a pale-blue linen handkerchief into the garter around her thigh.

Ethan's image came into view behind her. He wore a tailored tuxedo with a silk rose-pink tie and boutonniere that matched the delicate pink lilies in her bouquet.

He winked at her. "Are you talking yourself out of going through with it?"

Faith, a vision in white satin, turned to face him. "You do know it's bad luck to see the bride before the ceremony."

Ethan reached over and adjusted the fall of tulle attached

to a jeweled comb in her raven-black curls. "Doesn't that apply only if the couple isn't married?"

"I don't know."

Lowering his head, he pressed his mouth to her bare, scented shoulders. "Are you sure you're feeling all right?"

"I'm good now." Earlier that morning she'd experienced premarital jitters, and the normally unflappable Faith McMillan née Whitfield had taken to her bed for several hours until it was time for to ready herself for her church wedding.

"Ethan, you know you shouldn't be in here."

Recognizing Simone Whitfield's husky voice, Ethan turned and smiled. Her trademark curls were missing, her tawny brown hair pulled into a chignon and secured at the nape of her neck with jeweled pins and an enormous fresh magenta peony that was the exact shade of her strapless satin gown with flowing soft-rose-pink bow. Faith had selected Simone to be her maid of honor. Before he could explain why he'd come to see his bride, Tessa walked in, wearing a satin gown with narrow straps crisscrossing her back in alternating shades to those of her sister's gown. The rose-pink color shimmered warmly against her gold-brown skin. The sisters and their cousin called to mind the delicate flowers Simone grew and cultivated in the greenhouses on a portion of her White Plains property.

"What's he doing here?" Tessa asked her cousin. "You know it's bad luck for the groom to see his bride before time."

Throwing up both hands, Ethan walked out of the bedroom and closed the door. He didn't want to debate the silliness of the superstition or get into it with the Whitfield women that Faith may be his bride, but she was also his wife.

"Do you think he's pissed?" Simone asked conspiratorially.

Faith pressed a hand to her middle in an effort to stop the flutters in her belly. "No. There aren't too many things that can rattle Ethan."

Even when they didn't agree on something, he'd politely excuse himself and walk away, leaving her fuming. Once he believed she'd cooled off he would return, then they would have a quiet, rational discussion.

Simone fluffed up the layers of tulle in her veil, which ran the length of her hem in the flowing train. "I bet if you didn't show up at the church he'd blow a gasket."

"It wouldn't matter to him because, as he likes to remind me, we're already married."

Tessa adjusted the bodice of Faith's gown. "This style does wonders for your cleavage."

"What cleavage?" Simone quipped. "If I give her some of my chest, then you'd be able to talk about cleavage."

Faith narrowed her eyes at Simone. "I happen to have enough, thank you."

"Anything more than a hand or mouthful is too much," Tessa intoned, gesturing to her sister.

"Y'all just jealous," Simone countered.

"Not of double Ds," Faith said.

"I am not a double D, Mrs. McMillan. I happen to be a very full C cup."

A soft knock on the door ended the debate as to bra sizes. Edith Whitfield opened the door and entered the bedroom. The three younger women gasped. Edith looked every inch a mature model in a silk suit the color of pink champagne.

Faith blinked back the tears that seemed to come out of nowhere. "You look beautiful, Mom."

Edith smiled, nodding. "So you do, my darling." She smiled at her nieces. "I'm sorry to break up your little party, but it's time we leave for the church."

Holding her bouquet in one hand, Faith picked up the flowing skirt to her wedding gown and walked out of the bedroom, her attendants following.

"Are you ready, princess?"

Faith smiled at her father. "I've never been more ready." It was the same thing she'd said to Ethan in Las Vegas.

The organist played the opening bars to the "Wedding March," and everyone in the church stood up and turned to watch Henry Whitfield lead his daughter down the white carpet to where Ethan McMillan stood with his best man, former Air Force Academy roommate Lloyd Seymour, and William Raymond and his son William Raymond III as his groomsmen.

Faith stared straight ahead, her gaze fixed on her husband. A hint of a smile played at the corners of his mouth the closer she came. It was only when Henry placed her hand in his that his smile became a full grin. Several women close enough to see his expression gasped softly when the deep dimples slashed his lean cheeks.

Ethan and Faith had talked about writing their own vows, but then decided to use verses inspired from literature and the Bible. Faith had chosen a passage from Charlotte Brontë's *Jane Eyre* and he from the story of Ruth.

Faith, having handed off her bouquet to Simone, turned to face Ethan. Only the sound of breathing could be heard throughout the seventy-year-old church. "'I have for the first time found what I can truly love—I have found you. You are my sympathy, my better self, my good angel. I am bound to you with a strong attachment. I think you good, gifted; a fervent, a solemn passion is conceived in my heart; it leans to you, draws you to my center and spring of life, wraps my existence about you, and, kindling in pure, powerful flame, fuses you and me in one.'"

A muffled soft sob broke the silence, and Edith Whitfield wasn't the only one blotting away tears.

Ethan's deep baritone sliced throughout the church. "'Entreat me not to leave thee or to return from following after thee; for whither thou goest, I will go; and where thou lodgest, I will lodge. Thy people shall be my people and thy God my God. Where thou diest, will I die, and there will I be buried.'"

Simone lifted the bridal bouquet to hide the tears trickling down her face. She'd told Faith that Ethan would be the last man in her life, and his vow had just confirmed her prediction.

There came the exchange of rings, then it was over. When Ethan and Faith exchanged vows in Vegas it'd been before strangers. This time it was before God, family and friends.

Hand in hand they walked out of the church amid showers of rice, birdseed and orange blossoms. A cloudless sky and warm temperatures in early May made it a perfect day for a spring wedding.

Faith waved to her staff from the bakeshop as Ethan helped her into the backseat of the limousine. It wasn't often Let Them Eat Cake was closed on a Saturday, but today was the exception. Ethan hadn't booked any clients for his car or jet service, because he, too, wanted his employees to share in his very special day.

Resting an arm around his wife's shoulder, he pulled her closer. "When do you want to tell them?" he whispered.

"I'd like to wait until after we get back." They were

taking a week off for a brief honeymoon. She'd found a resort online in Oneonta that featured private villas that included an exclusive spa.

"You know your mother is going to go a little crazy when she discovers she's going to become a grandmother."

"I believe it's Daddy who's going to lose it. Unconsciously he and my uncle Malcolm have always competed with each other. It was Uncle Malcolm who had three children to his one, and once he became a grandfather it was like having a New York Yankees and Boston Red Sox fan in the same room."

Ethan lifted his eyebrows. "It was that critical?"

She smiled. "It was beyond critical."

Closing his eyes, Ethan tried imagining his mother's reaction once he told her that he was to become the father of another generation of Macs. Faith was now seven weeks pregnant, and her projected delivery date was January eighth—a year to the very day he encountered his sweetest temptation.

The driver stopped at the entrance to Whitfield Caterers, got out and came around to assist the newlyweds. Faith gasped when she saw Peter Demetrious standing in front of the massive doors holding a camera.

"Did you think I wouldn't come to take pictures of your wedding?"

She took the photographer's hand, leaned over and kissed his cheek. "I didn't tell you just because I wanted you to photograph me."

He affected a shrug of his shoulders that was purely European. "Do you think I'd miss the opportunity to shoot a beautiful woman?" He winked at her. "I'll make certain the photos get into the *New York Times*."

Faith turned and beckoned to her husband. She introduced the two men. Minutes later, the rest of the wedding party arrived and Peter ushered them around the rear of the property to a gazebo where he planned to begin shooting. The beauty of the landscape was breathtaking with sloping lawns and the pond filled with water lilies and a family of graceful white swans.

He stared at Faith McMillan, wondering if she knew how much her life was about to change. The photographs he'd taken of her cake designs were spectacular, and there was no doubt her coffee-table book would become a best-seller. Checking a light meter, he adjusted the lens on his camera and took several candid shots as Faith tilted her chin for her husband's kiss.

Peter knew instinctually that his first shot would become his favorite, and the one that would sit in a frame on a table or fireplace mantel for many decades to come. Without warning, Faith turned and stared over her shoulder at him. He got off another frame. Her large dark eyes shimmered like polished onyx, and the sensual curve of her mouth communicated that she was hiding a secret. She winked at him, and he returned it with one of his own.

He assembled the wedding party under the large gazebo and within seconds the overt love of Ethan for Faith Whitfield-McMillan was captured for eternity.

Every marriage has a secret—or three...

USA TODAY BESTSELLING AUTHOR

BRENDA JACKSON

JUST DESERTS

Book #3 in The Three Mrs. Fosters miniseries.

Danielle's husband's death shattered her dreams of
motherhood. Now she had a chance to salvage those dreams.
But would a marriage of convenience to Tristan repeat the
mistakes she'd made with her first, hasty marriage?

The Three Mrs. Fosters:

Alexandria, Renee and Danielle are three very different
women with one thing in common: their late husband!

Coming the first week of July wherever books are sold.

KIMANI™
ROMANCE

www.kimanipress.com   KPBJ0720708

GUARDING HIS
BODY

...as if it was her own!

Bestselling author

A.C. ARTHUR

Renny Bennett's new bodyguard just might be more
dangerous than any threat to his life. Petite Sabrina Dedune
has a feisty, take-no-prisoners attitude...and an irresistible
allure that's to die for. But after one searing kiss,
Renny's is not the only heart at risk.

TOP SECRET
ROMANCE ON THE RUN

Coming the first week of July wherever books are sold.

KIMANI
ROMANCE™

www.kimanipress.com

KPACA0730708

Welcome to the Black Stockings Society—
the invitation-only club for women determined
to turn their love lives around!

Power Play

Book #1 in a new miniseries

National bestselling author

DARA GIRARD

When mousy Mary Reyland discovers her inner vixen,
Edmund Davis isn't sure how to handle the challenge. Edmund
enjoys being in charge, but the new sultry, confident Mary
won't settle for less than she deserves, in business or pleasure....

Four women. One club.
And a secret that will make their
fantasies come true...

Coming the first week of July wherever books are sold.

www.kimanipress.com

KPDG0740708

The laws of attraction…

PROTECT
and SERVE

Favorite author

Gwyneth Bolton

Detective Jason Hightower has waited fifteen years to find
out why Penny Keys left him. Penny hasn't returned home
to face her difficult past…or the man she still loves.
But Jason wants answers, and this time nothing
will keep him from the truth.

HIGHTOWER HONORS

FOUR BROTHERS ON A MISSION TO PROTECT, SERVE AND LOVE.

Coming the first week of July wherever books are sold.

KIMANI™
ROMANCE

Bound by duty...or desire?

forget me not

NATIONAL BESTSELLING AUTHOR

ADRIANNE byrd

Detective Jaclyn Mason's investigation of her
partner's murder plunges her into a world of police
corruption—so she seeks help from her partner's
best friend, FBI agent Brad Williams. Brad ignites
passion beyond Jaclyn's wildest dreams...but can
he overcome her fragile trust to convince her that it's
true love?

**"Byrd proves once again that she's a wonderful
storyteller."—*Romantic Times BOOKreviews***

Available the first week of July wherever books are sold.

ARABESQUE®

www.kimanipress.com   KPAB1050708

These women are about to discover that every passion has a price...and some secrets are impossible to keep.

NATIONAL BESTSELLING AUTHOR

ROCHELLE ALERS

After Hours

A deliciously scandalous novel that brings together three very different women, united by the secret lives they lead. Adina, Sybil and Karla all lead seemingly charmed, luxurious lives, yet each also harbors a surprising secret that is about to spin out of control.

"Alers paints such vivid descriptions that when Jolene becomes the target of a murderer, you almost feel as though someone you know is in great danger."
—*Library Journal* on *No Compromise*

Coming the first week of March wherever books are sold.

sepia™

www.kimanipress.com   KPRA1220308